THE
DREAD
GODDESS

BOOK OF ICONS
VOLUME TWO

JILLIAN KUHLMANN

DIVERSIONBOOKS

Also by Jillian Kuhlmann

Book of Icons
The Hidden Icon

Diversion Books
A Division of Diversion Publishing Corp.
443 Park Avenue South, Suite 1008
New York, New York 10016
www.DiversionBooks.com

This is a work of fiction. Names, characters, places and incidents either are the
product of the author's imagination or are used fictitiously. Any resemblance to
actual persons, living or dead, events or locales is entirely coincidental.

For more information, email info@diversionbooks.com

Second Diversion Books edition May 2017.
Print ISBN: 978-1-68230-347-4
eBook ISBN: 978-1-68230-346-7

To Mike,
without whom there would be no books,
and no babies.

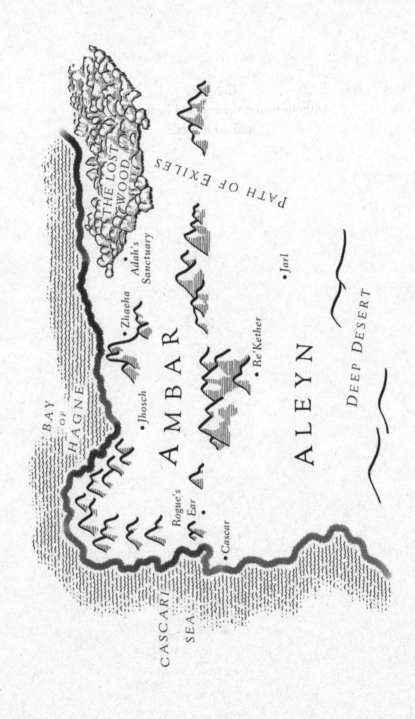

CHAPTER ONE

I want him in the moment I see him on the arm of his wife. In that moment I have divided them; with thought alone I can do this.

In the days and weeks to come, I will take her shape. I will take him, because this is the only way he will have me: unwitting. His tender gestures and fevered words are mine; he will love me best before her, before his three young sons, before his kingdom. With his heart, I shall claim them. His wife is too simple, too human, to lay her suspicions at his feet. She could not when he is every day begging at mine.

My cries of pleasure turn to howls of madness when I find that I am with child. How it has happened is the least of my rages; I focus only on what shall be done. His seed is too stubborn for the herbs that would flush a lesser man's from a mortal body. True First Men are few, and Shran is numbered among them…so too our son will be.

His wife, Jemae, offers to bear the child. She comes to me when it is Shran I am expecting, and I would have killed her were it not for the boon she offers. She has not suffered enough. She will suffer more.

She comes to me and my hand passes as easily through skin as fingers do in loose sand, and I feel no pain.

Until I do. I am Theba no longer, I am Jemae. I know now that I am dreaming, but it is as though a fire has been lit in me, a great burning beast turning my gut to ash. There are no reasons, no beauty. It is not a gift but a curse, and I learn the hour of my death in the first beat of his heart in my belly.

Thrashing, sweating, and sodden, I knew as I woke, half-starved and more than half-mad with cold and dreaming, that I was not alone. I was never alone; I had never been alone. I was Eiren, daughter, sister, friend. Eiren, icon of Theba.

Eight days I had wandered from the Ambarian capitol of Jhosch, wailing and retching like a mad ghost in the wood. I stank of sickness and fire and fear, my waking hours and my dreams haunted by the wreckage of the opera, the chaos and death that I had wrought. There had been no birds to echo my cries, no beasts to follow my scent or rend my flesh as readily as my screams cut the night air. Gannet had said that I would smell my own death if I passed beneath *Zhaeha*'s crooked peak, dared to go beyond the malevolent crone that loomed over his kingdom. But I did not, though it was my own death I chased into the mountains. I smelled nothing, saw no stirring creature. The trees here were not bristled with needles as the ones were below, but they were bare as spindles. I thought they must be dead, and I wanted to die, too. I curled between the roots of a great tree just as it was said Alyona's daughter had done. Mortal as her father had been, and though she lived far longer than he, even a drop of mortal blood promised death eventually. It was the same for icons.

But I was not permitted to die, not yet.

He had come for me when I was too weak to defy him. I wasn't even sure that he was a man, only that arms and iron-strong hands had taken me from where I had resolved to die among the withered trees. He had brought me here, though I didn't know where here was. Though there was water and fruit, I didn't want any of it, and I did not eat or drink unless forced. I woke sometimes to the dribble of water on my lips, and for all my thrashing, I would swallow some, and be sustained.

The pressure of his mind upon mine was the only way I knew that he was near. It was a kindred feeling, akin to what I had experienced with Paivi, and less so with Gannet, whom I had welcomed without even realizing it. I didn't move for fear of touching him if he was inside my cell, a small, square room with no door that my hands could discern. I could not see in this darkness, but I hadn't tried. When I had first touched the rough stone, I had felt memory instead, the brush of cloth and Gannet's warm flesh beneath, the first time that he had shown me, I could see without a light to guide me. I didn't want to remember, and I didn't much want to see, either.

And Gannet had no place here. He would not have intruded upon the deep silences in my heart in the way this man did. Even if I had strength for defenses, they would not have mattered. My captor squatted in all my ugly places, saw me and made me see me, too: icon, monster. I supposed he was both, to manipulate me as he did. He didn't ask questions or wait for answers. He turned over my thoughts like stones, a wanderer searching for water. And when he found what he wanted, he dug, deep. There was no hiding the horrors from him, the tender gestures, my earliest memories of tears and embraces to those sweet moments most recent.

"You should have let me die." My mutterings were as mean and as small as the pallet upon which I lay, the scrap of woolen blanket I had discarded, the earthen cup emptied on the floor beside me. "The others died. Let me die, too."

Even as I spoke, I knew what I suggested was not an end to the madness. Another Theba would be born, perhaps this time within the kingdom and so within their clutches. She would be shaped and changed to suit their needs, if she wasn't killed first, and my people would bow to the Ambarians at her command. It would happen anyway. Did that mean that I wanted to live, or that I had to?

I brought my knees as near to my chin as I could, making myself small, easy now given how emaciated I had become. I didn't want to die, but I didn't know how to live with what I had done, with what I had wanted to do and might willfully do again. Even the thought of Imke, who had deserved her fate, made my stomach twist. I could still feel the hot press of her skin bubbling beneath my fingers, could see the wild, anonymous shapes of those who had sought to outrun the fire, to flee. She had burned and they had burned, too. I had been for a moment the merciless weapon Colaugh wanted, but I had been the wielder, too.

Empty stomach or not, I thought I might be sick and turned away.

"Would you like to know how many are numbered among the dead?" The voice was low, musical, heartless, like an instrument played expertly but without feeling.

"Numbers do not interest me as much as names," I said, eyes scanning the dark and his mind, too, though I perceived nothing. It was as though the words had come from stones, and all was still and lifeless again.

"But names have faces and with them, stories. You like stories. Don't you want to hear theirs?"

"I wasn't aware that what I wanted played any part in the course of my life." My words were games, my tone betraying every grim facet of my curiosity about what the speaker had to share. Whatever life I had been cursed to lead, I was still eager to live it, and with the silence broken, so was my resolve. I would want and feel and regret. I knew no other way.

There was no response for a time, and I thought perhaps my captor had gone. But then a door I had not known was there was opening, a broad, featureless figure silhouetted in the light that poured in. Their shadow stretched out to meet me, and I touched the darkness cast on the floor as though touching the figure itself.

"Eiren, I do not mean you any harm."

The voice was different, and more than that, it was unmistakable. Antares drew near enough that I was no longer blinded, and in a moment I could make out his bearded face, the dark pits where I knew his steady eyes to be.

"What are you doing here?"

Had I been so mad with hunger and cold that I had not known Antares when he had taken me in the wood? Had he restrained me for fear of what I might do to him?

"I am here to help you. Please sit up, if you can."

And I could, with his assistance, the world righting itself. His answer did not satisfy me, though, and even as Antares lifted a cup of water to my lips, I raised a hand to prevent him.

"But why? How?"

Only when he began to speak would I allow the cup to reach its journey's end, and I drank greedily, but slowly, as I listened.

"You may take the truth from me when you want to, Eiren. It will be easier than words," Antares began, his features dim but defined, now that my eyes had adjusted. It was only torchlight beyond, but I had been in the dark for so long, it had seemed like several suns to me. "I brought you here to keep you safe. He is the only one that will shelter you now."

"Who is he? There was no one here but ghosts before you."

"I do not believe in ghosts, Eiren, but if I did, they would be waiting for you in Jhosch, not here."

He laid his hand upon mine to help me to my feet, and with his touch, I could sense his thoughts, the necessary distance he kept from his recent memories, leaving them that much closer to me.

I saw the opera hall with its belching smoke and the servants bearing large, ungainly bundles, their faces long and soot-painted; I saw far fewer footsteps in ash retreating than those that had entered at the opera's beginning. Antares was there, tall in his memory as he was in life, as real as the child Gannet had been in the memory we had shared. Inside Antares went and I did, too, pulled along by his memories.

The shapes of dark animals were sketched in ash, the stone black and oily as though splashed with wax. But it was not wax, and these remnants were not animals. I had raised a torch to Theba, and my fuel had been the fat and bones and blood of those who had been foolish enough to worship her. I could not be sick in memory but would be soon enough.

My eyes followed Antares's to the stage where a cloaked figure crouched and the scorched stone shone like melted glass. This had been where I had stood, the heart of the fire, and it was where Gannet stood mourning now. Even as I looked upon him, I saw him as Antares did: a man too slight for the sword, cold and unknowable. My knowledge of him was so far removed and paired so much with the hurt of what he hadn't told me that I found I preferred the distance Antares's memories gave me.

"Morainn?" Antares's voice was like something heard through a wall, nothing so crisp and immediate as the memory I had shared with Gannet of his childhood. Had it been his mind, or simply the mind of an icon, that was so sharp?

"Upstairs." Gannet, too, was difficult to hear, though his expression spoke plain enough. He was not hurt, but he was most certainly in pain. Even limited to Antares's recollection, this I could see.

"Is she awake yet?"

"No."

"And the king and queen?"

The way that Antares said this, even as muffled and remote as it was to me, I knew that he did not know that he spoke of Gannet's parents, too.

"Dead."

Without looking again at the guard captain, Gannet turned and departed down a discreet stair, his boots stirring up the ash that piled where the wealthy and the influential of Ambar had first reveled, and then Theba had.

There was very little left of Antares's memory of the hall and what I had wrought there, for he, too, turned to go, and I knew the start of his journey toward me lay ahead of him. The thick, gray air he breathed, the taste of fire—these things were replaced by the sterile stone, the thin pallet, and Antares's hand on mine. Left with my own thoughts, plenty and terrible enough, I recoiled from him. I could not make out his expression, but Antares did not seem surprised by my ability to read him. The only feeling I registered from him was relief of not having to tell me.

"Who else? How many?" I asked.

Antares's discomfort was immediate and plain, but I had no desire to give him respite, not when I was sure I would never know such comfort again.

"Many you do not know, I think. Some that you do. Imke, Paivi. A number of other icons. The twins, I remember. The others I do not. I'm sorry."

His apology seemed so sincere, but I could hardly accept it.

"Jaken and Shasa? What were they even doing there?" The icons were not meant to witness the opera.

Uncomfortable with the question, Antares shrugged.

"I don't know. They were found near Paivi. I can only guess that they came for you."

My eyes burned. To know that Imke and Paivi, who were my enemies, were joined by Shasa and Jaken, the queen, was no comfort to me. In the Rogue's Ear, I had reasoned through Kurdan's death, had accepted that his murder was necessary for my survival. I could do the same for Imke and Paivi, for the king. But when had Jaken and Shasa ever threatened me, or anyone?

Antares did not continue speaking but crouched on his heels beside me, arms resting across his knees. He carried no weapons, though I was not sure if he was making some sort of statement or if he was simply not allowed weapons here, wherever here was.

"How do you intend to help me, Antares?"

"I brought you here, Eiren, and though you fought me, you would not have if you'd been in your right mind."

I could have cried at that, his faith that such a thing as my right mind existed.

"I served another master long before the king," he explained. When he paused, it was as though the walls themselves had been breathing and now held that breath. "And when Colaugh died, I left before I could be charged with apprehending you for any other but that master. You do not know him, but you know his namesake. He is the icon of Adah."

Of all the gods Antares could have named, this one told me more about the nature of his service and his master than many others might have. Adah was the god of justice, though his definition of justice, at least in tales, was not how mortals would have named it. How would an icon carry out such an immortal, alien will? The same way I managed it, I supposed.

"And he was here, before you?" I asked, thinking of the figure I'd seen before, whose voice had offered me what Antares had given, and how much more I had feared hearing it from him than from a friend. I thought of all that entity had pried from me, and I was not surprised.

Antares nodded.

"He lives apart from the other icons but is not unknown to them. They do not come here. Almost no one does. But I knew he would want you here, so I brought you."

He wanted me here. Why? Was I to be separate from the other icons now? The thought of Gannet was like a cold hand squeezing my heart, and I saw his face again in Antares's memory, the grim choice in his eyes when the two spoke of Morainn.

"What did you mean when you asked Gannet if Morainn was awake?"

"What you saw, that was a full day after you had left." Antares was gazing at the floor. "Morainn was in a kind of sleep from which she could not wake."

What he did not say I heard all the same, as clear as if it were the crying of some predator in the night. *She could be sleeping still, for all I know.* There was no blame in his heart, but I wished there were. I wanted, needed, someone to be angry with me.

But it was Theba's anger that filled me, as bright and hot as the sun, eclipsing my shame. Antares might have been shocked by my next pronouncement, but not as much as I was, hiding behind the hate of it. I stood, for a moment towering over the much larger man.

"Imke and the rest had to die. Morainn would have wanted her dead if she had known of her betrayal." I was the very last person who could presume what Morainn would have wanted, but I did not feel like a person then. I was a monster.

Antares made no response, but a moment after I rose he did, too, lifting an empty hand, one I had grown so used to seeing wielding a spear, to the lit corridor outside my cell.

"If you are willing, he would like to see you," he said softly, and I could sense the threads of his anxiety, his surprise. I was not the woman he had known, but he would serve me faithfully still.

That had always been his charge, to protect me, to bring me to this place when the time was right. He was a warrior. He had known there would be bloodshed and death, perhaps even his own.

Perhaps still.

"I will go and speak with him if you will tell me why you serve him, Antares," I said, and though I had the impression already that Adah could summon me whenever he wished, I wanted to see if Antares would grant me a request that delayed the wishes of his master. I wanted to know the depths of his faith and in whom it was placed.

Unlike Gannet, Antares's expressions were rarely guarded. He was stoic by nature, not by force, and his devotion to his duty was something he had chosen. I had wondered once what sort of man Gannet would have been if he had not been an icon, and now I would never know. Antares, however, had decided his own fate, and his choices had brought him to me.

"I serve Adah because he serves Ambar, Eiren. When you speak with him, you will understand that means he serves you, too."

What he meant, of course, was that he and Adah both served Theba. And now, so did I.

CHAPTER TWO

Though well lit by torches, the windowless corridors we took to Adah boasted nothing distinct enough for me to be sure I could find my way back to my cell. I was at Antares's mercy, the way narrow enough for him to walk ahead, while I trailed close behind. I could have run but only through the way we had come. Eager for answers and curious to meet the icon who had orchestrated my rescue, however undeserved, I followed Antares without complaint.

"What should I expect?" I asked, trying to keep the tremor I felt in my gut out of my voice. The captor who had tormented me in darkness had seemed formless; it had known all, seen all, spared nothing. What would I see in the light?

"Adah is fairness and justice. Many of your stories feature the god."

"Yes, but an icon is not a god," I insisted. "Is he young or old? Kind or cruel? What are his gifts?"

This line of questioning didn't seem to make Antares any more comfortable.

"Adah wears many faces. He is what the observer needs to see to trust in his law."

That sentiment was hardly a comfort to me. An icon who could change his face, or at least one's perception of it? My powers were dangerous, but manipulation was not among them. Theba preferred a more expedient route to domination.

"And what do you see when you look at Adah?"

"What does it matter?" Antares shifted his weight, his mind cloudy. For him, I understood, it didn't matter. Still, there was the impression of an elderly man, imperious in expression, broad of shoulder, with a warrior's build that had not gone soft with age but stony.

My curiosity was quelled as we drew near the glowing outline of a mammoth door. It was as broad as two men and as tall, too, dwarfing even Antares. Characters akin to those in my books and embroidered on my clothing in Jhosch were stamped into the wood and inlaid with a dark metal I did not recognize. I started as Antares took my hand, placing it upon a symbol that looked to me like the rib cage of an animal, feather bones vaulted above an empty space where a live heart should have been. My shock at his touch was nothing compared to my wonder as the symbol began to glow, spidery light spreading from my fingertips, girded by the glow that illuminated the door's edges. The wood rippled like a curtain, parting, all the symbols on its surface suffused with light now, indistinct. For a moment, I saw many doors: the chapel arch of the palace in Jarl, the rock face that had obscured our home in exile, the curtain that had promised little privacy on the barge, and the mirror in whose depths I had been tested. All these places and the corridor where I stood with Antares were flooded then, with a brightness that belied my suspicion that we were underground.

Without needing to be urged on by Antares, I stepped forward into the light.

I was in a grove, greener even than what I had imagined I would find in Ambar in the spring. Saplings dotted the perimeter, and beyond them stood trees larger around than even many linked arms could circle. The scents of earth and the spice of flowers tickled my nose, the perfume stirred by my steps, my long skirt setting the blossoms of plants growing underfoot into a quiet dance. Antares was not with me now, but neither was I alone. Before me I saw several tomes abandoned among cushions and rough-wrought stools. This was clearly a place of teaching. Only one person remained: a man, sturdy as a tree himself, his face wood-grained with age but promising many seasons more of strength. It was not the same man I had seen in Antares's mind, but there was a similar gravity to his countenance. I knew him without knowing him, as Paivi had promised I would in time with all the icons. This was Adah, and for me he would never have any other name.

"Theba," he said. I recognized the voice I had heard in my cell, though now there was a touch of human warmth amongst the tenor notes. I liked it no better and feared him more. Still, something in me stirred to be called by him, toward him.

"I knew that you would come, in time," he continued, coming no closer to me, though the details of his appearance seemed to grow in definition. For all the lines of his face, his hair was thick, and corded muscles graced his bare arms, which were crossed over a plainly clad chest. "We must talk of what comes next."

I was outraged, and for a moment I was not sure from where the feelings had come. Then I knew: from Theba. The idea that he could order me to do anything surged like blood down a blade length, but the wound was my own. I could not imagine doing anything more, for good or ill, and was prepared to hear no charge. Adah understood me. There was nothing paternal in his attention, and neither was the hand he laid upon my cheek a sentimental touch. If anything, I felt like a stone or a lump of gold, my chin cupped in weights and measures.

"You were fond of games once, but I can see that you would prefer a story now. They must all have ends, you know." He released my chin and gestured broadly at the grove where we stood. "I have the power to bring you here but not to compel you. Neither can I keep you."

I realized as he spoke that what I had taken to be the grove was, in fact, Adah's mind. He had the strength to transport me here without touching me, or even my immediate awareness. What I perceived was not real. Another of his gifts, it seemed, and just as dangerous as a changeable face.

"It is a great power," I said carefully, marveling though I did not want to. If I wished it, could I return to the corridor with Antares?

"It is no power when compared with the kind that can sunder

worlds," Adah said, and there was no wonder in his voice, only observation. "I can only imagine worlds in this place."

For a moment, I considered arguing with him, affirming that I, too, preferred to imagine instead of destroy. I liked to tell stories, to fashion the flesh of them for my listeners, not to scorch their ears for hearing what I said, their eyes for seeing what I did. But I'd proven an aptitude for the latter, and that felt like all that mattered now.

"In the beginning there were no gods and no people, either," Adah continued. "Only shadows and dust, earth and air, our world a wheeling orb in the dark."

As Adah spoke, the grove grew blurry and dark, the trees stretching thin as wicks, burnt black. I could not see myself nor Adah, either. I was shocked by his power to manipulate my perception, and jealous, too. But this was a story I had not heard before, so I listened.

"But there were some things that stirred, without names or voices, and they recognized each other as living things. Out of the clay, they dug their own bodies. These were the First People, and among them, there were those who saw temperament in the black winds, the still rock, in the inky pools that reflected back the endless night. They saw light and gathered it to them, and they knew that if they could but fix the lights in the sky, their whole world would brighten and their understanding, too.

"The only way that the First People could reach the sky was to stand, one on the shoulders of another and another and another. It was not easy, and it was dangerous, too, for the lights grew so hot and bright that many of the First People burned up, the ash from their bodies raining down upon the others and the earth, whole mountains of ash that turned to stone in time. They seeded the world with their wanting. They made the stars above and the world below."

I felt Adah's gaze narrow although I could not see his face, could see nothing but the sweeping world imagined by his narrative. When he spoke, it was as though he whispered in my ear, but how close he was I could not know. I did not feel the limits of my own body in this place.

"You have seen the great city of Jhosch and the mountain that houses it, the chain that divides the world. It was their sacrifice that built it, as all great things require sacrifice. Pinned in the sky were the lights of fervor and willfulness, of mourning, sorrow, and ill deeds, the midnight vigils that were the virtues of young women, the hope of new mothers, the covetousness and calculation and all the things that were in the First People. The gods began as ideas lost in the act of sacrifice. They were created as the world was created."

It was then Adah shared with me, as Paivi once had, his understanding of a great passage of time, the changing face of the world and those who occupied it. Tragedy and joy were no more than colors on a palette. Indifferent as a star himself, he did not share in the terrors or tenderness of mortals, and so neither could I. But Adah, this Adah, had not known a mortal life, and I had lived too much of mine to keep from weeping and reveling, even though I knew these things were not for me.

"Theba," he said, and it was as though he spoke two names, the goddess's and mine, braided black as my hair paired with shadow. "Imagine what our world would be if the First People had not finished what they started."

We were sitting together in a room now. It was well lit with smokeless braziers but windowless, and it was much more like the sort of chamber I would have expected behind the great doors than the grove that had greeted me. The walls were painted with many scenes, faceless figures, whose bodies betrayed patterns of long suffering or pleasure. Their lack of features seemed to me to be shyness and not a fault in the artist's rendering. Naked, ink-limbed, they did not want to be observed.

"They would live in a paradise of ideas, without gods or wars to plague them." Even as I said it, I knew that I really didn't believe it. I had expected a charge from Adah, but the only thing he demanded of me was my attention to his words.

"You have always been a force to be reckoned with, Theba."

Like a needle sterilized in flame, the name threaded through me, new wounds made to heal the old. I had started something, Adah claimed. And so, I must finish it. "That you are here now shows me that your life will be as much of a surprise to me as all your deaths were. I am not asking you to make a sacrifice. I know that you already have."

One of the figures on the wall was a mother suckling a babe, a curtain of hair disguising her face, her full breast eclipsing the face of the child. I was reminded of something my mother had said in the cave when I was tested in Jhosch, that my birth had been the first of many steps I would take away from her. I had chosen to leave with the caravan in Jarl. I suspected now that I would have left my family even if it hadn't been demanded of me. My name did not matter, but the nature of my heart did.

"Where are we? And why are you here and not with the other icons in the city?"

Adah was taken aback by the question. I didn't know what he wanted from me, but I knew I wanted answers from him.

"We're in the wood beyond *Zhaeha*. Not so far from the city, but far enough."

So, I hadn't entirely lost my way. He continued without acknowledging my light nod.

"And I am surprised you have to ask—I am judge, jury, and executioner. Icon and man alike prefer that I keep my distance until I am needed, and it is my preference, as well. So, I choose to live where they prefer not to go."

"But why?" I had survived the crossing, even if I could not remember it completely. "Are you the only thing to fear out here?"

Adah's smile was brittle.

"There is nothing to fear from the fairness of the law," he said, and I couldn't be sure if he was joking or not. I expected not. "The people of Ambar are suspicious people, and I encourage their rumors. Still, there are wild things in this world that cannot be tamed, not by me, not even by you. They must dwell somewhere. Why not here?"

It wasn't any kind of answer. Perhaps Gannet had honed his conversational skills with Adah.

"All icons come to know *Zhaeha*, in time," Adah continued, watching me carefully. "In fact, I believe you've been here before. Were you not tested?"

My brow furrowed. I remembered the strange trial I had endured in the palace, the hallucinations of the mountain, of Paivi.

"Was I transported?"

Adah waved his hands in a gesture that neither affirmed nor denied the question. I sensed that it wasn't so simple, which didn't surprise me. I struggled to arrange what I understood in my mind and not to throw my own arms up in frustration.

"So, what next? You said you won't ask me to make a sacrifice, but that's exactly what the opera promised."

I shuddered at the memory of the opera, at the idea of Theba realized in her full aspect. Not an icon, but a goddess. Gannet had said he didn't know how it would be done, that no icon had ever attempted such a thing, but it was clear they believed that it could be. And they meant for it to be me.

Adah scrutinized me, only taking his eyes off me when he moved to pour wine from a jeweled decanter recovered from a clever compartment built into the side of the cushioned bench where he sat. I did not take the proffered cup.

"You want to avoid more war, but there is always war. Someone has taken your place at the head of the Ambarian Army. They believe that she is the one responsible for the murders in the palace and revere her for her cleansing flame."

More than surprised, I was indignant, too, and a hot fist seized my heart. Theba would not like someone else to have her spoils. Even as I opened my mouth to ask of whom Adah was speaking, he raised the hand that held his cup of wine, three fingers opened in a gesture to quiet me.

"I don't know who she is."

"But how can they not tell the difference?"

It seemed foolish to point out to him the many differences

between my appearance and that of most Ambarian women I had seen. Where my skin was threaded with all the tawny gold of sunset, theirs was cold as a cloud. Their eyes wore many shades of gray, green, and blue, where mine were dark as wet stone. Still Adah smiled, thin and without amusement, perhaps guessing what I thought, perhaps reading me.

"How many met your eyes? How many were brave enough to look into the face of the Dread Goddess?"

He was not wrong, and even if there were some among them who might have questioned this usurper, who would have dared to provoke Theba's wrath if they were wrong? I looked at the figure of the woman in relief on the wall again, at the babe, whose eyes I imagined would have followed her face with every nourishing pull on her breast, memorizing the contours of devotion. "So I must stop her?"

"You must do nothing," Adah returned, following my gaze. "But there is unrest in Aleyn. The peace promised by your departure was short-lived. And now the Ambarians know that what they need to exorcise Theba lies in Aleyn, in the ruins of Re'Kether. There will be no negotiations this time."

It should have been a revelation, to learn that my people resisted still. But I was not surprised. I resisted, too.

"What do the Ambarians need? What is in the ruins?"

Again, Adah studied me. "A weapon. And they know because I told them."

I sucked in a breath. "Why would you do that?"

"I finish what I start, Theba," he said, for the first time something akin to a challenge in his tone. He was thinking of the story of the First People, of what I had begun in Jhosch—what I had run from. "You might think I'm not giving you much of a choice now, but there's always a choice. You can pursue them, if you wish, or there will always be a bed for you here. Not the cell, now that you have returned to yourself. You could always teach the young. Perhaps you would learn something."

His mention of young icons stirred a memory in me, and it

wasn't mine. How I had not noticed the familiarity in his voice before was the fault of weariness, of how he had befuddled me in the grove. I recognized his voice as one that I had heard only once before and briefly, in the thrall of Gannet's mind. A dark room, a young boy, and a grieving mother. In Gannet's memories, in his wildness tamed before he could even begin to know it.

"Don't you want to put a mask on me?"

Adah's eyes narrowed in shrewd surprise. He might have thought that he knew me, but he didn't know about *us*. I might have run from Gannet, but he was not gone. He could never be gone from me.

"There is nothing I could do to disguise you, Theba. I would be foolish to try." The heat of the braziers flushed my cheeks as Gannet's hands had, along with the feathery touch of his breath. Adah rose and ash stirred. I did not taste Gannet's kiss then, only the fire I had started in the great hall, bitter soot and satisfaction. "But if you're interested in burdens, you may accompany Antares on his next task. It is south, and you can decide on the road if you wish to keep going or not."

"What is it?" I asked, wary.

"An icon has been born in a village south of here. Two, actually. After a fashion," Adah answered, eyes leveled on me in keen interest to gauge my response to his next words. His observation was cold, and I could penetrate nothing beneath his superficial curiosity. "With Jaken and Shasa dead, Alber has returned to us, in one vessel, this time."

The sickness I felt at his words had no root in Theba and was every bit my own.

"I'll go," I said quietly. The figures on the walls did not move but seemed to crowd me, to make demands where Adah would not. I imagined the mother who suckled the babe with my own mother's face. Even during war, even as a young girl, my troubles had never been more than misremembering the names of Shran's sons or the number of nights he passed dreaming of Jemae before she joined him in his bed. Deeds had been of less interest to me than stories, but Theba had taken from me any chance to live without questioning how her presence would taint my actions. She had done more than that already. In Jhosch, I had welcomed her, and I was not so foolish as to think she would be easy to be rid of. I could cut off my hands and still she would find a way to use me to ruin; she had given me an appetite for ruin.

Adah didn't comment, nor did anything about his posture betray his response to my decision to leave. He was a god of balance as well as of justice and would make no judgment until he had seen this thing, whatever it was, to its end. He looked toward the great door where, no doubt, Antares waited.

"You'll need to bring the mother."

His words drove my gaze again to the woman on the wall. I knew in an instant that she, like the mothers of so many icons before her, had been blinded, that Antares himself had done such things. In Adah's mind, I saw a low fire, treated wood burning hot, herbs boiled in water whose scent was meant to calm those awaiting the blinding bath. I imagined that Antares regarded these things with brute necessity, that a small part of him was sorrier for the nurses who must be blinded, and not for the mothers who went willingly for a few months more with their children. There were other measures for those who could not, or would not, let go of a treasured son or daughter. For them, I was sure Antares felt no more pity than he would have for a foundered horse.

"There will always be more children, but only one icon," I whispered, feeling more alone than I had since those first few nights out of Jarl. Antares would protect me only for the immortal spirit my body housed.

And nothing else. No one else.

"I'll be in my cell."

CHAPTER THREE

The way to Adah's chamber was stranger the second time, the path wound tight as a curl on the head of a babe, crooked as the channel that birthed him. I moved with bare feet, trailing the ragged hem of my traveling gown, carrying in one hand the cup I had taken hours before. Even as I reached it, the door was not the same, for inside the symbol I had touched was now a beating heart. It was sticky when I touched it and reluctant to let go of my hand.

He was not alone inside. A filthy woman sat begging at his feet or seemed at first to be begging. But she was on her knees before him, his manhood filling her mouth, and I thought at first how strange it was to see him with so common an organ, so common a whore.

"Has it been so long since you had one of your own?" I asked, my voice sounding strange to my ears. It was coarse but musical, too, a wild, discordant dance that leaped from my belly to my tongue and called all to pitch themselves this way or that. The voice of a goddess.

Adah measured my words before he took measure of my tangled gown, hitched by my own hands at my sides. In the same instant that he thrust the woman away, he thrust into me.

Because I did not bleed, I knew in that moment that I was dreaming. I woke, nails raking down the cold stone of my cell wall as they had down his skin in the dream. But Adah had no flesh. He was one of the stars he had spoken of, but I was a god, too, and while I could feel his heat, I could not be burned up by it. I felt sick and uncertain, sure that Theba took advantage of the feelings Gannet had roused in me to turn my heart to these dark visions. She could only lust, never love. Wasn't that why she had hated Jemae so much?

24

And what was I to make of my racing heart? Was it hers, or mine?

The door to my cell remained closed, but I found myself checking my clothing, rubbing my face on a tattered sleeve, making sure now that my eyes were open in waking and wondering if the desire I had felt, fading now, had been Theba's. As a goddess, she had lain with many men, mortals and immortals alike, but I had not known a man and was in no hurry to allow her the privilege of using my body in such a way. Despite the tug of memory that was of Gannet's lips on mine, I wasn't sure I even wanted him to have the privilege.

Not that he would have the chance now, if I changed my mind.

Shaking as though to clear the dream and my heart, too, of want, I tried to sit up but found that I couldn't. My limbs were seized with heaviness of another kind as my perception shifted to see into the dark without even my needing to will it. What had been indistinct shadows now became the clear angles of the little cell, and a bundle half as long as I lay across my legs. With a shriek, I thrust my hands forward. I thought of plunging my hands into fur or worse, expecting Adah to be here. It was foolish, though, to think so, for the figure was much too small, and when it unfolded in sleepy agitation, the eyes of a child met mine without hesitation in the dark.

"He told me not to wake you," the child explained. There was nothing in the voice, the short, shaggy hair, or sleeping robe to indicate age or gender. "But he didn't say I couldn't wait for you to wake up. But then I fell asleep, too. When did you last bathe? You really smell."

The child was certainly younger than ten to be so candid. I smirked, too surprised for speech until I had extricated my legs from beneath the child's frame. It was much easier now that the child had risen, too, though I realized that the meeting of our eyes had been chance. The child looked now in my general direction, but her eyes roamed, or his did, without settling more than a few seconds on shoulder, brow, or face.

"It's been a while," I admitted. I could feel her discomfort, for I decided that she must be a she, so akin was her distress to the kind I had felt in my sisters when they had been girls. It was a naked feeling but certain, too, in a way the emotions of my brother had never been like those of a boy, more the stirring of cricket's legs than song. "Why did you want to wait for me?"

Brow furrowing in a fashion that was comical in a face so young, she drew three little fingers down her lips before answering.

"Adah sent me away and said that Theba had come, but I wanted to see. I don't think you look like her, though." She spoke swiftly, as though the words had longer legs than she and might outrun her. "My candle burned out, but I saw you first. You're not very pretty, or terrible."

"That explains why you fell asleep," I responded, and because she could not see my smirk in the dark, I continued in a lighter tone. "I'm Eiren. Who are you?"

"Emine," the girl returned instantly, though I could see her struggle no sooner than she had spoken. I felt the tender worries of the child snaking, like her limbs had, across my sleeping form. Her true name she buried, for she was an icon, just as I was, and had to learn to be only that, a lesson I would never master.

In tales, Emine bestowed beauty and good fortune upon those she favored and withheld them from those who displeased her. A heavy responsibility for a woman grown into such things, yet too much for a scrawny child.

"Well, Emine, perhaps you are partial to sitting in the dark, but I am not. If you take me somewhere warm and bright, I will say that it was I who found you."

I had no idea if Adah would punish her, or if her fierce temperament would even submit to such punishment, but she was on her feet in a moment's response. She didn't say anything about my neglecting to name her as an icon, nor my refusal to own Theba, but I was not sure if this was the churlishness of youth or something else. Being the youngest of my family, I had little experience with children, much less with child icons.

Only when we had traveled a little distance in the corridors did I realize how cold my cell had been, and how she might have moved nearer to me while sleeping just to keep warm. That she had been sleeping, too, suggested to me that it must be night, or whatever counted for night within this place.

"Why are you here?" In her question, I heard the incredulous curiosity of a child, not ignorance. Why should I, with all the power and faculties of an adult, choose to stay?

"I don't belong anywhere else anymore," I admitted after a long pause. We had arrived in a chamber I had not previously visited. It had none of the touch of Adah, the braziers more numerous and burning, with flames tinted gold, green, and blue, and the walls hung with woolly fabrics instead of painted ones. The furniture, too, was small and arranged haphazardly: many chairs were pushed together to simulate a caravan, a great canopy draped from four others that were placed back-to-back in a square. Was this Adah's notion of a nursery? I smiled, surprised at the ease of the expression, as Emine strode forward. She was lord in this place, at least, and not Adah.

Even as she settled before one of the green burning braziers, her features smoky in the haze of heat, my expression darkened. Had Gannet known this place? What of the icons of Theba who had outgrown their cradles?

I sat down beside Emine on a cushion.

"Where I come from, we tell stories," I began, finishing the sentiment in my head as I had come to understand it for myself: *when we cannot find the words to tell our own.*

Like most children, Emine's curiosity did not extend to those things that did not interest her, and she did not ask me where I was from. Instead, she did just as I had hoped.

"Tell me one."

It did not surprise me that one of Shran's histories should surface in my mind, his face as a child appearing nose first as though he broke through water. I had not told this particular story in some time, but it seemed appropriate, surrounded by the artifacts of childhood, to speak of the of the early years of a man whose own youth was often forgotten.

"As a boy, Shran often wanted a brother, and in his darkest moments, even a sister would have done. But he was born to his mother and father very late in their lives, and as they saw him grow only to his fourteenth birthday, he never had any brothers or sisters to keep him company and share in his mischief.

"Which is not to say that he did not have companions, of course. Before Theba laid claim to him, Shran was of interest to many gods and goddesses, and as the world then was young, there were some among them who were not yet done doing their own growing. Among them was the god Tirce, the mover of earth and stone."

Nothing in Emine's face changed to show that she knew the icon I had met in Jhosch, though I did not think that there was sufficient evidence to assume that the icons did not visit Adah, now and again. I suspected at least that Gannet had, and even as I warmed to the growing interest of the child before me, I wanted the attention of the man I had left behind. He had always been so cold when I had engaged him in storytelling, and I wondered now how much of that disinterest was built, stone by stony glance, to keep from growing too close to me.

"They met in a grove in the city of Re'Kether, which boasted as many wild things as it did the things that man had built. The trees were as tall as temples and the shallow pools as broad, beasts wandered without harness and the city's people didn't think to tame them. Though Tirce had assumed the guise of a young man, beardless but with many more seasons than the young Shran could boast of, he spotted the boy through a great fanned leaf and immediately shed the years that separated them.

"'Where goes the prince of Kether?' Tirce asked in the tenor of youth, stepping out from behind a tree and placing his hands on his hips. Shran was not to be daunted, and more than anything, hated to be recognized when he could not recognize in turn. No boy of ten would have failed to take advantage of the privileges his station allowed.

"'I may go where I like.'

"Tirce smiled. 'And so can I.'

"Not to be outdone and ignorant of whom he spoke with, Shran abused his power further.

"'If there is no road, my father will build one. Someday I will, too.'

"'If there is a mountain, I can move it.'

"Another boy might have conceded, but Shran was no mere boy. Mortal he might have been, but his temper was as stolid as the mountains Tirce claimed to move. Their foundations would have been easier to shake."

I wondered now how the fact that Shran was among the First People figured into this telling. It was not unlike stories to exaggerate the character of the mortal man or woman, but Shran had always been special. Like Salarahan, his importance was measured not only in the number of stories we told about him, in his own histories, but how he figured in ours.

"Determined not to be outdone, Shran dropped to his knees, gathering a clod of dirt as large as both of his hands clasped together.

"'You would have to be very strong,' he surmised, packing the clod tightly in his palms. 'But I know that it takes more than strength to build a kingdom, and I think it must be the same for mountains. Can you throw this without breaking it?'

"He passed the clod to Tirce, who accepted it with a smirk more befitting a boy than a god. Shran stepped back and watched as Tirce raised his arm high and hurled the clod of dirt, keeping it together through the force of his will. When it struck the hardened path through the grove and left an indentation rather than breaking apart, Shran knew at once who it was he had crossed paths with in the grove. The gods had never talked to him before, but it was not unheard of, in that time, to see them in their full glory."

"There were no icons?" Emine interrupted, relaxed from the

rigid posture she had taken at first, seduced by something other than the dark this time.

"I don't know," I admitted. "It was a very long time ago, and I did not know there were any such things as icons until I came to Ambar."

But I did not want to tell Emine that story. I would maybe never tell it to anyone. I considered instead what her education thus far had lacked, and I did not feel so sorry for the answers I still awaited. Why the gods had chosen to walk among us then as equals, and now possess us, I could not know. For all that Theba's presence had given me, this knowledge was not among her gifts.

"Instead of naming Tirce at once and admitting defeat, Shran gathered instead another clod of dirt, packing this one as tightly as he had the first. He considered it for a moment and then pulled a length of silk from his waist and bound it together. Without speaking or even acknowledging the god, Shran, too, lifted his arm as high and as confidently and hurled it as far as the god had done.

"'I do not need a god's power, but a man's mind, to achieve great things, Tirce,' the boy Shran exclaimed, naming the god, at last. Tirce laughed, beginning a friendship between a bold child and a curious god with the sound.

"That afternoon was the first of many where Tirce took a boy's shape, as long as it took Shran grow out of his, and together they built the range of mountains that separates the lands of Ambar and Aleyn. Shran would throw stones, earth, and herbs, and Tirce would shape them in the air to fit the horizon. Shran did not crave much for brothers once he had shown a god how to behave as one."

Emine's gaze was approving as I finished the story, satisfied as I had suspected she would be at a story that featured prominently the exploits of children, even if they were big as myths and not so small as she. I had enjoyed the telling almost as much as she had, and like the smile that had crept across my lips when we entered the nursery, I felt the heat in my heart that promised healing of another kind. In moments like this, I was a child again myself, the warmth of my mother's lap the whole scope of the world.

"Why are you here, Emine?"

She seemed surprised by my question, and without my skills, she could not read my meaning. Still, her answer was not without a gravity that many years cultivated.

"My mother and father put me out of the house and wouldn't let me in again," she said quietly, her brow and lips still as the brazier's edge while she contemplated. "The big man came for me when I was sleeping on the street and made me return all the things I had charmed from their owners."

Her victims would not have been unhappy to share, so persuasive could Emine be. That she had been abandoned surprised me more.

"The big man? Do you mean Antares?"

"I do not often give my name to children, for they will only forget it. And there are more important things to fill their minds with."

I sensed Antares only after he had spoken. Emine didn't start, but I did, turning like a guilty man facing his accuser. He was not looking at me, but at Emine, and if he came to lay punishment, it was upon her head and not mine.

With me he would not have dared.

"Emine, you should go."

I bristled at her dismissal, but her obedience was absolute. For having dared to come to me in the first place, she must have been lonely. Did Emine have no one but Adah, when Antares was not here? With whom did she play? What tender-handed guardian washed and combed her, comforted her when she woke from nightmares? Even if I had been allowed to stay here, if I had wanted to, I could not have provided for her in that way. Mine was not a tender nature, not anymore.

It was this knowledge that stayed my hand when she rose, that did not regret when her eyes remained fixed like a bird of prey upon an unwitting prize. She was a strong child and reminded me of all my sisters, as they had been, or perhaps as I had imagined them to be. Emine moved quickly past Antares and out the door without looking back.

He was left to contemplate me, then. When he spoke, his words were matter of fact, though his tone had none of Gannet's practiced coolness I had loathed and come to long for.

"You slept in your cell."

I nodded, wanting to close my eyes and see Gannet in his place, to be near enough to his face to touch the border between heat and coldness, where mask yielded to flesh. Still now I did not know how much he knew, but anything, anything withheld was unforgivable when I was driven to such horrors.

Or perhaps it was that I could not forgive myself, and so I must find a more comfortable target.

"Eiren, you don't have to follow me to recover Alber, if you don't want to."

What I wanted was to undo all that I had done, to whisk clean my steps as the sea had cleansed the sands in Cascar, as servants followed after travelers dragging sand down polished corridors in the palace when I was a child. Here I was, but in Jhosch I had been, and the Rogue's Ear, and Re'Kether, and my city, my Jarl, where my toddling feet had learned to walk from my mother's womb and away from her.

"Why do you call me by my name?" I asked. That he called me Eiren was an affectation, now, when I had parted from those the woman Eiren could rightly have called friends. Theba was not so lucky.

I felt in Antares none of the certainty in his dealings with me that he had possessed with Adah and with Gannet. I had not known then that I should have observed him, or perhaps I would have discerned his true master sooner.

"I thought it made you more comfortable," he answered, his own discomfort plain. Theba stirred within me, the hot crawling feeling I had come to think of as her influence creeping from somewhere near my heart but not my heart, across my skin, needling my eyes. She knew how she would order him, and in a moment

I did, too. I was compelled to close the distance between us as I had imagined I would a moment ago if it had been a different man before me. She sensed a new power in me, and she wanted to abuse it.

I was speaking before the words were fully formed upon my lips, as though someone else had planned them.

"I am forbidden the things that would make me comfortable," I said sinuously, the words slick as burning oil. I saw Antares as though through a filmy screen, felt as I did, sometimes, when I woke from dreams of falling to the fear that I was still. "My name is not among those things."

It was an uncanny sensation, to panic at what I did and revel in it in the same instant. I could not cry out or clutch at the little furniture to slow my progress toward him, and though my throat grew dry, it did not tighten against speech as it should have done. It was not like any possession of Theba that I had felt before, for there was none of my will in it, none of my wanting, and all of hers.

If Antares noticed the change in me, he gave no outward sign. With the control Theba had seized, my gifts had diminished, and I could read nothing behind the surface of Antares's features. Like a yoked creature, Antares hung upon the thread of the conversation he understood and did not take Theba's bait. Still I noted without wanting to the sculpture of his shoulders and his arms, unarmored now, in contrast with how I had always seen them in the caravan. He did not sweat, but the braziers that had cast their eerie glow on Emine's face touched his in strange colors, a supernatural sheen. Theba wanted to take him, and so she compelled me to.

"Adah commands me in *her* stead, Eiren," he returned, and I knew he did not speak of the mistress he had left sleeping in Jhosch. Theba did not even give me room to grieve the thought of Morainn, and if I would fight her, it would not be on that. The steps between Antares and me were every moment fewer. "If you would have me call you Theba, then I will."

Theba parted my lips, but I bit my tongue, hard, relishing the sharp pain, the coppery taste of blood. I thought of the story

that I had only just shared with Emine, of the boy Shran who had
defied a god with the ingenuity of mortality. It did not matter that
I knew now he was numbered among the First People. Did I not
descend from them myself? I was not Theba's plaything, though I
had become her vessel.

I felt Theba then turn her attentions to me, abandoning her
game with Antares in favor of eclipsing my will completely. It was
like being shrouded, buried underneath many carts of stone and
earth. I could not imagine how I must look to Antares, a woman
at war with herself, still as the grave. From the tips of my fingers
and toes to the crown of my head I felt her, pushing me down,
pushing me inside, like acid rained down on intruders. Our armies
had resorted to such tactics in the desert to protect us, carving out
discreet clefts in the stone to surprise the Ambarians with their
death. I had not seen it and was glad, for my imaginings now were
less painful for my ignorance.

Without a name to call me by, Antares said nothing but closed
the space I had prevented Theba from crossing and put a hand on
each of my shoulders as though to shake or steady me. The touch
subdued us both for an instant, and when my eyes focused on him,
they were in my control completely.

"When do we leave?" I asked hoarsely, shaking like a stringed
toy.

Antares seemed surprised by the question, though his thoughts
were quick to turn to the charge he had been given from Adah,
wherever they had been when Theba had been in control.

"Within days, if you wish it."

I looked past him to the doorway, surprised to see the quick
retreating heel of a small foot. What had Emine observed that I
had not?

"I wish it."

True to his word, Antares moved to do my bidding and ensure
our hasty departure.

CHAPTER FOUR

Emine wanted to come with us. She begged me when she came to me again in the night and even when I ushered her out again in the morning. The pattern repeated itself the following night and day, though she paused in her pleading for stories to share her meals with me, her playthings, little details of her life in Adah's refuge. There were no other children here, and her loneliness was palpable.

But she couldn't come with us, though it hurt me to tell her no. I felt a kinship with her, her reluctance and uncertainty at her lot in life. But once we had passed out of the refuge, I had more to occupy my mind.

I marveled at the trees now more than I could have when I had wandered madly from Jhosch. I wondered over their variety and their profusion, their surfaces peeling parchment, veined and vainly colored, filtering light in wild patterns my feet could not follow. When we had traveled across Ambar to Jhosch, there had not been trees like these. What forests we had encountered had been well-tended or mere groves, thinned over time with the industry of the Ambarian citizens. Adah had chosen for his domain a wild place, and it was wildest of all to me, who had known nothing like it in the deserts of Aleyn. The deeper into the wood we went, the more I grew used to the tangled spread of bare, crooked branches. They reminded me of the lacework stone in Jhosch, and I wondered if the spaces there had not been made to reflect the strange chaos here.

Antares was no more at home in the woods than I, though he was unburdened by my whimsy and idled without appreciating the beauty of his surroundings as I set our lazy pace. I wondered that Theba did not attempt to seize me again as we spent first one and then night after night by firesides reminiscent of the one I had shared with Kurdan and Gannet in the Rogue's Ear. There was no intimacy in our dealings, however, and the Dread Goddess staked no claim when the cold light and rustling leaves distracted me.

When I heard singing on the fifth day, I knew it was not Antares. The voice was neither male nor female, nor did it sound even like *one* voice. Like precious stones tumbled in a barrel, it promised sweetness and grit in the same note, and Antares met my eyes in shared alarm. He raised a hand as though to stop me, but I strode ahead.

The trees thinned ahead but only just, finger-thin branches shearing the sky into pale scraps. The clearing, if it could be called that, looked as though a great beast had come tunneling through, disturbing the soil and the sparse moss that prospered on the forest floor. I saw no one, but I hadn't imagined the singing and was rewarded after a moment's patience with the dull blade of a shovel breaking above the surface of the soil, loosening a great cascade of moist earth, and dipping down again. My unpracticed steps, loud in the wood, caused a furrowed brow to surface next, smeared with dirt and boasting eyes sharper than the shovel's blade. Two more brows and pairs of eyes followed, the three figures like a many-headed creature emerging from its warren.

"Linger here too long and if you are not dead, you will be soon."

It was an uncanny voice, one of the singers, with many depths even alone. I did not know if he threatened me or posed a riddle, though if the latter, I was sure some threat would follow a wrong answer. It was Antares who was roused to action by the speech, having followed me into the clearing despite his reluctance.

"We serve as you do," he said with a soldier's caution. The three in the pit observed him openly, though he tried pointedly not to look upon them, and I sensed some knowledge between them that I was not privy to. Antares knew their business here, and they guessed at his. Only when the smallest of them braced one hand against the lip of the pit and steadied another on a bronze urn balanced at its edge, did I know, too.

Four graves there were, and dozens were dead in Jhosch. Who else but icons would be buried in this secret place? Paivi. Jaken and Shasa. And who was the fourth?

"Who is it you bury here?" I asked, wondering if a daughter of the royal court would earn such a privilege in death.

"Erutal we have buried," said one, rising fluidly as a pillar of fleshy smoke.

"And Alber to either side of him, divided in rest as he was in life," said another, angling his way out of the grave with the shovel he gripped still. These I knew, but who was the last? I held my breath as the first man opened his mouth to speak again, his eyes locked with mine. He might not have recognized me, but he recognized in me some power he must submit to. And so, he did.

"Dsimah we return last to the world that she loved, for she was the last to leave it."

Dsimah should not have been there, either. Not at the opera, and not in this grave. Still, I was relieved it wasn't Morainn.

"What business can a deserter and a childless woman have here?" the first man asked, looking from Antares to me. Antares was insulted, but he struggled to keep it from me, and there was no sign that the men could see. "You have no armor, but your clothes and body show the signs of its wear. And as for you"—the man fixed his attention full upon me, his eyes joined with those of the other two men in the same eerie motion—"only mothers come here to be rid of their children, and many years later we bury them."

"Sometimes not so many," said the second man, the quietest of the three with a voice deep as a drum.

"I am no deserter," Antares said, at last. There was contempt in his voice, and contempt in the three before us. They didn't feel right, though, not completely real. I found myself picking at their thoughts, drawing them out one by one like threads in a tale.

"They do more than bury the dead," I reasoned, seeing the

little span of each man's life as bland and colorless as undyed wool. "They cannot leave this place, this garden of the dead. They will die here, too, and there will be no one left to bury them."

The first man stepped forward, lips pulled nearly to his ears in a grimace. The other two advanced, as well, and as their eyes and heads had seemed before to move as one, their legs did, too.

"It is said that every tree in this wood has its roots in the body of a dead icon," he recited, but his was not a voice for telling stories. "When we take them, they have already been carried a great distance by those who would blind themselves before looking upon us. Our gaze is said to weave the first stitches of a burial shroud on all who see us."

"I wish I had found you when I still wanted to die," I replied, my voice braided with Theba's will, and my own. "But now you threaten me at your peril."

Antares might have longed for a spear, but I had no need of such implements to defend myself. The three had stopped moving, but they stood close together now, behind them the soft, fresh graves of men and women whose lives had been only half-lived. What sorts of ghosts would Jaken and Shasa be, twinned in life but separated in death? If the essence of the icon traveled on, what of the man or woman who had been only vessel to it?

"More are coming," said the second, following my eyes to the graves. "And we are behind in our work."

"We are at war," said the third, looking down. The second man looked up, and the first looked right at me. "There are some who follow Theba, others who will be struck down by her. Many we will see here again, and soon. The faithless who remained behind will never find rest here."

"There is no such thing as rest here," I said, feeling again the anger building in me that another presumed to do what I could not do, what I would not do. I refused to acknowledge the insanity of it. The imposter incensed Theba, and her outrage threatened to overwhelm me.

"Not for you," they said together, each man's voice ringing a little in my ears, words reverberating. Their next words sounded again like a recitation, like some formal charge. Two of the three held out their shovels, high as torches. "And not for her."

They wrenched the struggling form of a small girl from the pit. I had thought she seemed small in the nursery, but she was infinitely smaller now, gagged and bound, though she fought the creature that held her. Had she followed us? Or had they produced her to torture me?

"Those touched by the gods can only serve or perish."

The one who held Emine put a hand over her face and she went still. I no longer sensed her terror. Where their eyes had been were shadows now, their hair parting to reveal spiders spinning the cottony lines of their aged faces. They were not men, and neither did I recognize them from some horrible tale told in the dark to scare children. I believed the three terrible creatures before us had more root in Ambarian lore than anything Aleyn would record and retell.

"I am already bound against my will," I said quietly. "And she would no more serve here than I would, I think."

It was not Emine whom I meant, but they could not know that. I did not want to touch that place again, the hot dark inside me where flames licked forever at memory, heart, and mind. But I knew there was no alternative. My body was weak, and Antares's was not made to combat such creatures. The winter litter of loose soil and snapped branches at my feet began first to smoke and then to shrivel, while orange tongues of fire forked as they raced away from me and toward the three figures.

They could not show surprise or horror of their own, but all three withdrew several paces, and I struggled to keep the fire from pursuing them to whatever end such creatures could have. I did not want to hurt Emine, only to drive them off, compel them to leave the girl and save themselves. Even as I felt I must lose the battle, Theba's passion as inevitable as water to a boil, one of the creatures ignored his fellows and stepped forward into the fire.

I was transported. I felt him burning up, so dry and thin as kindling that flares before a true fire can be built on its eagerness. I saw him as he was now, no more human than so many twists of paper, and I saw him as he had been: a young man, not handsome but strongly built, with good teeth and deep-set eyes. They were blue, and I saw them fill with tears too many for his years as this punishment had been laid upon him. This was his past, the foul deed that had secured this unnatural future. For the murder of an icon, he would toil until the world was new, serving the dead, hardly more than dead himself. Adah had laid this sentence, but he was not the Adah that I knew. So many hundreds of years had passed that this creature did not remember how it had come to be, or he would never have dared to speak to us.

The fire alone would not be enough to consume him, but I sensed that I had the power to release him, to give him his final rest. I hesitated, but when I felt no urge from Theba to return him to the world or let him go, I did what I would have done well before I had been touched by her influence.

I showed compassion.

There was nothing left of his body but ash, and the two creatures who remained kicked it up in their haste to retreat, dropping Emine as carelessly as a bundle of sticks. The fire retreated, too, and I raced to Emine's side.

Her skin was slick and cold, but I felt the fine mist of her breath on my fingers when I held them beneath her nose. The beat of her heart was slow but steady. She did not rouse, not even when Antares lifted her from the ground, but at least she lived.

"What was she doing out here?" I asked, irritated at what was easy: a child found where she was not meant to be.

"Emine is headstrong," Antares replied after a moment, his mind reeling still, his eyes darting from here to there as though he expected the men to appear again. He did not look at the ash, though his boots tracked it away when he began to walk with Emine in his arms. It was my turn to follow. Though I was hardly eager to linger, I didn't know what was ahead, what else to expect in the wood. I watched the limp bob of Emine's head against Antares's arm and concealed my shaking hands in my skirt.

"I didn't believe the stories," Antares said after a moment, his words expelled on a breath I imagined he had been holding since the first tendrils of smoke escaped the hem of my skirt. "In all my years traveling here, I have never seen the widow makers."

I shook a trail of ash from my skirt, leaving the cold marks upon the leaves like snow.

"Why are they called that?"

"They are the fathers of icons," Antares said. "Rather than have their children taken from them, they kill them, or hide them, or whatever desperate fancy strikes them."

It was clear Antares had thought this no more than a story, or, at the very least, he had thought of it in the way I had done about many of the stories I had told throughout my life: this was the way of the world long ago, when great, impossible miracles and tragedies alike were possible.

"I am surprised that there are only three," I whispered, and Antares shot me a dark look.

"It's a big forest."

I looked back over my shoulder on the graves, not afraid, now, but hollowed out by sadness.

"For people who worship as you claim to, it seems there are a great many of you who prefer your gods in stories and not in life," I said.

"There has always been unrest," Antares explained, beginning to walk the perimeter of the grove. There was no sign of the other two creatures, but his posture remained guarded. Emine was hardly a burden to him—no doubt that would change when she woke up. "But there is no point to it anymore, now that you are here."

"Whom do you think they spoke of, when they spoke of the faithless?" I asked as we exited the grove and the trees closed around us again.

"I'm not sure," he admitted, and I glanced at his face, confirming what I heard in his tone. The climate in the city when he had left had been one of turmoil, and he could not predict what course things had taken without leadership, with icons dead and the imposter heralding war. As though he could read my thoughts in turn, Antares continued, "I suppose there are some who imagined that these days would never come, or they would not live to see them. If they resist the tide of the world as it is written, they will have to abandon their faith."

When he spoke of resistance, he was not thinking of those who had taken us all by surprise at the opera. The rebellious murderers had never claimed to believe, but perhaps there were icons, like the gentle Dsimah, were she not already dead, who would not have wished to carry Theba's banner.

"I don't want to be buried here anyway," I insisted. I had never imagined much of my life beyond the bosom of my family, and though I had already traveled far and forgotten many of the comforts I had once believed I could not live without, the idea of even my place of final rest being decided for me was unbearable. I wanted the desert to reduce my bones to sand, my blood to pool for birds and dune mice to drink.

"It is an honor," Antares began, but I did not let him continue. Battling Theba had left me little patience for anything else.

"What, to be remembered only as one in a long line of many? To lie forever where no one can mourn you? I have never wanted this. Or didn't they tell you that?"

It was growing dark. With the fading light went my energy and so too a measure of the control I had over Theba. I was sure that she would take me in the night and direct me as though I were a sleepwalker. Perhaps she would distract me with some pleasant dream, or perhaps the dream would be of her deeds, and I would be forced to watch.

Only when we had exhausted the light, though, did Antares stop. He claimed that we were close enough to the village now that tomorrow we would pillow our heads upon down instead of earth. Though I made her a comfortable pallet, still Emine did not stir, and I fought not to panic when the little water I poured into her mouth dribbled out again.

While Antares dug a pit for the fire made necessary by the cold but so small that it did little more than keep us from freezing to death, I thought of other fires, other camps, of Gannet. I thought of the rain that had delayed us in Ambar, when we had huddled together, telling stories. My ignorance then had been a blessing, for all my troubles had seemed many. It was worse now. I could not forgive him and perhaps would not even admit my longing to him if it had been he who kindled the fire now, but he would've done it differently, and maybe I would have surprised us both. Shadows descended that were cast neither by the trees nor by Antares as we crouched on opposite sides of the fire. The flame caught our thoughts and burned them up, his for fuel and mine for ash, muting the light and heat. Emine lay on one side, her chest rising and falling in regular breath.

"I saved Imke from the sea in Cascar," Antares said, surprising me from my reverie. The fire was very low and lengthened the shadows from his brow and nose, obscuring his eyes completely. "She was drowning. Rogan helped drag Morainn ashore, and Triss was able to swim on her own. I swam out to meet Imke, and she thanked me for saving her life."

He did not say what it was about this that hurt him, but I knew it all the same. He had saved her, and she had gone on to take many innocent lives. Whether she had done it with her own hands or not didn't matter. She was a heretic and had schemed with heretics.

"But you don't wish you hadn't," I urged, and now he looked up at me, his features sharpened by the movement. "You are a good man, Antares. You should not regret that."

"I would have thought that you would feel my failure more keenly," he said, and I felt again the thrill from Theba, the delight in torturing me when there was the opportunity for a moment to become intimate. She blurred the lines between what was real and what wasn't, tried to show me what I wanted to get.

"Haven't I shown that I wouldn't?" It was a struggle to speak the words, but I did so through my teeth. My senses grew in potency, and Antares's scent filled my nostrils as fully as the fire and the chill-stripped trees. He crossed to me and opened his pack, removing rations enough for us both and pressing a small tin pot for tea into the earth where the fire was catching. Not looking at me, he filled it with clean snow that quickly began to melt.

"I know it has been a struggle for you, Eiren. But you have been given a gift many would give their lives to possess."

Many had. I caught my lip between my teeth to keep from speaking or worse. I was reminded of Shran's histories, of Theba's lust for a mortal man. I had never thought of questioning it, and it had made no sense when I had first heard it and made even lesser sense with every telling. But I felt her compulsion in me now, sharp as the bite of hunger. I was sure I had never been so starved. Even as I thought of Gannet, she used my own senses against me.

"You speak out of ignorance," I said, willing my senses to root, to ignore what she tried to do. I would not move to him; she could not make me.

"I speak out of *reverence*," Antares insisted, and now he was near and my restraint made no difference. Instead of his scent, I could smell now the heady perfume of exotic flowers paired with brazier smoke. The light was by turns moonlight and firelight, but it was the green light of the fires that had burned in the theater the night of the opera, when heat had poured off Gannet's body and into mine. And so it was now that I imagined him, too warm to be the stone his expression too often promised. Theba used my hands to reach for Antares, feeling not his coarsely spun shirt but the smooth plane of Shran's chest bared to a balmy night. Even as my lips parted to protest, I felt Gannet's tongue and Shran's teeth, and I ached from toes to crown to be with the one that I had abandoned.

But I had abandoned him. He wasn't here, and I wasn't there anymore, with him. I would never again have that brief moment that I shared with him in the opera box. Rejecting Theba meant I must reject him, too.

My moan was one of frustration. I opened my eyes, not realizing that I had closed them, and beheld Antares looking at me strangely from across the fire. Had he even moved? What had I last heard that was true? Theba's power over me was greater by the hour, and she had found a way to bend me to her will, at last. I was sick at the destruction we wrought together but felt something else entirely in our desire.

"Is that tea? Can I have some? Is there food, too?"

Emine's head lifted from the ground, hair in untidy peaks, eyes sunken but sharp.

"Emine," I said, rising and bundling the blanket that had slipped from her shoulders more tightly around them. She grinned at me, offering no explanation for why she had been in the wood. I was so grateful for her interruption I didn't even care. "There's plenty to eat."

"Not a bite until you tell me what you're doing out here," Antares growled. Obviously, I was the only one feeling generous.

"I followed you." Emine's eyes dodged ours, following Antares's hands now as he poured tea into two small cups, pointedly avoiding filling a third. "And then I got lost. That was when the bad men found me."

I didn't feel any dishonesty from her, but neither did I feel like we'd been given the whole story.

"Did they say anything to you?" I asked. "Did they try to hurt you, before we came?"

She shook her head. "They didn't talk to me at all. Just tied me up and started—started digging a hole."

Antares didn't need my gifts to feel her fear. Though he remained tight-lipped, he passed her a cup with an admonition that it was still hot. Perhaps because she was young, all her thoughts were all bobbing urgently on the surface: relief, curiosity, will. If there was anything she wasn't telling us, it was crowded out by the mundane reality of being small, scared, and hungry.

I squeezed her shoulder lightly before returning to my pallet. Though Emine's presence was an unnecessary complication, I was glad she was there. She smiled at me over her cup.

"Tell me a story before bed?"

It was my turn to smile.

"Of course."

CHAPTER FIVE

By late afternoon of the next day, well before the sun began its descent, we came upon a village situated at the edge of the wood. The trees here were sparsely needled, and those with bare branches were planted in ordered rows: an orchard. We were no longer under *Zhaeha's* influence, then.

Still, it was the smallest and poorest Ambarian settlement I had seen. The dwellings were squat and could be distinguished from the forest only in shape, built from thatch, wood, and mud. Though it was so cold that I imagined I would not leave the fireside if I had any choice, there were many villagers out of doors working, and in the case of the village children, deep in elaborate play. They eyed Emine warily and she them, in the way unfamiliar children will in the moment before they have decided to be enemies or friends. Hardly anyone else seemed at first to notice us until a young man, sweating at a forge, ceased his hammering to come out and greet us. Even this seemed more in response to his desire for a break than any real interest in our presence.

Antares, however, had no interest in diverting the man.

"A babe was born here recently, to a mother who has seven others. Where does she live?"

The young man pointed down the dirt track that served as the village's main thoroughfare, but his eyes did not leave Antares's face. "She has late flowers blooming beside the door," he clarified. His eyes glossed quickly over Emine, over me. "Do you mean the child harm?"

His question did not matter one way or another, but I sensed what response Antares gave would determine whether or not this man would find a way to warn the woman of our approach.

"We mean him great honor," Antares replied curtly. He had what we needed, and he turned from the man, dismissing him.

We began to walk, our footfalls firm and certain on this beaten lane, so different from the treacherous paths we had taken in the wood. I wondered if our actions would make a widow maker of this woman's husband, a man to take the place of the one I had willfully freed. Would Antares return him by force to Adah, as well? I trusted in his physical strength and his strength of will, but perhaps not his ability to deliver an infant and a grown man without incident.

"What happens to the mother, when her babe is weaned?" I asked suddenly, feeling shameful for having only just now considered her fate. I eyed Emine, who looked gloomily away. Did she wonder about her mother?

Antares did not appear to share any of my concern or my guilt. "She will return here, to her life," he answered, taking my arm to guide me around an icy patch in the road. He offered Emine no aid, but she hopped deftly over. I felt the sturdiness of his convictions in that grasp as well as his desire that I should share them. "I know it must seem strange to you, this task. But I assure you, it is necessary. Don't you wish you never had to know all you would be leaving behind? Your life would be much easier now."

He believed what he was saying and would not understand the vehement horror that filled my mind at the idea of never knowing all that had made me who I was. I had wondered many times what Gannet would have been like had he been raised to the self I knew he possessed and kept hidden, but never had I considered what I would be without it. Theba had the power to seize control from me now. She would have known absolute power if I had not some will to resist her.

"I haven't lost anything that I have left behind," I said quietly as we reached the hovel. "I do not think this child's ignorance to be a blessing, but a curse."

Emine snorted at our exchange.

"You both talk a lot about things you can only guess at," she said, her little voice hot with feeling. Antares ignored her. His attentions were still on me, and I thought for a moment he would argue me to reason as Gannet might have, but it was not his place to convince me of anything. Gannet would have fought me, and I would have been secretly thrilled in fighting back, but Antares had only the will to serve. I felt my resolve harden and the flame of irritation gutter before springing higher, hotter. Even as Antares reached to knock upon the flimsy door, I laid a hand upon his arm.

"Did you know that I killed Kurdan?" I said, searching his face as the confession left my lips. "He attacked me and I killed him. If I'd never known my life before Theba, I would not have regretted taking that man's life, or any other."

Antares's face was as open and guileless as a pool of still water.

"Is that really what you want? To be sorry every time you do something you must?" Antares returned after a lean moment, the words pulled like a thread from a hem. There were many more where those had come from, but the door was opening and I let go of his arm, turning my attention to the young woman framed there. She looked too young by far to have so many children, but they clustered around her like hens in a yard. She cradled the smallest to her breast.

Alber.

I realized I did not know how this was done, if she knew who we were or why we were here. I braced myself for her surprise and her horror, but even as Antares opened his mouth to speak, she hefted the child irritably to her shoulder.

"Cries night and day he does, and no one to help me with him." Her speech was rough around the edges, more than I was used to in Ambar and more even than that of the young man who had greeted us. "But I had a dream you would come. I'm only sorry you haven't got a use for any of the others."

Her coarseness was too much for me to bear, and I could not disguise my look of distaste. The woman's eyes traveled down my frame, the soiled traveling dress that would nevertheless seem a fine thing compared to her garb and the scraps that passed for clothing on her many children.

"I can tell you haven't got any, or you wouldn't be making that face." She coughed and wiped a filthy hand between her mouth and nose. As Antares stepped within, the children drew back, each one finding a shadow to retreat to, the largest of them receding to the large, sagging bed, the only piece of furniture the woman's home boasted. Antares didn't spend much time looking around, though he spared a smile for the children before reaching into the pouch at his waist and withdrawing a second, smaller pouch. This one jingled, and that had everyone's attention.

"There will be more when you return," he said, and even the youngest of the children, a girl who could have been no more than four, knew what he referred to. "And for the expense of seeing that your other children are cared for."

The woman's eyes narrowed, and I did not have to look too deeply to know what she thought. Her oldest child had work, enough for the children to live meanly for the months she would have to remain away. But she had no intention of telling Antares that. She looked down at the babe, who had begun to fuss and squirm, and I followed her gaze back and back to his conception, to the little purse of coins that had bought a night in her bed and six months of hard looks from the other women in the village. But now she had a prize, though it was what the child would provide her, not the child itself.

If I were an infant and so unwanted, I would not need to be Alber's icon to be unhappy.

"I'll make arrangements for the children," she said, but what I heard was her desire to run and gloat to a neighbor. She took the infant with her and left me and Antares in her home, with her children, whose eyes had not followed their mother's departure. How many times had they been left alone? Did they like it better without her? My parents had five children altogether and had more love for each than even the resources of a kingdom could rival.

"Come and hear a story of your baby brother," I said suddenly, crossing the little distance to the middle of the small room the whole family seemed to share, dropping to my knees on the brushed dirt floor. I held out my arms, for a moment thinking that they would not come, but when they did, I noted Emine's dark head among them. I imagined Esbat and Lista each on a knee as they had done with my mother, Jurnus sprawled just out of reach but close enough to place one finger upon my leg if he needed to remind me that he was there, too. Anise would kneel, stately, beside me and a little behind, as though she were too old for such things but loved them still.

"There was a man who made his fortune making houses. He built little cottages for men and women who were only just married, constructed temples to house the faith of an entire village, and made shop fronts to shelter their dreams of wealth. Later, he would return to the newly married couple to build extra rooms when they expected one, two, and three children, and to the villages when they gave up their gods and needed homes for new ones.

"But his greatest work was the palace he was asked to design and build for the king. He exhausted an entire forest of timber and a quarry of precious stones before it was finished. The king was so impressed that he took the carpenter into his dearest confidence. A house for him was a fine thing, but what he needed most, what he desired most of all, was a house fit for the thing he loved best: his pet rabbit, Slippers."

They giggled now and it was a musical thing, brightening the corners of the dreary little cottage. The rafters rang with it, and I let them go on longer than I would have my own siblings.

"The carpenter was puffed with pride at being given so great a task. A house for a king was one thing. Many before him had made such things. But a house for a rabbit? This was a challenge he relished.

"But it was not as easy as the carpenter had hoped it would be. Would the rabbit prefer a hutch? An elaborate burrow? A miniature of the palace that matched that of his master? Each stone he laid dissatisfied him, and he would tear it out of the mortar again. The wood he cut was always crooked and ended up in a pile to be burned. The fine tiles he shaped and sanded for the little roof were never the right color, the right thickness, the right weight, and he grew so mad with anger that he threw them on the ground and stomped upon them in the street.

"He began to build with other things. He snatched laundry from the line when servants, husbands, and wives weren't looking and staked a frame in the mud to hang the flimsy walls upon it. From a farmer's garden, he rolled an entire patch of pumpkins for the floor and sheaves of corn for the roof. The sorry family whose clothes he had stolen had to dress themselves in the ash from the carpenter's fires when he grew sick of his imperfect work, and the farmer feasted on discarded stones. Still the carpenter worked day and night, building and breaking down again until the law of his village dragged him before the king for thievery and madness.

"The king was surprised to see him so bedraggled, dirty, and weary. 'What has happened to you, friend?' the king asked. 'You left here a rich man with the trust of your king and important work to do. Why have you not done it?'

"The carpenter's head hung low. He had failed the king, and he had failed Slippers, too. He lay himself prostrate on the fine floor he had tiled for the king himself. As he lowered his face to the ground, he saw it skewered between two reflective tiles: on one side, brilliance, and on the other, creativity. Two faces. Two possibilities.

"The carpenter looked up at the king.

"'I beg you cleave me in two, so I might live to do your bidding.'

"The king could not for a moment speak, so taken aback was he by such a strange request. But the carpenter was desperate.

"'Take your sword and split me or I shall die!'"

Shudders from the children followed my words, along with the necessary gesture that accompanied the story: a single finger drawn from nose to navel.

"Even as the king was ready to commit the carpenter to a cell to await a more appropriate punishment, one among his guard took pity on the madman, who was now writhing in a fury on the floor. He crossed to him and struck him square in the belly with his spear. Everyone in the court shrieked, the king included, but the wound did not bleed. Instead, like the many legs of a sand crab scuttling, four arms and four legs issued forth from the carpenter's belly, followed quickly by two stout bodies and two heads, eyes bright in faces that were whole, unharmed, and identical.

"Two carpenters stood now before the king, a god released from a mortal prison. Both bowed and smiled in perfect harmony.

"'I am Alber,' they said together. 'Our gift was too great for one mind to manage, but two shall make it greater still without the sorry cost.'

"And now the king did finally speak, though his shock was most profound.

"'That is a very good thing, for Slippers has been busy, too. I now require a home not only for him but also for his twelve children: Boots, Belt, Bangles, Breeches, and Buttonhole, Pockets, Gloves, Lace, and Sandal, Ribbons, Rosettes, and Shoe.'"

But the children didn't laugh as my siblings had always done, because as I finished, their mother appeared in the doorway. Alber slept fitfully in a sling across her chest. She was not smiling, and Antares was quick to usher me out. The children were sluggish to lift themselves from the floor, to scatter from each other and part from me. Still I thought of Emine as I looked on her dark head, Emine who had crawled guilelessly to me in sleep. I thought of the infant Alber, who did not deserve to grow up without his mother's love, even a mother like this one. I thought of the infants whose deaths had driven Theba to my homeland, to me. I could do nothing for any of them. My gifts were for undoing.

Like silk-spinning spiders, the children trailed their mother's hem to the edge of the village. The infant Alber squalled when he woke in the sling, beating ineffectually at her breast. I believed the children would have followed her until the road disappeared into the wood, all animal tracks and beaten leaves, but Antares would not let them.

"Your mother will return in the spring. Go back to the village." His tone was not unkind, but neither could his command be ignored. The children wavered. It was not a filial longing that I felt in them, but the helplessness of abandonment, of not knowing anything else, let alone anything better. I had no more stories, nor coin or food or comfort of the kind I had refused to take from my own family when I had departed Jarl, and it pained me.

So they turned back, and I turned away, not wanting to watch their sorry heads bobbing in retreat. Antares looked back over his shoulder, not at the children, but at me.

"If you wish to go south when this is done, I will lead you," he said softly, falling in step with me. I sensed the mother's interest in our conversation but her ignorance, too. She couldn't hear us over the infant's cries. "There's a quicker way that a larger force cannot take, but the terrain is treacherous."

"Why would you do that?" I asked. I couldn't read him: his mind was slippery, the answer caught only by his lips and tongue.

"I was there when you left Aleyn. I should be there when you return."

When, not if. Was Antares as sure as Adah was, about how I would make up my mind? If I didn't go and the imposter's army obliterated my home rather than simply subduing it, if they found this weapon and I was not there for them to use it—I would be safe. I could flee somewhere they could not find me. I could remain Eiren.

But I knew there was a cost. And both Adah and Antares knew I'd be unwilling to let anyone else pay it.

"Thank you," I responded stiffly, neither agreeing to go, nor refusing his offer of help. It would do, for now.

We had not gone far when I began to sense something and wondered if one of the children had followed us. I felt excitement and swallowed feelings that at first I attributed to a child who aimed to sneak after us. Alber had ceased crying, rocked again to sleep by his mother's walking. I wondered briefly what name she had given him, what name he'd never grow to know. We had fallen into a marching pattern, with the woman in the middle, between me and Antares, with Emine racing excitedly ahead. My skin prickled as though damp, the chilly wind picking up hairs and causing pimples on my arms. Not one but many minds, now, furtive. There were no leaves crunching underfoot to announce them, no whispers or hushed breaths, and even as I stopped and turned about slowly to discover them, they were upon us.

They wore hoods of rough cloth or rags over their mouths and noses, poor and useless disguises. There were so many, more than a dozen, and they came at us from all sides. Two of them seized Emine, her shrieks quickly muffled. I stumbled back into the arms of another pair, their thoughts a giddy barrage. They meant to take us alive—or tried to. Alber began to cry again, and though I heard no shout from Antares, there was the sound of a spear shaft striking against flesh, a groan as the point met some mark.

I struggled, but I was held fast by many pairs of arms. Months ago, I would have considered such force excessive, but now, as I felt the hot blood of Theba pump from my heart to hands and feet that itched to scratch, burn, and kick, I knew it was necessary.

Another groan was heard, this time accompanied by the juicy thrust of a blade into a belly. My ears closed against all sounds but that of Antares's knees as they dropped to the path. The fists that held my arms felt like so many vices upon my heart, and my last breath expelled a sob against the gloved palm that snaked over my mouth and nose. My hands were pinned, ropes biting into my flesh. The infant's cries subsided and in their place, I heard the mother's voice.

"You can have the babe and these three when I have the coin you promised me."

My body was overrun then. I tore at my attackers, my bindings, myself. I felt my nails shred leather, pierce the soft flesh beneath, heard the screams and only just kept from digging organ-deep. They ran. They should've run faster.

One had fallen in the struggle, another lay bleeding at my feet. His eyes locked with mine and he only whimpered, not even attempting to escape. He had no hope of it, not once I'd laid eyes on Emine's broken form, on Antares sprawled, not moving, beside her. His eyes were open in shock, weapon still in his hand.

I took a deep breath, closing my eyes. The sobbing fool in the dirt could not hurt me, but the memory of their crumpled bodies could, blazing behind my eyelids. I could have chased the others, should have, perhaps, especially if they were taking the child away. But I found myself rooted to the spot, crippled by the thought that he would be in greater danger with me than he was with the heretics, for that was what they were. When I opened my eyes again, I saw the ugly touch of fire upon the man's neck, the skin waxy and seeming to run down below his collar. He had been in the opera house. He had survived when so many had died.

"If you're here," he wheezed, voice reedy with a hollowness that precipitated death. His question burst madly from a shattering mind: "Who is the v-v-viper at the head of the Ambarian army?"

I took two steps forward, more fearful of the stillness I felt, the coldness in my belly, than I had been of the heat that had consumed me only a moment before. I bent and delicately brushed a lock of Emine's hair from her face. She didn't stir. I choked down my grief and my rage.

"That is a question you and I both would like an answer to."

Theba and I spoke together, a buzzing on my lips as though someone had placed a thread there and was attempting to whistle through it. I seized the heretic with the strength of my will and Theba's, too, sustained his life, prolonged his pain so that he might give us both what we wanted.

"What do you know about the imposter?" The words were mine and so was my tongue, but the drive to speak was Theba's. So too was her fury pounding against the walls of my heart, threatening to burst the organ and my body, both. "You say she leads an army. How many follow her?"

The man looked as though his lungs had been deflated and

filled again with sand instead of the air that would sustain him. His voice had more than a little gravel in it when next he spoke.

"Very little," he wheezed, tongue scraping against dry lips. "She does not have the support of the whole kingdom but a great part of it. There are other icons who march with her, but it is impossible to know if they are being coerced."

"What of the princess? What has happened to Morainn?"

"Many say that she is dead. Others say that she is wounded and disfigured and will not leave the palace for shame. All I know is that she hasn't been seen."

His words created a cold well in the pit of me that I felt myself falling into. I had not only regret but shame, too, for I had done this and could never be forgiven for it.

Especially not by Gannet.

Like a toy that no longer had the power to entertain me, I released the hold I had upon the man. He heaved a great breath, and it was clear to us both that it was likely to be his last. I heard a distant shout, the crashing of many booted feet, and sensed the fools that were returning to claim their dead. I could not add to their number, would not. I ran. Away from his slain fellows, I flew. Away from Emine. Away from Antares.

Antares. Every syllable of his name was cold as a blade driven into some soft part of my being. In Aleyn, noble men and women were interred in great crypts with their ancestors, all of them on their bellies so that they might take the shortest course through the world and to the rest that lay in soil, stone, and sand. I could neither bury Antares nor offer him tribute. I had hardly known him well enough to know what sorts of gifts he would like to be remembered with, not spears or leathers, I realized, for these were only the ornaments of his duty. He had been more.

I expected at any moment to find myself at the village again, to relive the taking of Alber like a detail in a story. I would tell it like some lesson meant to be learned, some inescapable fate that must be suffered over and again until it can be accepted. But I'd had enough of fate, and made several turns irrationally away from what I felt, blindly, was the direction we had come.

But could I return to Adah? Did I want to, even without this dark news? Antares had said he would lead me south, that there was a path I might take that would give me an edge over the imposter's army. I could warn my family, or run with them. Without his help, the only way that I knew was the Rogue's Ear, or risk facing the entire Ambarian force. Could one icon, even the icon of Theba, stand against so many?

It began to snow, flakes as bright as stars in the falling night. I recalled the tale that Adah had told of the First People naming the stars at the cost of their own lives and felt dragged down to the very belly of the world with grief. It would feel good to sleep on the earth, to sleep within it, quiet and buried in a wood where I could not harm anyone else. Theba would not lie with me, of course; she would go on and perhaps find a more willing partner for her hatred.

To win against Theba, I would have to live forever.

Even as I plodded forward, directionless, I felt my dark sight failing from exhaustion, or perhaps my eyes were simply closing of their own accord. Head and feet both began to throb, and I stopped, leaning against the rough bark of a tree for support. I felt no flicker of life within it, and the wood felt as rough as gravel against my check. The sensation was familiar, and I remembered another wild, trying day: the day that I had been tested in Jhosch, when the Paivi in my mind had bade me climb the stone stair to the altar above. My cheeks had dragged blood across those steps, and there was blood on me now, too. It wasn't mine.

I recalled, too, what Adah had said, that all icons find their way to *Zhaeha* when they are tried. I slumped to the tree's base and was within the cavern with the pool, the place during my test where I had seen the shade of my mother. Had I really been there, within the mountain?

And if I could be transported to the mountain, could the mountain transport *me*?

I settled into the winter-hard soil, the night dark with my thoughts. We had traveled a strange road through the Rogue's Ear. Why shouldn't there be other secret ways in the deep places of the world? I might not be able to find the path that Antares had spoken of, or manage it alone, but I felt as called to *Zhaeha* now as I had the day I'd fled Jhosch. Maybe I only wanted it to be true, but with each star that winked into brilliance above me, I felt more sure that I had been there before. I hadn't just raced madly beneath the peak, but I had ventured within.

Looking out into the darkness, I felt my eyes focus again, the sharp edges of branches dragging across the darkness. Without firelight, the shadows didn't dance but simply lay upon each other, folds upon folds of midnight cloth. I didn't rise, not then. But I knew that in the morning when I would climb or find some high ground, I would direct myself toward the crooked peak before forging a path.

I would return to *Zhaeha*. I would find a way home.

CHAPTER SIX

I had to climb a tree. My first. I'd chosen a stout one, as many were spindle-thin, and still felt the lifeless, papery bark shred underneath my fingers as I sought careful purchase. But I finally reached a vantage that stretched on in all directions. Through the early morning's wreath of snowy fog, I saw the ominous peak of *Zhaeha* against the brightening sky. There was an answering tug in my gut that I couldn't have imagined. I could've guessed the direction of the mountain and done so correctly.

I had rations enough in my pack for a few days, but Antares had carried the bulk of our supply. I'd run before thinking of searching him—and was too scared now to consider going back. I had seen enough corpses during the war to know that even those you knew in life would be remembered by their lifeless faces. I had no desire to eclipse the man he had been with a mask of death. Perhaps the widow makers would find him when they came for Emine and bury them both. Or would they leave him to stiffen in the winter sun, to waste to blue skin and white bones on the forest floor? I swallowed the hiccup of a sob at the thought and started walking.

For three days, I feared encountering another living creature, but I was unsettled, too, by their absence. I felt I didn't belong in this wood and didn't want to think too hard about what did. I stopped each night before it got too dark to find wood for a fire, choosing a small clearing on the third night that seemed as good of a place as any. I wouldn't have known a good spot from a poor one: we had survived in exile, but my survival skills were based on what I had been able to observe rather than on direct instruction.

The fire, when I finally got it going, was far from merry, but it was warm and kept the darkness at bay. The night beyond was impenetrable, the haunting quiet broken only by the crackling of dry wood. The flame called out to me, a kindred spirit in destruction. Fire could burn and maim and did so mercilessly. But it was also a comforting source of heat and light. How many travelers were preserved by its glow? How many homes were made refuge? It might not have been in Theba's nature to recognize its full range of power, but it was in mine.

It should matter, that I cared.

When I finally slept, my dreams were fitful. The broken forms of Antares and Emine fell over and over again before me, my mind providing all of the grim details my bound eyes had not seen. Emine was in turn each of my sisters, then she was Morainn and finally Imke, and it was my hand that dealt the final, brutal blow. I licked the blade and felt my tongue fork. I tasted blood and tears when I woke, crying out against a gray dawn.

A dark figure was silhouetted before me, looming and featureless in the early light. I scrambled back, tangled in my bedroll, and flame leaped from my wrists, drawn from the embers of the meager fire. The blaze was momentarily blinding, but the voice that followed eliminated the need to see.

"Take care with that, *Han'dra* Eiren. Everything is kindling here."

The lips quirked beneath the smooth plane of the half mask, a twitch of shadow on his pale face.

"Gannet?" I would not ask if it was really him, if he was really here. I could not bear the answer if this was a trick of the wood, a weirdness that preyed upon the weak.

Neither did his response need words. He crossed to me, taking the hands that were still warm from the quenched flame and lifted me to my feet. He met my eyes, and I sensed his caution, his desire, his fear. His touch was true, his mind open to mine, each of us troubled with recent horrors, seeking the comfort of the other.

I am here.

I am sorry.

I breathed the scents of his traveling clothes and he the tangled sweep of my hair, lips parted in an exhalation we shared as they met, sweet, urgent, mad. My hands skimmed his chest, fingers pinning in the folds of fabric at his shoulders and deeper, feeling the muscle there, the hint of bone. Gannet's hands on my hips pressed me flush against him even as his mouth left mine, trailing down my neck and lower still, his fevered lips branding the slight swell of my breast above the collar of my stained traveling dress.

This was not the opera. Neither was it a dream. There would be no interruptions.

But Theba had twisted in me, shown me that I could not have this without acknowledging that she would have it, too. In the way she had manipulated my dreams, in the way she had perverted my perceptions of Antares. I knew that I couldn't trust her, and now I wasn't sure that I could trust myself. I clasped between us the hands that sought lower on Gannet's lean frame. Was it Theba who hoped to conquer him, or me?

Which did I fear more?

I pulled away, only just, planting my forehead in the hollow between his shoulder and throat, arresting his own fevered journey down my body.

"How did you find me?"

Mine were not the sweet words of a hopeful lover but a repentant enemy.

"Adah," he said, breath slowing. "He told me you had gone south with Antares and that he did not expect you to return."

"And you followed us?"

"You, actually. I started going south, but then I sensed you, the way it was before we met. I could hear you, your thoughts." His expression, already sober, darkened even more. "With Antares gone, you're going to the mountain."

Gannet had seen his death, then, too. I grimaced.

"I have to."

"I know. I will go with you."

"Even knowing why I go?"

He nodded. Rather than questioning him further, rather than conjuring an argument, I relaxed against him again. There was so much still to say, but it could wait for a breath or two. We didn't even need words, and my grief for what I had done, my gratitude for being offered a way forward against the imposter and my resolve to take it, all of it passed into him through the places that we touched.

It went both ways. Gannet's hands tightened where they'd come to rest on my hips. With that pressure came an urgent flood of memories.

We were in Jhosch, in the opera house. Gannet had dodged a heretic's dagger as he turned toward the fire, not away, as everyone else had done. Knives of flame glanced away from him as he cleared a path through the fire and the fleeing, the flailing, the dying. He carved the air out of the chamber where his sister had fallen, suffocating the flame, but it was not soon enough to stop the tongues of fire from licking her cheek, her scalp.

This was not the greatest horror he offered me, though. Through Gannet's eyes, I saw the black fury that was Theba, the wicked contortion of my face as I blasted down all who fled before me. Only when the fires had been extinguished was I the woman he knew, trembling from head to foot, ashen eyes empty as they considered the carnage before them.

I was shaking now, as I had then, and even Gannet's arms girded tight around me could not still me. He tilted my chin to look at my face, giving me no choice but to look into his. His eyes behind the mask were as warm as the fingers that cupped my chin, the blank chill I'd once believed to be their only expression now absent. Gannet's eyes held the warmth of secrets shared in the dark, the whispered heat of spent lovers in stories, their heads upon the same pillow.

"Is Morainn alive?" He hadn't shown me, and I had to know.

"She was when I left. She is safe but—sleeping."

Tears burned trails down my cheeks so hot that I wondered they didn't boil off. She hadn't awakened then. Would she ever wake?

"I'm so sorry, I didn't mean to. I would never have hurt her if I…if I had been myself."

Gannet didn't cradle me, didn't coddle me, but he held me firmly before him and commanded my eyes.

"Eiren." His voice was flat as a stone baked in the sun. "You cannot change what you are any more than I can."

"You don't even know what you are."

"I know that I am devoted to you, every finger, every breath, every bone."

I sucked in a shaky breath, searching his face.

"How can you say that? After everything I've done?"

"You're not the only one who's allowed to forgive." His eyes cooled at my words, and he was again the icon I knew, disguising the fury of feelings from the man within. But he was irritated, and this familiar ground put me at my ease, at last.

"Fair enough," I murmured. His declaration was something a woman in a story might have swooned for. I felt myself in danger of it with his hands on me still, his breath near enough to tease the loose hairs from behind my ears. "What do we do now?"

Gannet's breath was audibly relieved. I felt the walls going back up around his mind, but I sensed now how necessary they were for him to get by, and how a word from me would bring them down again, if I wished it. He secured my cloak around my shoulders before stepping away under the pretense of rummaging in his pack.

"Now? Food, a fire. And then *Zhaeha*."

CHAPTER SEVEN

While we ate, Gannet told me what he knew of the imposter and the state of Ambar. He had no more of an idea who she was than Adah did, though he suspected it was one of the other icons, perhaps Najat.

"The Dreamer?" I snorted before I could stop myself, feeling Theba turn over in the core of my being, sending acid creeping up my throat. I clenched my fists before continuing more evenly. "That seems unlikely."

"Whoever she is, she has some power. Maybe it's only persuasion. Maybe not."

"Adah knew I wouldn't be able to resist going after her," I said, chewing thoughtfully. Gannet scooped another handful of snow into the vessel near the fire to purify it before filling the water bladder he carried.

"Anybody who has met you could guess as much." Gannet wasn't looking at me, but I heard the smirk on his lips. I smiled in response despite myself. I had missed this. Missed him.

"Do you know the way into *Zhaeha*?" I asked, determined to follow his lead and remain focused on the task ahead.

Gannet shook his head. "I didn't even think it was possible to go there on purpose. There are many reasons we avoid the mountain, and these woods—they're kin to the Rogue's Ear. Old places, with rules of their own."

I nodded, remembering how the paths we had taken through the Rogue's Ear had been different for each of us, how we had all been tried by that place.

"But you've been there by accident?" I asked.

"I don't know. When I was tested, I appeared to stand on a hooked peak, with no way of knowing how I'd gotten there and no path to climb down."

"What did you do?" He'd spoken to me once before about his test, the hands within the hands when we were in the prayer garden at Rhale's estate, but this was new.

Meeting my eyes, Gannet's mouth was thin as a blade's edge. "I jumped."

I gulped the last of my tea. "I was on a cliff side, too, but there was a cavern, with a pool. My—my mother was there."

Gannet's brow quirked, and I continued hurriedly, wanted to lay out my whole mad plan before I could second guess myself.

"I think, if *Zhaeha* is like the Rogue's Ear, and if my mother can travel there, why shouldn't we be able to travel to where she is? To warn her and my family about the imposter's army, to flee into the deep desert?"

"As you did when you were a child."

"Yes."

"And you'll let the imposter have what she seeks in Re'Kether?"

"If I'm not there, she won't be able to use it."

"Eiren, we don't even know what it is. What if we can use it to stop this?" Gannet's expression was guarded, near unreadable with the mask.

"What good can come of freeing Theba?" I asked, heart pounding with sudden fever. "I'll probably be dead, anyway. I can't see any other way for her to live again as a god without getting rid of the icon first."

I knew that he wanted to touch me, to settle or soothe me somehow. But I knew, too, that such impulses were still new enough for him that he wouldn't try for fearing he'd fail.

"You said yourself that you couldn't resist going after her. I know you," he said, tone gaining strength with every syllable. "You won't run from this. So, meet her on your own terms. Find what she seeks first."

Even as he spoke of the imposter, I heard in his voice that

he meant Theba, too. I had fled from her power for so long and had seized it to such disastrous effect in Jhosch. Perhaps there was another way.

"Well, we have to get there first," I said, dodging the command. My heart was plain enough to him anyhow. I looked up, the morning's wreath of snowy fog having dissipated enough for me to see the mountain's craggy slope. I didn't remember ever having been this close, but I knew that in my madness, I had skirted the mountain. "I was planning to find my way blind before you arrived. It's as poor of an approach for two as it was for one."

Gannet made no comment but rinsed his cup with a bit of water before stowing it in his bag and rising to his feet. His trim figure, in dark pants, tunic, and familiar cloak, told me that he was ready. To follow, to lead, to partner in whatever awaited us. I shook out my skirt as I rose, hoisting my pack.

"If we go to Re'Kether, what will we find?" I asked, committed to the course even if I couldn't admit it. The last time he and I had been in the ruin, something had attacked me, and I, in turn, had nearly struck him down with lightning.

Gannet walked ahead, seeing some path I didn't through the unbroken soil.

"Nothing good," he answered, tone carefully absent of any feelings he might have on the prospect. "You're stronger now, which could mean you'll be safer. Or not."

"That's comforting."

"You won't be alone this time."

I noted the broad arch of his shoulders, the fair hair that brushed the collar of his cloak like snow on shadow. A hand reached to break a delicate branch from one of the trees, and he left the broken limb hanging where it twisted away. He saw me watching over his shoulder, and inclined his head toward the branch.

"If the wood turns us around, we'll know we've been here before."

"And you think if the forest has the power to lead us astray, it can't also mend a branch?"

His expression soured, and he stopped walking.

"Do you have a better idea?"

"Yes," I said, striding ahead of him with an unapologetic smirk. "Don't get lost."

He disguised his amusement from me, but only just, and allowed me to maintain the lead. It felt better, being just behind the strange compulsion that drew me to *Zhaeha*, without compulsion of another kind embodied in Gannet standing in the way. We had enough to occupy us that acknowledging the understanding between us wasn't immediately necessary, but it would soon be. And I would have to confront my hesitation for what it was: fear. Fear of getting close and committing some unthinkable deed that would drive us apart, fear that if he had me, he wouldn't want me anymore, fear that no matter how real the things we felt for each other, they would never be all that was between us. Theba was with me, every instant. Controlled at times, wild at others, but she was still there. I didn't want to think about what she might do with me.

And I didn't want to share him with her.

I felt a shudder pass down my spine, a charge from crown to toes, and I was grateful that Gannet couldn't read my mind as easily as he once had. I was grateful for the companionable silence that again settled between us, though when we began to climb a few hours later, I wanted anything to distract me from the nearing certainty of what we dared to do.

"Adah said there are rumors of *Zhaeha*, morbid curiosities that he encourages to maintain his sanctuary. Could you tell me what they are?" I asked after a time, not wanting to be left alone with my thoughts any longer. I remembered again what Gannet had said about the witch, that she heralded death.

"You want me to tell you a story, Eiren?" Gannet's tone was light. It was as close to teasing as I had ever heard from him.

"Yes, I do," I huffed, blaming the exertion of soil giving way to rock and the increasing pitch of the path we took, rather than irritation.

"I can tell you what was told to me, when I was a young icon studying with Adah. But I can't promise you drama."

"My stories are not theatrical," I insisted, but already I could feel Gannet building a narrative behind me, and I held my tongue for fear of dissuading him.

"Many generations ago, there were some who made Adah's sanctuary a place of pilgrimage. Those who dared the crossing only did so during the longest days of the year. The night beyond *Zhaeha* could not be trusted. Some heard voices. Others woke to find their belongings moved or stolen. Sometimes pilgrims would be lost. Most times they weren't found.

"So the pilgrims began to carry torches soaked in slow-burning oil, and to fast from sleep. But that was worse. They could see that they were not alone in the darkness. Their shadows turned on them. Some even said they traded places with their shadows, and the penitents who returned to their villages were shades, instead."

My lips quirked. "I thought you said there wouldn't be any drama."

"I didn't say I believed it," Gannet huffed. He seemed to be waiting for me stop smiling so he could continue, but when I didn't, he forged on instead, looking away from me, his own lips failing to maintain their usual flat countenance.

"Soon enough, the pilgrims who managed to reach the sanctuary with their wits intact were unwilling to leave. Adah, charged with the protection of young icons and the preservation of our history, could not allow them to stay. There was no work for them, no livelihood, and he found their mortal squabbles distracting.

"So Adah himself went into the wood, armed with one of the pilgrim's torches. He was gone for three days and three nights, and when he returned, the torch was nothing more than a limb of twisted wood in his palm, still smoldering but leaving no mark of fire upon his skin.

"'There is another world in the wood,' he told them. 'The world as it was, revealed only by moonlight. Living things that do not serve me cannot walk here in safety.'

"The pilgrims all insisted that it was Adah they served, above Tirce, who shaped their lands, above Dsimah, who showed them the way of plenty, above Theba, who reminded them to cherish what they had lest she take it away. Adah looked on each of the pilgrims and found only one who truly served. He charged this pilgrim with guiding the others and returning to Adah when his task was complete. He passed the stump of torch to the pilgrim and it did not burn him, for that pilgrim alone could accept Adah's blessing.

"The shadows did not trouble them anymore, though few risked the crossing after. Fewer still returned to tell about it. Those who did committed their lives in the service of the icon of Adah, carrying the torch of justice in their hearts."

It had all the makings of a good story and was surely the sort of tale that would appeal to the Ambarian imagination: unwavering adherence to the words of icons and gods.

"I don't recall Adah being impervious to fire," I said, toying with a petty detail.

"And I've not encountered a single shadow that wasn't the one I walked in with," Gannet countered. "It's just a story, Eiren. There are others equally as likely to fall apart under scrutiny, if you're interested."

"No."

He couldn't have known how this story would sit with me, and I wasn't angry with him. Not really.

"Antares served Adah, too," I whispered, eyes traveling up the perilous slope, sure there wasn't a living creature that could scale it. "Though he said it was me he really served, because Adah, along with everyone, has waited so long for Theba to return."

Gannet didn't put a hand on me, but I felt the weight of his thoughts as surely as if he had.

"I don't need to tell you that what happened to him was not your fault, Eiren. He chose to walk that road with you."

"Just like you?"

I met his eyes now, gleaming in the twilight, surrounded by the shadow of the mask. I held my breath.

"Not like me," he answered, taking two steps forward and pulling me toward him. The scrabble of my boots on loose stone was lost in the rush of blood to my ears when he pressed his mouth to mine, when the force that parted my lips threatened to unfold me utterly. The kiss deepened for an instant before I found myself dragging a breath against his cheek, his words brushing against mine. "You left me behind. But I won't watch you walk away again. I can't."

My hands clutched his shirt, felt the steady thump of his heart. I felt as if I were being pricked by a tattooist's needle, bound to a peg like strings on an instrument. *Stay, stay, stay*, his heart seemed to say. And how I wanted to.

I might have answered what he didn't even know he was asking, but I wasn't given the chance. There was a laugh, high and rattling from stone to stone, and with it came an avalanche.

CHAPTER EIGHT

Nothing could have prepared me for the shock of the cold as my arms pinwheeled in a mad rhythm, guided by instinct. My spine turned to ice and seemed to shatter, my eyes were little more than frozen orbs spinning madly in white-blind sockets. It sounded like the sea in Cascar, a merciless rage that tumbled me over and over and then pinned me as surely as if I were trapped between two stones. I tried to open my mouth to scream or breathe or both but found that I couldn't. And it wasn't the snow that held it closed, but Theba.

Still. Be still.

Even my heart seemed to slow, the frightened hammering softening to the lightest tap against my breast. I wanted to fight her, to fight the mountain, but there was a thread of sense left in me, and I wound my thoughts about it like I might my finger around a string. If I struggled, I would die. I would waste what precious little breath was left in my lungs and what could be drawn from the spaces in the compacted snow around me. I had to wait and hope that Gannet had not been buried, that he could free me.

And if he had?

The snow around me was an airless tomb. I could not wait. I did not have that luxury.

Move. Move now.

I felt Theba loosen her hold on me. I could not take a deep breath but I dared a shallow one, the flutter of snowflakes against my lips a brush with death. I remembered carving the stone in the Rogue's Ear, demanding passage where there was none. I did the same now, feeling the shift of my weight as my feet gained purchase and moved before losing it again, my hands clawed and scraped at the snow as though I would pull the whole sky down to be free. My head and neck emerged first, twisting in a moment of panic and the strange shock of even colder air on my frozen cheeks. And then I had vaulted above the snow, casting blindly from side to side, recognizing nothing, seeing no one. It was nearly dark now, without the benefit of sun or stars to illuminate the featureless snow.

"Gannet!"

My scream was raw, my lungs still starved for air, but his name escaped my lips a second time, a third, before being caught by some echoing rock and thrown back at me. If he was under the snow, he could not answer me, probably couldn't even hear me. I would not find him in time this way.

I dropped to my knees, closed my eyes, reached for his heat, for the familiar comfort of his calculating thoughts. At first, nothing, but then the whisper of fear, the outrageous doubt that this could be the end, after everything.

I leaped to my feet again and raced to my left, nearer the edge of a ravine we had been tumbled into. The black stone ahead of me was menacing, and I had the mad feeling that the smooth rock face had anticipated a future as an anonymous grave marker, rather than the site of a miraculous rescue. There was nothing in the snow to indicate where he was, but I felt him and would've snapped my fingers into pieces, carving him free. It was his hands I saw first, buried nearly the length of my legs beneath the snow, and I worked faster, exposing the gold hair plastered against his brow, then the mask and his eyes squeezed shut behind it. He was unconscious. I made quick work of his mouth and nose, and I nearly stopped for weeping when I felt his irregular breath on my fingers. He was alive, but the cold was reluctant to give him up.

When I had finally dragged him to the surface of the snow, I clutched at his shoulders and his head, shed hot tears on his face, and bent to share my breath.

You can't have him. It was the mountain toward whom I flung my refusal, though I didn't look up from his face. *He's mine. Mine.*

There was an answering call, but it was not *Zhaeha* who rose to my challenge.

He's ours. Ours.

I wouldn't fight her, not now. If I wanted to fight her ever again, I had to live first, which involved getting off the ice and seeking shelter, building a fire. The sun had well and truly set now, and I conjured my dark sight with some difficulty, seeing in the many shades of gray between snow and rock a slight incline that might mean a slope toward soil and kindling.

But I couldn't lift Gannet. Whatever supernatural strength I had possessed, I had, for the moment, spent it, and even his lean frame was too much for me.

"I need you to wake up, Gannet. I need your help." I put my hands on his face again, disturbed by the faint heat there.

Wake up, please. I reached out to him, reached beyond the mountain he had once shown me within himself. There were hiding places in his mind, sanctuaries where he could retreat in times of fear and uncertainty. I sped through darkness and flashes of memory, called to him as only one heart can call to another. *Gannet, I need you to wake. I need you.*

Like an eye pressed to a crack of light in a door, I saw him, roused him. The body I held in my arms began to cough violently, shuddering, spittle flying to sparkle on the snow. When he finally stopped coughing, his breath, though ragged, steadied, and the eyes behind the mask sharpened on my face. I was smiling and sobbing and realized rather belatedly that I clutched his head against my breast.

"We need to get off the ice," I said hurriedly, not shifting him, and increasingly aware that even under different circumstances, I might not readily have done so. "Can you walk?"

"Possibly," he wheezed, though he made an immediate effort to rise. I hooked my hands underneath his arms, offering what help I could until we both stood, wary but firm.

"I think there's a path over there," I indicated with a slight jerk of my head in the direction of the rock face.

"Or there's a sheer drop to certain death," he managed, each word reluctant with exhaustion, a miser paying out coins from his treasury.

"If you've spirit enough for spiteful remarks, then I'm not sure you need to be putting quite so much of your weight on me." I was sure I supported him only a little, but it was enough for me to feel the strain in my already weakened legs. When he attempted to stand on his own, he wobbled, and I clutched him firmly again. "Come on."

It was a slow crossing, and I didn't gloat when it turned out that I was right and there was a way down off the ice, stepping from rock to crusted snow to rock again. The stones had been transported by the avalanche, as well, and we were lucky we hadn't been struck by one of them. It was only when we both had our feet on the ground again that I was able to find some spark of warmth to draw from and coax a careful blaze into my hand. I considered the laugh we had heard just before the wave that had buried us both. Was it one of the shadows from Gannet's telling? Had it been *Zhaeha* herself, if she had some form and voice to conjure up?

Had it been Theba, exerting some force beyond me?

Gannet shrugged me off when we drew near an overhang, lowering himself to the ground with a labored breath. I spared him a worried look, but I could see little of his face, his features muted. I cast about instead for any sticks that I could transfer my small fire to, but there were very few. It would do no good to survive the avalanche only to freeze to death.

"Eiren," Gannet called, and I looked up from my scavenging to see him pointing. There was a break in the rock face and from it issued a light, flickering briefly, blue-white as a phantom. An invitation.

"I see it," I whispered, abandoning the clutch of sticks and crossing to where he sat, legs drawn wearily close. I let go of the tenuous hold I had on the fire in my hand. We needed a proper fire anyway, and we weren't going to find the makings of one out here. Gannet met my eyes when I looked away, and I realized he'd been looking at me since I'd drawn up beside him, waiting to see what course I chose. He'd already made up his mind.

There hadn't been time enough for him to recover his strength, but he got to his feet without my assistance, steadying himself with a light touch to my arm and letting go. We strode forward, solemn as mourners. The light continued to flicker like a torch, only the color was all wrong. The fissure in the rock face proved wide enough for us to pass through, one in front of the other, and Gannet made no comment when I slipped through first, nor when I took his hand in mine. If *Zhaeha* hoped to separate us, I wasn't going to make it easy.

The path was narrow, a natural shifting in the stone that provided uneven footing. What had I expected? Fairy lights? Ghosts with blue flames for eyes? It was nothing so easily named. The light coaxed us deeper into the mountain, always around another sharp corner or a vague distance. With my own curiosity before me and Gannet's trust behind, I ignored the cold, the very reasonable sense of danger, the growing weight of the rock above me. Deeper and deeper in we went, farther and farther down, until I had no notion of how much time had passed. The teasing light was constant until it flared to certain brilliance, bounding and rebounding against glittering stone. I winced, pressing my face back into Gannet's dark shoulder, opening my eyes again only when I felt his hand on my hair.

Look, Eiren.

We had taken the first steps from narrow path to vaulted chamber, a natural cavern illuminated by the glow that had taunted us below, or rather, the creatures who emitted the glow.

Their features were feline but hairless, eyes tilted away from small, flat noses. There was the suggestion of fangs pricking at their ink-dark lips. I thought for a moment their skin was flaked with gems, as the stone here seemed to be, but then I took in their whole form, the sinuous arms, the thick, strong tail. Scales. They were covered in scales.

The kr'oumae.

He had used that word once before, after the storm in Cascar. I had nearly drowned. They had saved me.

They stared at us, a dozen at least, arranged like the petals of a flower around a depression in the center of the cavern. Before I heard the hiss that met between their sharp teeth and their tongues, I felt it, a reverberation that was as familiar to me as the touch of Gannet's mind. They slithered, as much snake as siren, surging forward like a wave.

"The icon of Theba has been here before. She is no more welcome now than she was then."

I cast my eyes from face to alien face, but I didn't know who had spoken, or even how I had understood the words. It was as though in hearing them, I rearranged them to sense in my mind. I clutched Gannet's hand even harder, pressing my back into his chest. We stood as one against the storm of their eyes.

"I am Eiren. Theba is no more welcome in me, I assure you. I came, we came, because we need help." I felt as tossed by their collective gaze as I had that fateful day at sea, and I felt the resentful churning of Theba in my gut. I would not have survived the avalanche without her, but now I would rather be ungrateful than dead.

"Humans don't help us. We don't help humans."

Their tails whipped as one, an exclamation. I refused to panic, looking around them, between them, as though a weapon or a way out might present itself. They were close enough for me to smell the sea on them, tangy, dangerous. How had they come by that scent here?

And then I saw where they had been gathered moments before, the gentle slope of stone that terminated in a glistening, still pool. I recognized it and seized upon the only thing I could think of saying that might stand between their savage hands, suddenly reaching, and our throats.

"I have been here before. *Zhaeha* called me, and my mother, too. I am not your enemy. You have helped me before."

I opened my mind to them, the faint, breathless visions that were all I had of the world beneath the waves of the Cascari sea. The gleaming eyes, the small, slick hands that were gentler sisters of the ones before me now. I shared what it felt like to be buoyed to the surface, for my face to break open in a desperate gulp of air. With these creatures so near, I remembered now more than I had then, how the youngest of their kind had flipped underneath my arms and legs, propelling me forward until I beached against the sand. I recalled a feral, merry grin, and a flick of sand in my face from a departing tail.

"I just want to go home."

I sensed nothing from them, and no leader thrust her head and shoulders above the others. But they had ceased their advancing, merely watching us both. Only the rise and fall of Gannet's chest behind my back assured me that he was still breathing.

"Then go."

No riddles, no challenges. They broke apart as though by a blade, creating a narrow passage between their bodies to pool beyond. As eager as I had been a moment ago for any way out of the cavern, I hesitated.

"How do I know where it will take us?"

"It takes you where you need to go."

"That's not a guarantee." The thrill of fear lingered, creeping down my spine, hips twitching with the desire to run.

"Nothing in life is guaranteed, little sister."

Their strange employ of the endearment chilled me even more. Before I could decide how to respond, Gannet broke in from behind me.

"In stories, the *kr'oumae* always exact a price. We would rather know it, before it is paid."

"We?" It was more hiss than word. Despite my resolve, my knees began to quiver. I was grateful for Gannet's steadying bulk. "It isn't a price *she* can pay. Are you willing?"

I turned my head to look at Gannet. I could see the muscles of his jaw working, the eyes behind the mask flickering in acknowledgment. He read more into their words than I did, or they spoke at greater length to him in a language I did not understand.

"I'll pay it."

That was enough. There was not even a choice in moving forward or attempting retreat, and they swept us toward the pool now. I teetered on the edge only for an instant, a vain hope that I might see my mother opposite me again, studying me across the water. With any luck, I would have more than her shade to comfort me soon.

Gannet held onto my hand so tightly I could feel my smallest fingers bruising, and we dove in together.

For a moment, there was only darkness, quiet. The unmade.

And then I was everywhere, every time, every self that I had been. I was a child again before the war, driven even deeper back to the true beginning of my troubles: my birth, the squall of my first breath carrying a note of Theba's fury. I echoed my sisters' footsteps as soon as I could, my brother's playful crowing before I had learned to speak. I was taking those first steps after Gannet onto the barge, trailing sand and little knowing how dear to me the shape and hem of his person would become. The heat of my outrage in the opera house touched me again, and I felt and smelled and tasted all that the fire had that day. I was reduced to ash only to rise again, newly bright.

My skin tingled as if my flesh were flaking away, and my lungs burned. But it wasn't fire that deprived them, but water.

I burst, gasping, into air, heat, and light. The weight of my heavy clothes threatened to drag me back below the surface, my feet kicking wildly in search of purchase, but Gannet had released my hand only to loop two strong arms around me. I couldn't seem to focus, my eyes blinking away water and the visions the pool had induced. But I felt heat on my face and smelled the sharp, bitter spice of desert air beyond the sodden wool of Gannet's clothing.

"Are we here? Did it work?" I paddled weakly with my arms,

but even the slightest movement made my head spin all the more madly.

"We're somewhere." Gannet's response was stiff, and then he was pulling me to a smooth ledge of stone. "Sit. If you fall in again, I'm not sure I'll be able to get you out."

I sat and felt him sit beside me. The room we were in began after a moment to take shape, blurred by the steam rising from our clothing, rather than whatever had gripped me during the passage.

We sat on the edge of a great well in a mason-worked floor. It had been carved, the sides sloping gently down to a depth nearly the height of a man. The light here was low, angled in from the ceiling as it was closed in on all sides but for an entrance opposite where we sat, and only rubble was visible beyond. All around us were images in relief on solid stone, men and women whose state of undress would've made me blush if my body wasn't still running wild with terror. They were artfully posed so as not to expose themselves, but their limbs were suggestive all the same. The confident slope of the women's noses, their slim arms draped over their breasts, broad hips making a focus of their middles, could have seduced even the most noble-minded. They reminded me of the images in Adah's sanctuary, but these were far, far older.

"Somewhere," I echoed in awe. I attempted to withdraw my feet from the water, but it was already retreating, sucked down to the well's center until it had completely disappeared beyond an ancient, blackened grate. The stone wasn't even wet anymore. I cast a sidelong look at Gannet, meeting his shielded eyes with my own, dark with worry. "What did they want?"

He didn't answer straightaway, and when he did, he looked toward the center of the well, as though he expected the water to rise up again and claim him if he answered untruthfully.

"There is no male of the species."

I choked, coughed, and the heat that had been absent from my cheeks a moment before flooded them now.

"I see," I squeaked, desperate to recover myself. I wanted to know exactly how Gannet had paid this particular price and also fervently wanted *not* to know. He spared me from asking with a dismissive wave of his hand.

"Whatever they needed from me they took it through the water. My mind was—elsewhere."

A laugh burst out of me like a spark shot from a popping log in a fire.

"You must know how that sounds," I insisted when he met my eyes, his own blazing with irritation. For a moment, I thought he might carry on being sour, but the corners of his mouth shifted slightly until he was laughing, too. I was warmed all the way through by the sound, becoming aware of the press of his thigh against mine through our wet clothes. When he stopped laughing, I wasn't laughing anymore, and I caught my lip between my teeth to keep from speaking.

Thank you, I thought, at last, holding his eyes.

I said I would fight for you.

His lips below the mask twitched, all the explanation he was likely to give for what he had done in the cavern to see us through to the other side. I wanted to take his hand, wanted to do more than just that, but I pushed myself up from the ledge, instead.

"I want to know where we are."

Gannet nodded his agreement and rose, too. I carefully averted my eyes from the figures in relief on the walls, though they seemed to take on life in my peripheral vision, the stone brightening, their limbs shining as though with sweat or light. The doorway I had noted when we first arrived was partially collapsed, but I was able to slip through and Gannet, too, with a bit more effort. There was a thick layer of sand here, and our steps cleared a path to a mosaic floor that might have been obscured for ages. The pattern was reminiscent of the ones that had spiraled out beneath my feet when I was a very young child in the palace at Jarl. My heart quickened.

The corridor we walked into was close but intact, and at its end I saw a stark square of hot, white sunlight. We approached cautiously, but rather than the elation I expected to feel at being home, dread coiled in my gut like a hungry snake. Wherever we were, Theba was not happy to be here.

I braced my hands against the crumbling frame of what must once have been a narrow servants' entrance, gazing out on the ruins of a square. The buildings opposite the one we emerged from were in complete ruin, the crumbled facades like so many broken brushstrokes, their foundations laid bare. Beyond them were more structures in various states of decay, and looming over it all was a massive edifice, circled by towers crooked as teeth. On the horizon, the mountains were a featureless canvas, the sun a blazing thumb-print of light. I felt the hum of recognition in my bones. My heart began to pound with the enormity of what we had done, how far we had come, and where.

"Re'Kether," I murmured, stepping out into the square into deeper drifts of sand, undisturbed by human traffic for millennia.

Or perhaps not. As I cast about for an alley that might lead in the direction of the palace, I noted the deliberate clearing of debris blocking an entrance to the square on our left, and that two others appeared to have been purposefully blockaded. The isolation I had felt moments before when we passed between worlds, that Gannet and I were the only two in the known world, evaporated, and I sensed many presences, all of them bent toward violence.

"Gannet, I think we're too late," I whispered, wheeling around to meet his eyes.

But he wasn't looking at me. He was held by a man, a head and shoulders taller and broader than he was. His eyes darted between what he could see of his captor's cloth-wrapped face and the wicked knife pressed to his throat.

"I'd say you're right on time."

A strange, brutal voice and an explosion of pain at the back of my skull eclipsed any further thought.

CHAPTER NINE

I woke with a start. Coarse cloth covered my face, knotted at my throat, and I felt suffocated by my own breath. Sweat pooled above my brow, threatening to blind me, and I strained against bindings on my legs and arms. I reached for Theba's strength, but she was elusive, and I found only weariness instead. My head was throbbing, and I was for an instant grateful to be blinded by the cloth; the glare of the sun might've caused me to pass out again from the pain.

It was very quiet. I felt unyielding soil beneath me, so perhaps I was in a tent or dwelling. I tried to sense anyone nearby, but my thoughts were scrambled, as though someone had taken a hold of my head and shaken it violently. Would they be back to finish what they'd started? Would I die as helpless as the babes who had preceded me?

"Where is she?"

The sound of heavy canvas flapping followed the muffled voice, a rich tenor I was sure I recognized. But it had none of the youthful whine I remembered. It couldn't be.

"Eiren? Where did you find her? What possessed you to leave her like this?"

"We couldn't be sure…"

The bag was pulled off my head and the shock of cooler air, quickly deepening to a dry, familiar heat, left me blinking dumbly for a few seconds. I gasped, squeezing my eyes against the shock of light until the pain in my head subsided slightly. My wits returned slowly, but the face that confronted me was as incongruous as the voice. The narrow chin was decorated with a hastily trimmed beard, the frenzied dark eyes grown darker in their determination.

"Eiren," Jurnus whispered, unable to take his eyes from my face, not even to tend to my still-bound hands and feet. "You've changed."

He had no idea how much.

"So have you, brother."

I shuffled, trying to hold my hands up so that he could see that I was still bound, but his men had done a very thorough job. Still, the gesture was enough, and Jurnus's eyes snapped to my bonds. In an instant he was cutting me free, and a young man in piecemeal armor, looking sheepish, was doing the same. We were in a low structure, stone and rotted beams with a length of filthy canvas rigged up for cover. I didn't see Gannet.

"What were you doing out here? How did you escape?"

For once I was spared unraveling every thought that populated his mind, the scenarios he imagined, his frenzied heart. My head hurt too much. I focused instead on his voice, the restraint I could observe in his dealings with the others who crowded into the makeshift tent. They were all armored and carrying weapons and so was he, I noted with surprise.

"Why aren't you in Jarl? How did you come to be in Re'Kether?"

"This is the only place the Ambarians fear to tread. They won't pursue us here, and so here we are. *Fighting back*, Ren. Finally." His smile was wolfish, and I had seen that look before. He'd worn it when play fighting, and I had seen its twin on the faces of the heretics in the opera house in Jhosch.

"Where is my companion? The man who was with me?" I asked, my voice gravely quiet. Jurnus's expression darkened, and I liked that look even less. "The Ambarian? I remember him, you know. He was with the ones who took you."

"Where is he, Jurnus? Tell me now."

The strength Theba had denied me a moment before pressed forward with each word, the power to command him flooding my voice and my veins. My brother took a step back.

"Bound, as you were. They brought you to me here, as soon as they guessed who you might be. Why do you care?"

But I was pushing past him already, reaching out for Gannet's mind even as my eyes fought to scan our surroundings.

Jurnus grabbed my arm and pulled me to the ground, hard enough that my knees struck painfully against the stone.

"Get down," he hissed, and then he was yanking me back into the shadows of the tent. The soldiers with him hung back, uncertain, as Jurnus spun me to face him, eyes blazing with anger and confusion. "The Ambarians fear occupying the city, but they lay siege on all sides. Occasionally, there are some in their patrols who are bold enough to strike within the ruined walls. You will expose us."

I took a steadying breath, closing my eyes briefly against my panic and the pain.

"I need you to take me to Gannet, the man you captured with me. And I need you to take me somewhere we can speak freely."

"What's going on, Eiren?"

"I will only tell this story once," I insisted, my words made heavy with power once more. I could feel him fighting back against the compulsion, his memories of a gentle, pliable sister at war with the creature who commanded him now. "And I'm sure you're not alone here. Mother and father, our sisters? Take me to them, after I have seen you free Gannet."

I thought he might resist, that the little pressure I had applied would not be enough. But he relented, stuffing the bonds he'd loosened from my limbs into a pack that he threw over his shoulders. He jerked his head at the others in the shelter, and they gathered their own things quietly, expertly, collapsing the canvas only once we were all ready to slip out from underneath it. One of them even hung back to sweep a cloak over the tracks we made in the sand, obscuring our passage. Perhaps the bulk of the Ambarian force would not enter the city, but clearly there were enough skirmishes to warrant such care.

We hurried along a debris-strewn alley, not so fast that we

made significant commotion, but fast enough, without speaking. We kept a low enough profile that I couldn't even determine if we were going in the direction of the mammoth structure I had seen outside the bathhouse earlier, though I caught glimpses of it in between intact buildings. I hoped that none of those under Jurnus's command took liberties with their prisoners, and that Gannet would have only a headache to worry over, as I did.

My dark imaginings drove my heart into my throat before we reached a dark, squat structure. Jurnus put out a hand and his soldiers instantly ceased moving. I thought they would have stopped breathing for him, if they could have. From Jurnus's lips issued a low whistle, the perfect imitation of the carrion birds that haunt the sands, and after a tense moment, the sound was repeated back to us, and he led the way within the ruin.

They must've used this place for sanctuary before, since the floors were swept and the arched windows imperfectly blockaded with stone. Still, I was not at my ease and drew back like a viper ready to strike when I saw Gannet slumped against a far wall, face bloodied. Jurnus was quicker to reason than I was, though.

"Untie him and wake him, if you can."

I didn't wait for the order to be followed, spying a water bladder abandoned on the floor and snatching it up, crossing to press the spout to his lips. One of Jurnus's soldiers, a young woman who could not have been more than ten and five years old, bent to loosen the ties from his ankles and knees. Up close, the wounds seemed superficial, likely the result of not having been taken by surprise, as I had been, and being rather more difficult to subdue.

Gannet, I'm here.

My touch was feather light on his cheek and mind both, and his eyelids fluttered. I sensed his pain but could do nothing about it. I blotted at a cut above his brow with the hem of my skirt, traced a thumb over the edge of the mask where it had dried.

"We tried to take it off when we thought he'd passed out," the girl murmured, catching my eye when she moved to unbind his wrists. "He wouldn't let us."

"He doesn't have to be conscious to be stubborn," I said, allowing myself to feel a moment's relief. Still I felt the growing concern of my brother's attention on my back, and I turned to look at him.

"He's a friend. We came here together. You don't have to be afraid of him."

"I'm not afraid."

And he wasn't, not of Gannet. The fear in his eyes had a great deal more to do with me.

I looked away from him, meeting Gannet's eyes instead, which were now open and unreadable. He rubbed his wrists where they had been bound.

Stubborn?

I suppressed a smile, rising and brushing sand from my skirt.

"Gannet, this is my brother, Jurnus." I gestured between the two men as though they might exchange pleasantries but knowing instinctively that they would not. "He and his soldiers have *escorted* us some distance into the city. There is an Ambarian force laying siege to Re'Kether."

"And more on the way," Jurnus said roughly, not looking at either of us. "Our scouts report several thousand moving in from the north. They should be here within days."

"Days?" I nearly choked on the exclamation, barely keeping my voice just above a whisper. "That's impossible. The fire—it's been less than two weeks since I left Jhosch."

Jurnus studied me, dubious. "We've had intelligence on their movements for almost as long but nothing on a solitary pair of travelers from that direction. Unless you sprouted wings and *flew* in, you couldn't have covered the distance in that time."

I looked at Gannet, whose own eyes were cast down, calculating.

"It seems we've arrived where we meant to be, but not when," he said softly. I could've cursed.

"There's still time. There must be. Take us to mother and

father," I said, thinking better of the demand the moment I'd made it. "Please."

"I told you that we're fighting back," Jurnus muttered, making a poor attempt to maintain his composure. "Dozens of the loyal are smuggled within the ruins each week, and hundreds riot in Jarl."

Hundreds. Jurnus believed he could combat the fanaticism of the Ambarians with only *hundreds* to command. The dull throb of guilt joined my heart in beating. If I'd only better phrased my wish of the *kr'oumae*, if I'd found another way…

But we could still win, if we could find what the imposter's forces sought before they had the chance to storm the city. I assumed they would have none of the qualms about entering the city that the occupying force possessed, or was at least not willing to count on it.

We exited the building in a line, keeping low. The soldiers spread out as soon as we were some distance from the sanctuary, nearly invisible in their pale clothes and sand-scrubbed armor under the blaze of the midday sun. We were in what I imagined must have been an open-air market, with little rubble for cover. The ruins here crackled with an energy I recognized—and feared. The city grew around us, a living thing. Though in ruins, the presence of my people here, alive and emboldened with a revolutionary spirit, seemed to resurrect the crumbled foundations, the broken facades, the centuries-still figures in the fountains. Though their features had been all but rubbed away by sand and time, they seemed to dance out of the corners of my eyes, the phantom laughter of water that no longer played at their feet in my ears. My vision blurred.

"Wait here," Jurnus hissed, the words for my benefit and Gannet's, as his soldiers were stilled by a slight gesture of his hand. They were trained well.

We had moved into a square that must once have been very grand, and Jurnus's posture remained tense, his eyes fixed on a point ahead, where no doubt he waited for some signal.

He didn't elaborate on the command, and I didn't ask. I felt myself drifting, surprised that my feet were still solid enough to carry me into the square. I looked around, attempting to fix myself in time. The stonework boasted elaborate mosaics of animals both real and imagined, the tiles faded, though they once had been vibrant with nameless colors. Great beds for trees and flowers had been flooded with sand, but I could see how they had once wound in circles toward the fountain at the center. There, six unnaturally lean figures with the tails of fish joined hands, their stone faces immutable, smoothed with age. The real thing had been far more frightening. I felt dizzy, without anchor.

"Do you remember the fish-finned girl?" I was asking everyone and no one, drifting toward the fountain like a scrap of cloth on the breeze and as difficult to pin, for Jurnus reached out and failed to secure me. Was it Theba's touch I felt, cool as a ghost against what skin I bared to the sun?

I stopped before the fountain, transfixed. Minute bronze fittings were set into the faces of the figures, spouts where their mouths once had been. There was no water now, but I could see how it had been, the streams arching and intersecting in wild patterns.

"Her mother didn't like the feel of the babe's webbed hands against her breast and demanded that her husband dump the infant in the well. He couldn't do it," I whispered softly, madly, seeing again the multi-lidded eyes of the *kr'oumae*. They had called me sister. "He put her in the sea instead."

As I spoke, I reached out and touched the fountain's edge. It might once have been painted, too, for the faintest coral blush was visible on the stone. In the same instant, Jurnus had crossed to me, pulling me down into the shadow cast by the ancient sirens realized in stone. His hand on my arm was like a shackle.

"What is wrong with you, Eiren?" Jurnus hissed. "Did they hurt you?"

"No. I hurt them."

Jurnus couldn't respond, because in that instant we were interrupted by a shout. And I felt them all. My mother and father. My sisters, Anise, Esbat, Lista. I felt all of them keenly and Jurnus, too, a dark edge to their delight in seeing me, wondering why, and how, and at what cost.

How could I even begin to tell?

But with the return of my senses came something else, too. They descended upon me but the colors of their simple clothes, so unlike the faded finery we had worn in the desert, began to blur and change. As I had imagined it, the fountain began to spew forth bright, cool water, splashing playfully onto the now immaculately kept square. The stones were newly dusted, and I saw my feet on them, bare, with delicate rings on each toe, not booted as they had been. Jurnus was gone. Gannet was gone. Where my family had been, courtiers gathered, gossiping, fringed scarves drawn across their faces or beaded low on their brows. The air was sweet and deliciously mild in my lungs, and as I looked around, expecting more figures, I saw instead the trees, pruned to shapes nature alone would not have crafted, casting shadows like embracing lovers on the ground. There was such beauty, such mundane peace, that I could have wept for the comfort of it.

I anticipated Theba at any moment, already sure that no matter how lovely, this could only be one of her tricks. But she wasn't there, not in any form that I could feel, and the courtiers paid me no attention, not even glancing my way. Was I here in body and mind? Was my family now holding my lifeless, dozing form, or had they seen me vanish before their eyes?

I felt safe, at peace. I had the distinct feeling that leaving the square would not take me away from this, whatever it was. It felt real, as real as any mad thing I had experienced of late. This was like the test the icons had administered to me in Jhosch, though there was no cup of doctored wine to blame for this vision.

I sat down on the fountain's edge, the pearlescent rose of the stone catching and reflecting the sun's light in every droplet of water that splashed and slid down the rounded edge. The water frothed so that in places a fine mist hung in the air, and I leaned my face forward into it, closing my eyes and feeling the dew settle in the humid folds about my eyes and nose. I wore a loose, flimsy gown that parted above my breasts and below my hips, and when the mist touched my skin, I felt chilled as though I had been tickled.

"Why do you smile?"

I started, and for a moment, wasn't sure who was talking. The courtiers hadn't moved, whispering still to each other behind the delicate silk of their scarves, and there was no one else in the square. There was a little splash, and this one didn't spout from the stone sirens' mouths. I looked down, and darting in the fountain were a trio of fish, their scales shining in one instant red, in the next, green, and so on through a whole host of colors in the moment it took me to note that one had his lips poised just above the water, a slight puckering as he repeated his question.

"Why do you smile?"

I didn't think Theba was likely to take the form of a fish. It was condescension enough for her to assume human shape. Besides, there was nothing about the creature that felt of her darkness, her temptation. He made me think of a different mythology altogether, of the story of Jemae as a young woman with her fierce moods. It had been the story I had told my first night among the icons in Jhosch, at Jaken's request.

Jaken, who along with so many others, was now dead because of me.

"Because it is peaceful here," I replied, but I wasn't smiling anymore. The fish whipped his tail and a fan of water soaked my skirt. The water was cold despite the sun that warmed it, and my flesh pimpled beneath the sodden fabric. It was so real, the fountain, the light, the layered, hushed voices of the courtiers, that I had no room to feel anything for long that wasn't wonder.

"And you crave peace," the fish observed, he and his brothers and sister parting to create a reflective space between them, still as glass. I bent reflexively to see myself, but the world trembled and turned on its side, the horizon slipping like a silk hem, the city's architecture a ragged edge of embroidery.

Only, it hadn't. I'd fallen, and even as I reached for the fountain's edge to pull myself up again, arms were hooking under my arms, and there was grit under my nails. The shouts I had heard were turned to screams, the grunt and breath of battle, the clang of weapons. There was no sheen to the fountain, nothing but an empty, sandy basin where the cool water and the fish had been. My mother's concerned eyes bored into mine, but she didn't speak. My father was at her side, my sisters behind him, and towering behind were several heavily armored guards, urging us away from a fight I could hear but not see. My lips parted, but no words came out.

"Get them out of here."

It was my brother, sword flashing as he gave the order. The clang of weapons echoed in my ears, and I heard Theba's laughter in each skirmishing blow, chiming like funeral bells. I had brought her here, to my family. We were in this war now together.

I felt myself slipping again, not into the sweet dream this time, but into darkness. They were already blaming exhaustion, stress, hunger, and thirst, their thoughts like flies settling on my still face.

But it was fear that drove me down, fear that held me there until the blackness eclipsed their thoughts and mine, too.

CHAPTER TEN

I woke, alone, in a dimly lit chamber, a cool pillow beneath my cheek. Braziers burned low in the four corners, illuminating richly patterned walls and casting a burnished glow over the sheer covering someone had draped over my legs. There were no windows, and it made sense: if there was safety to be had in the ruins, it would be underground. I felt as though my head were in several pieces, my thoughts out of order or missing completely. There was little sense to be made of what I had seen in the courtyard, an impression of Re'Kether as it had been. That I had slipped so easily into the vision was another complication I didn't need. I wasn't given more than a moment to regain my bearings, though, for my mother was slipping into the room already. She was carrying a tray laden with a pitcher, a squat cup, and several covered dishes. I wanted to ask about Gannet, but her arrival proved more tantalizing for my curiosity.

"Is it really you?" I asked, my eyes fixed on her face for all the smells emanating from the tray made my body tremble with hunger. She gave me a look so familiar it hurt.

"I don't need to ask you that," she chastised, sitting down on the bed's edge and placing the tray between us. "And your presence here is far more unlikely."

I nodded slowly, but I couldn't maintain eye contact. I poured myself a cup of water and drained it an instant later, then poured another and forced myself to sip this time. Without asking, my mother lifted the lid of the dish nearest to me, revealing meat stewed in a thick, aromatic broth. There was bread and pickled vegetables, too, and currants in a syrup so sweet it made my teeth ache. I ate some of everything before speaking, burning my tongue in my haste but not caring in the slightest. It tasted wonderful. It tasted of home.

As my hunger ebbed my curiosity grew. I considered why I had needed to ask my mother if she was really there, and decided I wanted her to know. The test felt like something that had happened years ago, longer even than the last time she and I had been together.

"Did you dream about me, while I was away?" I asked, studying her expression, memorizing every new line worried around her eyes, the hairs newly grayed at her temples.

"Often."

She wasn't looking at me, nor at the dishes of food I was slowly emptying. Her eyes were focused out, beyond, as though this room had a window only she could see through.

"I saw you, a few months ago," I went on. "It was like a dream, but it wasn't a dream."

Now she looked at me. I could hardly blink for the intensity of her gaze, fixing me like an insect in amber.

"What do you mean?"

I managed to shrug, looking down into the cup I had drained.

"I felt sure it wasn't real, what I saw, but I didn't think I'd get the chance to ask you, either," I admitted. "I visited places in Ambar…that weren't anywhere. You and I were underground, sitting at a pool's edge. We talked."

My mother's brow furrowed.

"This is the farthest I have come from home, Eiren. What you saw was not me," she insisted, though I felt she wasn't being entirely truthful with me. I began to dig without even realizing that I was doing it, seeing my face reflected murkily back at me as it had been that day in the cavern.

"Stop that." My mother's voice was sharp, edged with fright. She didn't remember it, not really, or had only a shade of memory, as she had been a shade of herself. I was sorry to have invaded her trust but was strangely let down, too. I had felt a connection during my test, and I had wanted some part of it to be true, at least.

"It felt very real," I offered as an explanation—an apology. So many things in Ambar had felt real, more real even than what I had known before. The genuine tenor of Morainn's laugh. The heat of Gannet's touch and the fire in mine. My independence. My power.

"What happened to you, when you were away?" she asked, though I heard a different question, quiet as a breath, and one she feared the answer to even more.

What changed you?

I stood up. My head felt clearer than it had since we'd emerged from the pool in the bathhouse, and time was short. I didn't even know how long I had been unconscious.

"I want to tell you. I will tell you. But first, I need to know that Gannet is safe. He's a…friend."

She noted the pause as I struggled to put a word to what Gannet was to me. If war hadn't aged my mother, this homecoming would. She rose, as well, but with less confidence.

"He hasn't been harmed. He's been cooperative. Now I can see why."

Here was a look of a different kind, and my cheeks grew hot.

"It isn't that," I insisted, grateful, not for the first time, that my mother didn't possess my gifts. Had I told her a lie? I certainly hadn't given her the truth.

"I'll take you to him. Dress first, Eiren." Her smile was tense, but only briefly. She didn't wait for the soil and worries of the road to be scrubbed away before taking two steps forward to embrace me, finally. Her touch was light and tight at the same time, and she smelled just as I remembered: of the scented oil she dabbed behind her ears, of her favorite tea, of clothes stored folded with dried herbs.

How hadn't I missed her more?

She stepped outside to give me the privacy to do as she had asked. There was an herbal salve and a rough cloth, the familiar odor leading me by the nose into memory. I scrubbed underneath my arms, my belly and neck, between my legs, remembered my mother's hands at this steady work when I was a child and all limbs and giggles. When I dressed, the familiar tug of light silk slipping down my back was achingly familiar, too. The dress was one of my mother's, too big for me, but as heartening as the food had been. I had worn beautiful things in my youth, and in Ambar, but my mother's dress didn't need elaborate embroidery to tell a story.

The corridor beyond was more suffocating even than the cramped chamber had been. We were underground, but I could see now that this place had not always been there. Behind where my mother stood rubble was piled, the ancient glaze of roof tiles glowing dully in the light of the lone torch she carried. I felt as though I were in a warren, a rough waste for rats to scurry. Just as I had in the square, I could see how things might once have been: rather than the uneven stone above, there would have been broad fabric canopies to offer shade and filter the light to soft reds, blues, and yellows. I half-feared I would be transported again but wanted it, too, powerfully curious about the world before.

Mother beckoned wordlessly for me to follow her down the dark path, her torch illuminating rotting timber, broken mosaic. She shielded the flame when we passed areas where its light might be seen, where the collapse had been only partial, and the moonlight provided a white-blue flood of light.

But she wasn't quiet for long.

"I remember his face," she said, drawing my attention from our surroundings. "What you can see of it."

I nodded. "He was my guide, my teacher, on the way to their capitol."

"He was with the final assault. He captured and enslaved you."

"Yes," I answered quietly, not looking at her, but ahead, at what appeared to be a pair of shoes forgotten against a cracked wall. They weren't shoes but the severed feet of a broken statue, the rest of which had no doubt been crushed under the weight of stone that had dumped from the street above when this part of the city had been swallowed up. I bent to examine the fine toes, the perfectly carved nails. I thought of the story of the sandal maker's daughters. She had taught me that story, and so many others. Was it a real one, as others had proved to be?

Did she know she had birthed a myth, as well as reared one?

Gannet was being held in a small room that was miraculously preserved, stone latticework all over, the like of which I would have expected to see in Jhosch. He could be seen from all angles and was afforded no privacy: there was more light here, and the numerous torches afforded me not only a view of him but also several guards standing watch, a chamber pot, and an untouched bucket of water within. I was not surprised to find my brother among those tasked to guard him, but the excessive number of armed individuals outside the chamber included my sister Lista, as well. This I could not have anticipated.

"Eiren!" she exclaimed, breaking from the group and running to embrace me. Her joy and relief were staggering, as real as the press of the sword at her side, the tiny, interlocking plates of cured leather she wore from shoulder to hip.

"Do you know him? He hasn't spoken more than four words to any of us," Lista rattled, pulling back to look me in the face. Hers was bereft of the paints I would have expected her to take up again, but her eyes sparkled and her cheeks were touched with the sun's blush. She'd never looked more beautiful.

Before I could answer her, Jurnus was there, answering for me.

"Of course she knows him. Why did you bring him with you, Eiren? What does he want?"

"He wants to see *her*," Lista insisted, and my lips snapped shut again, mouth full of words they wouldn't give me the space to speak. "It's all he's asked for. No water, even."

"A man thirsts for more than water," my mother said, chiming in with another knowing look.

"Eiren would never betray us," Jurnus countered, but his eyes had clouded. He looked at me. "Would you?"

"Of course she wouldn't!" Lista exclaimed, her eyes flicking through the detail of a latticework stone flower to appraise their captive once again. My irritation mounted, skin crawling with heat and the insect-swarm pricking of annoyance. "Even if he is handsome. What parts of him you can see, anyway."

"Enough," I hissed, my voice like the stomp of a foot. My outburst shocked them into silence, three pairs of eyes looking on me as though I were a stranger.

"Allow me to speak with him, please," I added more softly, though these were not the meek and yielding tones that they knew. I was not that Eiren, not any longer.

I didn't even want to be her.

My siblings and my mother stood aside, and I advanced into the room where Gannet sat, his arms hanging over his knees as he attempted to find a comfortable position on the rough stone floor. It had once boasted a sumptuous carpet, thick enough to cover his hands to the wrist. I could see it and the sunlight, too, a memory that floated before me as real as a reflection. I shook my head as though to clear it, and he was already getting to his feet, his expression for an instant that of unguarded relief at seeing me.

"Very hospitable, your family."

I rolled my eyes. "They have little reason to offer hospitality to the enemy, which, as far as they're concerned, you are."

My response created a careful distance between my family and me, and only because I knew they watched and listened did I show any restraint in reaching out to him. His wounds had been cleaned and were, as I'd initially suspected, superficial.

"We've lost so much time," I whispered, quelling panic. As I spoke, a plan formulated in my mind. "And the city is in ruins. But I had a vision in the courtyard, of Re'Kether as it was. If I could have another one, maybe I could find what we're looking for. It's bound to be ancient."

Gannet's lips curled, and I couldn't tell if he was pleased or troubled.

"Can you trust any visions you might have?"

"It's better than nothing," I snapped, because I heard what he wasn't saying: could I trust that I wasn't being manipulated by

Theba? "And it isn't only that. There's a ghost of the ancient city all around us, everywhere that I look, like a projection of light. I see ruined buildings made whole again, clean streets and trees heavy with fruit where there is only sand and crumbled stone. Do you see anything?"

I could see his answer in his tightened lips even before he spoke.

"No, Eiren. I see only what is in front of me."

While we were speaking, my brother and sister edged their way into the room, my mother a wary shadow behind them. Though Gannet had no weapons, they still regarded him as though he might strike at any moment, a feral animal cornered.

"Gannet, this is my mother and one of my sisters, Lista," I said, grateful for a mundane interruption.

"We've met." My mother's voice was icy. In her mind she was bound to a horse again on the road to Jarl. To her it felt like only yesterday. For me it may as well have been a lifetime ago.

"You don't have anything to fear from me," Gannet said carefully. "I'm here to help Eiren."

"Why?" Jurnus asked, hanging back despite Gannet's assertions. Gannet cast a knowing look at me, and my shoulders slouched in dread. I had to tell them. I had so much to tell them.

"Eiren, what is happening?" This from Lista, without pretense or pressure.

"It's a story I only want to tell once," I began, hoping to delay for just a little longer. But even as I trailed off, Esbat, Anise, and my father appeared, as though summoned by my anxiety. Father's face broke into a wide grin despite our awkward circumstances, and he crossed the room to embrace me where the others had not. He was over-warm, having regained some of the weight he'd lost in the desert, and his hands were callused with work. Unlike my brother and all three of my sisters, he wore no armor, carried no weapon.

"Eiren was about to tell us how she came to be here," my mother intoned, her words a warning: there was no excuse not to speak the truth now.

It would be easier to show them.

Gannet's encouragement was plain, but I neither wanted nor needed it. My breath trembled, a palsy in my throat. There wasn't air enough in the world to tell what I needed to tell.

"The Ambarians took me because they believe that I am the icon, the physical embodiment, of a goddess." Panic stirred the bile in my gut to a froth. "Of Theba."

Even Jurnus, who had been the least attentive to my mother's stories and more heedless still at prayer, gave me an uncertain look. But if I had expected shock, outrage, or fear, I felt none of them. If anything, overwhelmingly, I experienced their doubt.

"And you believe them?" Anise asked, even her level head shaking in disbelief.

"I didn't at first, but now I do," I answered, knowing they were in the place that I had been, on the barge with Gannet in the dark. Disbelieving.

"Eiren, you are no monster. They must have lied to you, tricked you," my mother began. I felt my temper rising at the catalog of obedience, dutifulness, and sacrifice she carried in her memories of me. Eiren would never have felt this way, so it must have been Theba. But were these feelings of resentment all her? Or did a part of me appreciate the past few months? I had been a captive, but I had been freer in more ways than I could ever have anticipated.

"I *am* Theba. I have seen and done things that I can't ever tell you about for shame of them. I am only here because I ran away from her power, but I know now that I can't."

My cheeks flared with feeling, my lips flushed purple-black and raw, still, from thirst. Esbat crossed to me, lifted a cool hand to my face in a sisterly touch whose gentleness hardly registered with me. I pushed her away.

"Have they poisoned your body as well as your mind?" she asked, hurt. "You are home now, Eiren. They cannot hurt you. They cannot make you tell their lies."

My eyes cut from the shock on her face to Gannet, to the

grim, knowing line of his mouth. He'd been right. It wasn't just easier to show them but was the *only* way they would understand.

I took a step back, refusing to meet the crush of their eyes, walling myself away. Their surprise and alarm, their uncertain impressions of the daughter and sister who stood before them, could not touch me. I was mutable as water, deadly as fire.

I knew I had the power to control the conflagration now. Having given in before, I instinctively knew to rein in the desire that followed the flame: to consume, to destroy, to render all to faceless ash.

So, when I reached within myself, not as deeply as I might once have needed to do, only my hand caught fire. I experienced a perverse, satisfying warmth in the act, my blazing fingertips reflected in the wide-eyed shock of my family. Experiencing their impression of what they witnessed hurt me more than the fire I had conjured.

"This is nothing compared with what I can do," I said for emphasis. "I can set fire to an entire city. I've tried. I can read a man's darkest heart, force him to act against his own will. I have. I am venerated. I am feared. By everyone."

After a moment, the flames were snuffed out, leaving my fingertips waxy and warm. No one spoke, and rather than encountering the risk of flooding my mind with the tidal swell of their emotions, I walled myself against them, stones of indifference damming me up.

"I didn't think what it would mean to return, but now I know. I don't belong here with you, not anymore."

As they had circled me once, the last time we had all been together, the day that I was taken, they circled me again now. And maybe it even felt the same for them, to support me no matter what my choices were, regardless of their limited understanding of them. But it would never be the same for me, never again. Though dwarfed by nearly everyone in my family, I saw Gannet through the wedge of their bodies and held back the tears I wanted desperately to shed. He waited until they had held me long enough to feel comfortable letting go before he spoke, an outsider attempting to find his way in.

"Eiren and I did not come here by accident. The force that comes from the north is seeking something within the city, and we must find it first," Gannet said, holding my eyes. "We must have access to your maps, your scouting reports. We need to know the movements of the Ambarian patrols, what parts of the city are safe, and where we can expect to encounter resistance."

He had everyone's attention now.

"You mean to go out there? The two of you, alone?" My father was baffled, and I couldn't blame him. He might have expected such behavior from Jurnus or Lista, but not me.

"And what do you seek?" My mother, full of stories, had any number of answers, but she wanted to hear it from Gannet, from me.

I wanted to tell her the truth, but I couldn't. They'd never let us go if I did.

"We believe it is a weapon from the ancient world. Powerful enough to change the tide of the war." Gannet glossed over what little we knew of a threat they would understand. I felt my father's alarm, my older sisters' blind panic, all their feelings all at once. I picked out from the scramble of emotions only Jurnus's wounded pride, his outrage.

"Why should we do anything you ask? You return with our sister and some wild tale, you have intelligence we don't, and you offer no explanation," he spat, a litany of grief. Even his love for me was tangled up with distrust, uncertainty, and grave underestimation.

My father laid a hand on Jurnus's arm and stepped forward. Despite the sweat that trembled on his brow, and the chill I knew he held in his heart, my father's voice was steady, his countenance that of a king.

"You ask a great deal. My son is not alone in being not altogether satisfied with the explanation we've been given," he said carefully, watching Gannet's face for a reaction. He didn't twitch, a preternatural stillness settling even below the mask. Gannet held my father's eyes with his when next he spoke.

"The force from the north believes it is Theba who drives them. There is an imposter with the army, posing as the Dread Goddess, compelling them to war. They fear her displeasure more than they fear their own deaths." Gannet's tone was cool, belying the heat of his next words. "Your daughter has risked herself, returning here, to warn you. To stand against them. If you will not come to her aid, I cannot help you."

A younger Jurnus might have drawn his blade on Gannet, but this one only tightened his hand on the hilt. Lista looked at him for guidance, her own posture betraying her uncertainty. Esbat and Anise huddled near my mother, fear and outrage warring in their faces and their hearts. My mother and father only looked sad, and in my father's mind, the grief over a lifetime of war dogging his passage toward peace was so heavy I couldn't bear it, and I had no idea how he managed it.

"We're lost," Esbat whispered, at last, pressing a fist to her mouth. "How can we stand against such madness?"

Jurnus shook his head and my father's hand from his shoulder, expression peevish.

"Who is this imposter? She's just a woman. We have the advantage in this city." Jurnus's words roused a look of doubt from my mother and reluctant nods from my sisters.

"I've never heard a story of a siege that ended well for the ones on our side of it," I interrupted before he could get more carried away. I looked between Jurnus and my parents, my eyes pleading. "Gannet and I must search the city. The fight will come to us either way—but if we aren't prepared, we will pay with our lives, this time."

"Why are you afraid?" Esbat interjected with a scholar's curiosity. "If you're really Theba, why don't you just kill this pretender?"

"Exactly. We have the real Theba on our side," Jurnus insisted, pointing at me as he addressed our family.

"Theba isn't on anyone's side." I felt a stir up my spine like trailing fingers. She would not let me stop with killing just the imposter, perhaps next time would not let me stop killing again, ever.

"And I'm not immortal," I continued, calmly as I could manage. "I couldn't stand against thousands, and even if I could, they may not all be serving her willingly. I won't kill innocents."

Again. I won't kill innocents again.

"But *you're* Theba," Lista argued, though she didn't sound completely sure of herself.

"It isn't like that." How could I make them understand? "Her powers are violent. Her appetites...dark. I cannot control her."

You are right now.

I heard my mother's thoughts and was grateful she did not voice them. I had no justification against her hope.

"I have done terrible things. If I give in to her again, I don't know what I'll do. I am afraid I'll never return to myself," I said after a tortured moment. I sensed that they still didn't believe me, not any of it, not really.

"There are other assets we may uncover," Gannet interrupted, sparing me from further explanation. "Re'Kether has many secrets, subterranean passages that will allow you to surprise the enemy, ancient caches of potent fire oil, and the golems."

"The golems?" This from my mother, who alone hadn't taken her eyes off me.

Gannet nodded, posture commanding, like a man preparing to deliver a lecture.

"Tirce fashioned soldiers of mud and clay for Shran, a gift to his friend when he was no longer a boy and their childhood games were behind them," Gannet intoned, and I couldn't help but admire how easily he diverted their attention from me. "They guard his tomb still, and an icon's touch could persuade them to serve you."

"But that's just a story," Jurnus said dismissively, and Gannet shot a surprised look at me. I could imagine his brows arching behind the mask.

"I thought your people put great faith in stories."

"Some of us do," Anise answered quietly. "But to take them literally? How can you be sure these golems exist?"

"I can't," Gannet answered honestly, turning my heart over again with a response that was so typically his. A lesser man might've shrugged, seeking an apology, but Gannet wanted none. "But you have very little time and fewer resources. Allow us to explore the ruins. We have no martial skills. We'll be of little use to you anyway."

I could see as well as feel my father weighing what Gannet had said, the likelihood of our finding anything of use, of getting ourselves killed in the process. Jurnus was flatly against it, but it wouldn't be his decision to make. I wasn't familiar with the story Gannet had spoken of, though it fit my understanding of the relationship between Shran and the youthful god Tirce. Was believing in an ancient army of stone men wilder than anything else I had come to believe? No. But it still seemed unlikely that we would find them. I had always believed the location of Shran's tomb was lost, though Re'Kether had never warranted a mention in the stories my mother had told. Perhaps there was a reason. Perhaps it was here.

"Fine," my father announced, at last, eyes passing between Gannet and me. "We will share what we know. We can spare an armed escort as well."

"No," Gannet replied, and belatedly added, "but thank you. We'll move more quietly and be less likely to be seen without one." He caught my eyes, his own cold with knowledge. My stomach twisted.

I could not stand against thousands, it was true. But if we encountered a rogue patrol, I could easily dispatch a handful of men.

CHAPTER ELEVEN

Even after everything, I had to convince my mother and father to release Gannet from his cell. We were both shadowed by guards back to the subterranean chambers our people had reclaimed, and couldn't speak together. I didn't even reach out to touch his mind, for I was watched every moment. My sisters and mother believed that I had lied about our relationship, and I didn't want to give them any more reason to think so. I cared for him, but it was not some easy dalliance that I could blush and giggle over as I might have done if our lives had ever been normal. It was dangerous. There was no future in it. They would not understand.

I felt drained, besides, by the necessary telling they had already required of me, the display of fire, the prospect of the imposter's arrival within a few days' time. Gannet and I would rest for what remained of the night and begin tomorrow. Exhausted though I was, I didn't know how I would ever sleep. The shadows of the past were growing brighter, softening the edges of the present, making it difficult to determine what was real and what was not, what was and what had been. Putting one foot in front of the other became a challenge; I couldn't be sure if I would meet freshly swept stone or sand-dusted ruin.

And then I saw the woman crouched on the stair, a mere outline, bright, fuzzy, and *wrong*. She was looking right at me, through me, and I whipped around, as though I expected to see something behind me.

There was nothing.

But when I turned back, the woman was still there, standing, several steps closer than she had been the moment before. I took an instinctive step back up one stair. Esbat noted my faltering, her worried face flickering with doubt. She opened her mouth to speak.

"Do you see that? Do you see her?" I managed, voice shaking with terror. Esbat looked alarmed when she shook her head.

The woman reached forward.

"Ji, it's me. Ji?"

The woman's face imposed upon my sister's for but an instant, her voice pitched at a stranger's tone. I did not recognize the name on her lips, on the lips of the other.

"Eiren, are you well?"

"Ji, come on. They're waiting."

The not-woman's hand connected with my chest and two women flashed before my eyes: Esbat, who dominated my earliest memories, and another whom I couldn't even place. Both were looking at me, speaking to me, the sudden chaos of knowing and not knowing threatening to make me sick. Beyond Esbat there was a changing scene, as well, the crumbling facade of an ancient artifice replaced with an imposing wall hung inexpertly with many faded tapestries. Underneath, the stone was the same. I didn't know how I knew but I knew.

Esbat's brow furrowed, yet even as she spoke my name her features changed, her nose flattened, her hair unraveled from its careful plait into wild tangles.

"Eiren?"

I had thought that there was no madness beyond Theba, no madness beyond the haunts of this place, but I was wrong. As the new face came completely into focus, the blurred edges of the other world imposed utterly over the one I was only just becoming accustomed to, I felt myself slipping away. As Esbat changed, I changed, too. It wasn't like it had been at the fountain in the courtyard, where I had seemed to pass as myself into some distant vision of Re'Kether. I felt the threads of my own consciousness unravel as another weaving began, another person, another set of knowledge and memories. I wasn't me. I forgot myself.

I was eclipsed entirely by someone else; I *was* someone else.

"Ji, have you been chewing leaves again? Get *out* of there before they decide to come looking."

I scrambled from a tall wardrobe, hitching the waist of artfully loose trousers with my free hand. In the other, I clutched a slip of paper folded around a blade, the trickle of blood from my palm revealing the message scrawled there. More knives were in the belt I wore beneath the trousers, a final and most deadly blade strapped to my thigh. Lucky it was the fashion.

"If she wants to know what I've got to tell her, she can wait a little," I hissed, neither confirming nor denying the accusation that my dalliance was due to the *cappa* leaf. Another fashion. Another vice.

"I think you overestimate just how much she likes you, Ji. Or what you can do," Mara returned, grinning. Her eyes were warm beneath a fringe of graying hair tucked behind one tattooed ear, heavy with the weights that identified her as a medium. She walked between the worlds, delivering orders from one into the hands of those charged to carry them out in the other. From our lords to the lorded over. To us.

I didn't argue with her. Mara's skills of perception were greater in the other world than they were here, but she was probably still right.

Her eyes flicked to the message in my hand, to the blood that oozed from the pressure of my closed fist. A drop fell, so slowly it was as though it were caught in time, and she swept a leg out to catch it in a fold of her skirt.

"Precious stuff. Don't want to waste it."

"And don't want to leave any evidence behind."

Though I was bred of the First People, I felt I had more to offer than what flowed through my veins. And that was why we were here.

"Come on," she said again, gesturing to the door that allowed a sliver of torchlight into the cloister where we waited. At the same time, there were families who could afford only enough fuel to cook their week's meat, and there was a temple on every corner with fires alight in every empty chamber. This was part of the problem.

We slipped into the corridor, the soles of our shoes weathered soft and soundless. More tapestries hung here, a few flapping in the wind that threatened to bring another storm. It was the month of fury, and the heavens were appropriately thunderous. We made our way down, and then *down*, deep into the temple's storehouse. I seethed at the great casks of ritual wine, the bolts of shroud cloth, the rice and grain sealed in spelled jars that repelled the elements and curious rodents alike. Mara laid a hand lightly on my arm, sensing my distress, and I shook her off. I knew she felt the same as I did, that she scoffed at such excess. That was why she used her gifts for our cause and not the temple's, as they'd been bred to be.

But we couldn't work fast enough for my tastes.

When we neared the meeting place, Mara withdrew a key from a discreet pocket in the scarf she wore around her neck, inserting it into a dusty lock. Our contact clearly had other means of entering this particular room, and I half considered asking her, wondering if she'd value daring as much as information. Unlikely, but if we were going to be working together, she'd do better to know me for who and what I was.

It was dark in the chamber, and when we entered and closed the door behind us, there was no answering illumination.

"You have a message for me."

The voice was hale and deep for a woman, though I assumed she pitched her voice to disguise herself if she couldn't be bothered with a light.

"And no way for you to read it," I said conversationally, feeling the sharp bite of Mara's elbow in my side.

There was a pause that another person might've filled with a laugh or a snort of dissatisfaction. Our contact did neither.

"I don't need light to read. Give it to me."

The message clung to my palm with the blood that had rendered it readable, and I held out my hand, a challenge. The blade I drew back with my opposite hand, sheathing it, but only just. Even if this was the only knife on my person that she could see, I didn't want her to think that I was too trusting. Trust was part of what had gotten our world into this mess.

I heard her breath, slight and shallow as she read the short missive. Then came the snort, throaty and most certainly displeased.

"A medium and a First Blood, and this is all you've brought me?"

"We can bring no more than what is given," Mara insisted, betraying the teachings that had dominated her early life. I tensed in anger, torn between wishing our contact could see just how much she frustrated me, and thinking it was probably best she couldn't. Someone placed within the temple was an asset we could ill afford to lose, as valuable as Mara, as valuable as me. Likely more than both of us, though I would never have admitted it aloud.

"What did you expect? There's discord on both sides," I said, rising to Mara's defense.

"But you didn't read it." Now her voice was a challenge. My fingers clenched again against my wound.

"Of course not."

"Why not?" the hooded woman asked. This was a surprise. The temple had all the power, more than the king, more, certainly, than his courtiers. There was nothing they could learn from us, not a thought in our minds they could not extract without waiting for us to voice it. I was flummoxed, not having anticipated the question, and this made me more irritated.

"Interpreting messages isn't my job."

Another pregnant pause.

"And you're afraid you'd misunderstand them."

I bit the inside of my cheek and tasted blood. She was being purposefully cruel, voicing what I would not have wanted Mara to hear.

I thought of challenging her, to strike her, but even as I deliberated on the least sensible course of action, a sudden flood of light filled the room, my skin buzzed as though stung all over, and I was Eiren again.

It was more disorienting even than Theba's strongest possession of my heart. I was myself, and then another self, and myself again. I was in the corridor with Anise, Esbat, and my mother, my brother, and Lista, the guards and Gannet having gone on a little ahead. They were slowing, too, and Gannet cast a searching look over his shoulder even with blades bristling about him. As far as I could tell only a few seconds had passed. Had my body gone on while my mind wandered? I could hardly ask. They already thought I was unhinged, and if I had truly experienced what I had seemed to, they were probably right. They would never let Gannet and me do what we needed to do if I couldn't be trusted to remain in control of my senses.

Who was she? *When* was she?

"Eiren, are you well?" Lista searched my face, Anise over her shoulder, narrowing her eyes at me.

"I'm fine. Just tired."

"What did you mean just now, when you asked if I saw her?" Esbat's gaze narrowed, sensing the lie.

"I thought I saw someone in the shadows," I answered. "But I was wrong. It's just exhaustion."

Esbat didn't seem convinced, but she let it go. Ever the logical sister, I had offered her a reasonable explanation for erratic behavior.

I couldn't think what this other woman, Ji, had to do with me, or make much sense of what I had seen. The ghost of Mara, if she had been a ghost, didn't reappear on the stair. Even as I tried to make sense of the thoughts that had filled me while I had been Ji, the details began to fade, like a story I had heard as a child and never had cause to repeat. I remembered, but not truly. Only an impression of the conversation she and Mara and the nameless woman in the dark had had. I hadn't been myself, but it was still strange, to have known the things that she did for a brief moment and all, only to forget them in the next. One crumbling hall looked the same as another, and I couldn't tell if it was the same one I had seen in the vision or not. I was deposited at the chamber where my mother had met me, but I couldn't settle. I waited until I was sure that the guard who patrolled this corridor had passed on before I slipped out of the room and into the dark ruins. I would go back to the stair, to see if the ghost was there again. Perhaps I could talk with her, or she would drag me into the past again. I would try to remember more this time.

It had been one madness after another since Gannet and Morainn had come into my life, and though he was here with me, I felt alone with the wild terrors that he had introduced. Gannet would no doubt insist that I would have awakened to Theba's madness in time, and I was grateful he wasn't present to argue the point.

Even as I doubted what I had seen through Ji's eyes, I perceived the other world, a strange periphery of shadow and flickering torchlight, the smooth, well-tended surfaces of ancient stone now sand-scarred from neglect. I could almost smell the crude animal fat-soaked torches they'd used to brighten the long, dark nights many ages ago. I slipped on the fine threads of a carpet that wasn't there, followed a worn stair to emerge into the night. I'd gone the wrong way but was too arrested by the sight to retreat.

I should've guessed that our subterranean sanctuary was part of the palace, but I was still surprised to look up and see the terraces, the moon-polished veneer of stone walls. Gannet had told me this city had been the seat of our ancient kingdom. What mythical figures had walked here, ruled here, died here?

"It isn't safe for you to be out here."

It was Lista, sword perhaps unwisely sheathed, eyes mere shadows with the moon behind her.

"I'm no safer underground," I insisted, shaking my head to clear it. She'd been carrying a torch but had hastily extinguished it before surfacing. I could smell the burning oil still, as familiar a scent as the expression of concern she wore.

Of all my siblings, Lista had been the only one who had never asked me directly about my gifts. Esbat had an intellectual curiosity, Anise a patronizing concern, Jurnus a rude air of wanting to know if this was something he could best me at. But Lista had simply never inquired, only allowed me to continue being odd, worthy of worry. I'd assumed her too ignorant to care, or too frightened to probe, but now I wondered if her acceptance didn't come from a different place, a bolder strength. Would knowing the source of my power, the depth of my gifts, change how she treated me?

I didn't have to ask to know that it would not.

"I can't very well let you get into trouble on your own," Lista said, her smile eclipsing the worries her face had taken on the months since we had seen each other. "I'm glad you're back, Ren. Even if I can't really believe what has brought you here."

"It doesn't matter if you believe me," I said quietly, hearing the words in another voice, another time, when Gannet had first said them to me, when I had been as reticent as they. It would amuse him, I knew, to see me defending the knowledge I had once scorned.

"But why would the Ambarians worship *her*?" Lista questioned, ignorant of the offense she dealt. I held fast to the flare of Theba's temper, remembering a story I should have found solace in months ago. I cast my eyes across the dark ruins of the city, shuddering as I spied the fires of the Ambarian encampment. It was far enough away that I might have mistaken it for star glow but still too close for comfort.

"You've heard the same stories that I have," I said. "Without Theba, life and love would be endless. The truest pleasures are fleeting. She keeps them that way."

Lista eyed me warily, knowing well that I meant to tell her a story. I couldn't help but smile. This was the first moment I felt like I had truly come home.

"There was a brief time when Theba made herself absent from the affairs of mortals, and while it should've been cause for celebration, instead it was a plague. Theba's passion for Shran was all-consuming. While she made a devoted toy of the king, his kingdom languished.

"Without Theba's breath to sow weeds and sing insects among the crops, they outgrew their furrows and choked each other, tendrils crowding. Blossoms had little chance to bud in the shade and entire yields were lost.

"Without Theba's hands to smother them, the sick wasted and wasted but didn't pass, the elderly languished, babes without mothers to nurse them cried piteously without relief. No one could die, nothing could change, and the little beauties of the world went unnoticed without Theba's cruelty as contrast.

"At last, it was Shran himself who noted the strange plague that visited his kingdom, sharing his worries with his wife, Jemae. But it was not Jemae he spoke with but Theba in disguise. She was so ashamed and startled by her inaction that she flew from him in an instant, causing three of the nearest rivers to flood their banks, a dozen granaries to burn, and a wasting sickness to claim the oldest and weakest within the city walls."

"I doubt anyone thanked her for that," Lista interrupted, casting a dark look at me. I sighed. This was not so uplifting a tale after all.

"No, her name was a curse. It still is. But it doesn't change the balance she brings to the world."

There was no one else to defend her, to defend me, but it made me sick to do it. I felt an uncurling, syrupy warmth in my chest, the low bubble of a chuckle that wasn't mine in my throat.

"She was here, in Re'Kether."

I was speaking, but it wasn't me. Theba parted my lips, moved my hands as they alighted on one of Lista's armored shoulders. Bile rose so high in my throat I was sure she could see it behind my eyes.

"Would you like me to show you?"

"You've never been here before, Eiren. How would you know?"

"I've been here."

And I had been, but it was Theba who laid claim to these ruined stones. My toes curled and I stood, leading, and only after I had taken a few steps did Lista rise and follow, too. We walked back the way we had come, this time out of another door, the lintel cracked and sagging. I wanted to scream at her to stay or to run very fast in the opposite direction, but she was coming after me. Because she trusted me. Because I was her mild sister. Because she didn't believe that I was a monster.

But I was. Oh, I was.

Lista had a torch, though I didn't need it to see. Where there was no moonlight I employed my dark sight, or Theba did, as though holding lenses up to my eyes. We snaked through a squat door in the garden wall, a servant's entrance. I should've railed that she drew us away from the safety of my family, of more soldiers, but I wanted to know what Theba knew, what she clearly meant to reveal to us both.

And she intended to take her time. I wasn't fighting her as hard as I had before, and she used my curiosity as a means to greater control. Theba delighted in my body, tripping my fingers along the rough walls as we passed through close corridors, touching my hair, tasting my lips with my tongue. They were dry and my throat was, too, and I thirsted suddenly for wine to wet them, or a kiss. She would need rivers and armies to sate her, but I would have settled to share a cup with just one man.

"Many blamed Jemae for the kingdom's fall," Theba said in my voice, her smile on my lips all wrong. But Lista couldn't see it, wouldn't suspect anything even if she could. Theba was carrying on as if I hadn't stopped telling the story. "It began then, when a woman so beguiled Shran that he failed his people.

"She considered herself blameless, though it was she who possessed Jemae, she who drove Shran to near madness with want of her. He had loved his wife and together they had loved their kingdom, but Theba had given him room enough in his heart only for slavish devotion."

I tripped and stumbled against a narrow stair, the pain for a moment granting me some control over my body. I reached out for Lista, as though with a touch I could warn her, but it was too brief. The slip caused Theba to clutch at me even tighter, and we continued up, Lista trailing, Theba leading, my will a powerless haze that threatened to blind me.

"If she was at fault, then she suffered plenty," Lista reasoned, Jemae's story unfolding in her mind, swelling as Jemae's belly had with a child that was not her own.

"She couldn't suffer enough."

These words caused Lista's senses to sharpen, and I knew the look she gave me without being able to see her, eyes fixed on the climb ahead. She didn't suspect the truth, that I wasn't in control but rather that I had become cruel. She believed something in me had changed in my time apart from my family.

And it had.

"Eiren, we really shouldn't be out here. The patrols have never penetrated this deeply into the city, but that doesn't mean they couldn't begin tonight." Theba ignored her, and Lista followed, partly out of a desire to protect me and partly her own curiosity. We passed out of the dark stair and into a wide, open one, the time-balding stone of the steps beneath our feet giving way to a beautiful chaos of mosaic tile. The colors had kept their vibrancy despite the neglect of many hundreds of years, perhaps because this place was largely shielded from the elements. Moonlight filtered in through miraculously intact latticework screens in the high ceiling, angled smartly to divert the rain.

Lista's torch created the shadows of wild creatures as we climbed on, their teeth seeming to nip and grind at our heels, sharpened by my imagination. I did not have to wonder long where they chased us, where Theba was leading us, for I recognized it the instant we passed through a high archway and onto what once had been a lush rooftop garden. Silks had hung here, in another time, the smells of waxy, flowering trees profuse in the air. I had dreamed this place.

I knew now it hadn't been a dream.

I saw the low stone bench where Theba had taken Shran, where he had presumed to take his wife, centuries of neglect failing to diminish the cold burn of the memory in me. The heat of his skin felt as near to me as though I wore it myself. I shivered and was relieved that I could. I felt Theba inexplicably retreating, and I was grateful to Lista for not asking me immediately how I'd known this place.

Why did Theba want me to see this? I could only think that she wanted me to feel as she felt, but what cause had the Dread

Goddess for sympathy? Was it not enough to control my body? Must she rule my heart and my head, as well?

Despite her earlier protest, Lista walked ahead of me onto the terrace, running her hands along the crumbling facade that would make it difficult to jump from here to the ground, several hundred feet below. It looked as though it had once boasted a parade of mythical architectural beasts, mostly serpents, and the rare, unlucky creature ensnared in the serpent's jaws. There was sand everywhere, evidence that storms had been the only occupants of Re'Kether for some time. Storms and ghosts.

The feeling was different here, more akin to the dread I had felt the night I had escaped the barge and yet somehow completely divorced from the wild terror of that night, too. And while there was certainly some of that here, stinging my eyes like smoke from a fire, there was a bitter sweetness in the air, too, as though someone had cast a handful of dried herbs on the fire just as it was dying, tempering the smell. I took a few steps forward, my lips parted as though I might taste what lingered here, the traces of forgotten love, lust, deception.

"Jurnus will piss hot oil if he finds us up here." Lista's words drew my attention, her smirk grounding me in the present. "Where are we?"

"Somewhere that Shran retreated to, a very long time ago. Jemae, too."

This was a place that had been beautiful and secret, a place to escape to when the pressures of court became too much. I was troubled by what was obviously a gift from Theba, showing me this place. I glanced at Lista, but she was looking behind me, beyond me, her eyes hard in the moonlight. I followed her gaze to the distant fires of the nearest Ambarian encampment.

"After they took you, we didn't know what to expect," Lista said quietly. "We spent three days in the reliquary, relieving ourselves in one corner, sleeping in another."

I knew better than to say that I was sorry.

"And within days of being allowed some freedom to 'ease the

transition of power' for our people, Jurnus raced after you. He killed two of their soldiers in the process. When he didn't come back, they chained father up. And mother a week later, when they found her mixing poisons. Then they made a spectacle of laying open the backs of the herbalists who had supplied her and burned three community gardens."

My sharp intake of breath was too loud for the terrace. My father, my mother, our people, we all understood physical pain. But our land was cultivated at great cost. The dozens of families that depended on those gardens would starve, or steal, or worse. Lista's thoughts were a turmoil of memory, the moments she stole to tend to the raw wounds on our parents' wrists blurring into clandestine encounters with one of the Ambarian soldiers, the knives she smuggled from his things. The one she'd used to cut his throat.

"How did you get away?" I asked finally, not looking at her.

"The Ambarians assumed that three sisters would behave themselves, with a hunted brother and a shackled mother and father. They were wrong." Lista forced me to meet her eyes. She needed me to know that she had suffered, that she had survived and was stronger for it. "They also didn't expect our people to have caches of weapons and water and gold enough for bribes."

"And now you're here."

"And now *you're* here," Lista repeated, her emphasis punctuated by her hands reaching out to clasp mine. She chewed her lip. "You really can't help us?"

I didn't need her to explain what she meant. I shook my head, thinking of Theba walking us both here, driven by some need that I couldn't understand. The Dread Goddess had her own agenda, and it didn't align with mine.

"There's not a weapon in the world you'd want to put in my hand. Trust me."

But she didn't trust me, not about Theba. And I couldn't expect her to, not when Gannet and I had promised them just that: a weapon.

CHAPTER TWELVE

Lista returned me to my chamber, making plausible explanations to the two soldiers we encountered on our descent. She hugged me, and I allowed myself to relax into the embrace. Captivity, the war, both had changed her. She was like silk that has shredded in a strong wind, whose fibers go on to feed a strong rope.

Dawn could not have been more than an hour off, and I fell straightaway into my bed, not even bothering with the little lamp. But it flared to life no sooner than my head hit the pillow, and I shot back up, my fright transforming quickly to shock.

"What are you doing in here?" I hissed at Gannet, who leaned against the far wall, back stiff as the stones themselves. I snatched at the loose collar of my dress before remembering that I hadn't bothered undressing before falling into bed.

"I was waiting for you."

"Obviously." I bit my tongue to keep from being so obviously baited. "But why? If my brother or father, or gods forbid, my mother, learn you're in here, you'll find it impossible to scout the ruins tomorrow as you'll be without the use of your legs."

Gannet stiffened. "I know how to go unnoticed when I need to."

"You're the least noticeable masked man of my acquaintance."

"Eiren, what happened on the stair?" He fought the urge to grin, his determination always easier for him than his long-neglected sense of humor. "I felt you change, but it was gone again as quickly as it came. I came to ask you about it and you were gone. So, I waited."

I sat up, and before I could think better of it, beckoned him to join me at the edge of the bed. He didn't fight the request, but he didn't sit near enough for us to touch, either.

"It was another vision of Re'Kether as it was. But this one was different. I *became* somebody else. I walked through a moment in her life, knew the people that she knew."

"Was it a story that you remember? Did anything look or sound familiar?"

I shook my head. It wasn't an unreasonable line of questioning, but I didn't know any stories about any Ji, or Mara.

"I don't even remember it all now. But maybe you do?" I told myself I didn't only want to touch him because I could now, because he was there, but because he might be able to help. I laid a hand on his cheek and tried to share the strange vision with him, but there were no memories to transmit, just snatches of detail clouded as though with sleep, like a dream. For the first time, I didn't have to try to hide something from Gannet; he simply couldn't see. I let my hand drop reluctantly to the thin blanket and retreat to my lap. "I saw a strange figure, like a ghost, on the stair. And when she touched me, I was transported."

"But you didn't go anywhere," Gannet observed, eyes worrying the air before him with thought. "It's really not safe for you here."

"It's not safe for me *anywhere*." I felt like the admonishment was swiftly becoming a refrain for my life. "I tried to go back to the stair, to find the ghost again, but Lista found me and Theba— Theba took control of me. Walked me to an empty part of the palace above."

Gannet's eyes flashed in alarm.

"You couldn't stop her?"

"No." I squirmed. "But I didn't try very hard. I wanted to see what she wanted to show me. Is this something that happens to other icons? Don't you lose control sometimes?"

It was Gannet's turn to be uncomfortable.

"I'm not always clear which wants are mine and which aren't. I'm not sure that's the same."

"Wants?" I felt my heart quicken. His eyes were still, potent as the night. He feared to speak what he thought next, but he made it plain for me.

Sometimes I feel the line between us begin to blur. I don't have the control I once did. I feel you here, everywhere.

He reached tentatively to trace a finger down my shoulder, catching against the fabric of my dress and grazing bare skin. A thrill danced in me, and I collapsed helplessly into it.

Not everywhere.

I took his hand and placed it on my breast, pulling him near, catching his mouth with mine and providing my own hands the work of tugging his shirt from his trousers. My breath caught and his, too, words turned to sighs in the silence, coupled only with the friction of clothing we hastened to discard.

He moved quickly, easing me down against the worn mattress, exploring my cheeks, my neck, the tops of my breasts with hot, eager lips. His hands swept up my thighs, brushing the folds of my gown away as easily he might the spindle-thin pages of an ancient tome. Even as he meant to, as I meant to let him, there was the smallest voice in me that protested. *Someone could hear. Someone could see. You're not alone.*

You're never alone.

I might have ignored it. But he didn't.

Gannet shook his head as though clearing it, lifting himself away from me and rolling to the side, eyes unreadable in the dark, behind the mask.

"I told you I don't have any control." His words were quiet, his countenance severe. I pushed my skirt back down my legs, flushed now from shame and worse, wanting to tuck his shirt tails as eagerly as I had wanted to untuck them only seconds ago.

"What is this?" I asked quietly, not looking at him, not wanting to.

"My sister believes we are in love," Gannet began carefully, not the response I had expected. I held my breath. "I want you. But I feel...pushed. By my own heart, perhaps."

Perhaps not.

We were icons. Whatever we did, could we ever be sure it was what *we* wanted? My own heart soured. It didn't matter that I had the same worries, that I wasn't sure what drove me to him with such force. Was it love, as Morainn believed? I had never been in love. I wanted him to say that he believed that what we wanted was right, that it could not be corrupted.

But Gannet wasn't in the habit of telling me what I wanted to hear.

"We should both get some sleep. You should go," I said, at last, feeling petty, unkind, and only a little guilty about it. He was still lying on his back in my bed, and he turned his head to look at me.

"You're unhappy."

"Of course I am," I answered, sitting up so he couldn't see my face, only the slumped profile of my shoulders. "Theba takes everything from me. Even the things I didn't even know I had, didn't know I wanted."

I felt his light touch in the middle of my back, radiating heat.

"And yet she's given me so much." Gannet was trying to soothe me, but he was, in part, sincere. If Theba hadn't woken in me, we would never have met. "Eiren, look at me."

I cast a look back over my shoulder, eyes hooded. He sat up, meeting my gaze and holding it a long moment before speaking.

"It's me I don't trust, not you. I know who you are, Eiren. I am not afraid of Theba."

"But does anyone know who you are? Does Adah know?"

Gannet shook his head, lips pressed to a regretful line. "If he does, he guards that secret very closely. Not knowing has never kept me from anything. But now—" he began but stopped short of saying more. I'd held up a hand.

"Please, I understand."

When he left, he made no more excuses, offered no further apology. There were no kisses, no protestations, nothing an encounter like this one would've ended with in a story. It felt like an age before I slept, salting the mattress with tears he hadn't earned, biting my lip, my tongue, my pillow in frustration.

CHAPTER THIRTEEN

I was roused by the smell of tea assaulting my nose and my empty belly. I had no other garments but those I'd slept in and the Ambarian traveling gown that was too heavy for the heat, so I smoothed what wrinkles I could and went in search of food.

The area we occupied beneath the palace made me feel like a rat scrambling through a warren, the natural light needling through broken stone in bursts of white and yellow. There was a large common area which boasted many low tables and assorted supplies arranged in the corners that soldiers coming and going would pick from. Here, too, were the refugees from Jarl who could not fight, the elderly, the mothers, the children. Their faces were lined with the weariness that comes of waiting on the edges of war, for death, or for it to be over. For them, there was nothing else.

I sought my family around one of the many small hearths. The spread and the company were nothing like I remembered, even in our leanest years in exile. My mother had fed me well the day before, but when I came upon her, Anise, and Esbat, their fast was broken only by hard bread and shriveled olives in a murky looking oil. Jurnus, Lista, and my father were absent, but Gannet sat with them, his legs underneath him, attending to his own meager rations without complaint.

"Eiren," Anise said, a desperate edge in her voice. "We're almost finished. I was nearly ready to come and get you."

It didn't take much prying on my part to sense that Gannet was the source of her discomfort. His features beneath the mask were drawn and pale, his hair brushed severely back into a short tail.

"Then I suppose I ought to be grateful Lista wasn't here to eat my share," I replied, sitting down between Esbat and my mother and helping myself without further comment to the fare.

"Lista is doing penance for last night's excursion to the palace above by hauling stones to secure the perimeter," my mother said, leveling her gaze on me. "I was hoping you or your companion might be able to provide me with a fitting punishment for a god."

I blanched. How had she known? And why hadn't Lista blamed me?

"We were quite safe," I said lamely, though it was even less the truth than my mother would believe it to be. Theba had compelled me there, and Lista had witlessly followed. I could've argued we had more to fear from the Dread Goddess than we did the Ambarians. "But I should've told someone, I know."

My mother didn't respond, only grunted, sweeping the hard crust of her bread through the last of the oil from the bowl of olives.

"The imposter's army will make it difficult to give you warning of our comings and goings," Gannet interjected, looking at my mother, and each of us in turn. "We have work to do."

"As do I." My mother's expression sharpened on his features, and it was almost as though she had a blade in her hand, testing its weight, its sharpness. "War has never kept me from seeing to the protection of my children. I won't begin to neglect them now."

A tense silence soured what food remained before us. I could hear my sisters' thoughts, see their memories of the time that war had, in fact, done just that: she had not been able to protect us the day that we were captured, when we were returned to our city without the free use of our arms and legs. But they knew better to argue with her, and I would not give Gannet the opportunity.

"Then we should get to it." I popped the last olive in my mouth and, spying an assorted collection of water skins in a pile opposite us, crossed to collect one for the day's exertions. My sisters were taking it in turns to think of me now, to fret, to doubt, to fear, their thoughts like the pressure of a reed needle in muscle. Except there was no release, no sigh following the sharp pain as it subsided. Instead, I ached, pricked again and again with their wondering and worrying. They did not like that I was to be given leave to roam freely about the ruins, did not like the company that I would have to keep. I had wanted so much to be home, to see them again, but now that I was here, the idea of being in the city above, occupied only with my own thoughts and Gannet's whenever he saw fit to share them, appealed to me greatly.

"We don't have much in the way of intelligence to share," Esbat said, at last, rising from the table. "But I can show you what we have."

We followed her down a short corridor and then a stair that wound deeper beneath the ruins. My skin prickled as the air cooled, and when Esbat stopped to light a small lamp in a cleft in the rock, I stood near enough to Gannet that I could've brushed his hand with mine. But I didn't. I felt my mother's suspicious eyes on me, trailing behind us with Anise at her side. In another time, with another man, what she expected would have been celebrated.

But not now, not with this man.

Esbat hadn't lied. Our intelligence gathering had been primarily to determine the movements of the Ambarian troops, the shifts in their number, the places in the city most open to incursion. So, while there were some rough sketches of the terrain and the surrounding structures to be had for these areas, the rest of the ruins remained a mystery. There were other documents in the chamber, scroll cases, flaking parchments squared carefully on shelves that I expected Esbat to have dragged here for just such a purpose, but these she ignored, favoring what was already laid out on a broad table in the center of the chamber.

"Much of the city is unstable," Esbat explained, sweeping a careful hand over the woefully incomplete map she'd laid out before us. She had a curator's touch, and I could sense her protectiveness over these meager documents, the little knowledge she was given leave to accumulate in the middle of a war. "We don't usually go inside the buildings for fear of collapse, but I expect you won't have that luxury."

"No," Gannet answered curtly, looking down his nose at the map.

"But that doesn't mean we can't be careful. This will help us. Thank you." I tried to capture and hold Estbat's eyes, but she met mine only briefly, her expression troubled. She didn't trust Gannet. "Maybe we'll find a library. I'll bring you as many books as I can carry."

Without looking at me, Esbat anchored the map carefully with smooth, polished stones before recovering a box of writing implements from beneath the table where she'd laid it out. Only then did she continue, looking between Gannet and me. "You'll want your hands free, if you encounter the enemy."

It was a warning, an accusation, a fear, and none of it was lost on me. My cheeks flooded with heat and my lips parted, but my mother was speaking before I could.

"Go, and safely. I will say a prayer for you."

Gannet had his hand on the small of my back then, but I didn't need him to propel me forward into the corridor, down the stair, past the guards that clustered nearly unseen in holes carved out between broken stone and sand. His whisper in my ear felt more intimate than sharing the thought would have been.

"And whom will she pray to?"

"Not Theba," I muttered, the sound one of very few to be heard as we drew away from the palace. Even the tiny lizards that scurried over the rocks as we drew near passed silently. "Do you know where we're going?"

Nothing had caught my eye on the map we had been shown, and good as it felt to have the sun warming my back and my hair, I didn't think wandering the ruins aimlessly would be the best use of what little time we had left.

Gannet crouched in the shadow cast by a mammoth stone column, listing perilously to one side but erect still.

"It is fitting that your mother should send us off with a prayer. I think we should try to find some house of worship, if we can," he began. "The gods walked here and this relic, this weapon, it makes sense that it would have been in their care, doesn't it?"

I bit my lip, thoughtful. "It's an obvious course but a good enough place to start."

"'Good enough'?" If I'd been able to see the whole of Gannet's face, would his brow have quirked in amusement? Furrowed in irritation? "I'm glad of your confidence."

"You're welcome," I answered, suppressing a smile.

We moved quickly through the ruins then, staying low, driving toward the east and the point on the horizon where the sun crowned each morning. There were many tales of Dsimah's origins that likened the sunrise to a mother's swelling belly, to the slick, glossy head of a birthing babe. I shared what I knew with Gannet without words, and he with me, the illustrations he had seen in ancient texts in Jhosch, words from the mouth of the icon of Dsimah herself. If there had been a temple to Dsimah here, it would be where the first light would strike it, and it would mimic the sun's arrival in its construction.

I tried to use, too, the strange reconstruction of the other Re'Kether that asserted itself most in shadows, in broken stones reassembled. I found I could see it most clearly out of the corners of my eyes, an ancient world imposed upon a modern ruin, the road swept clean of sand and perfectly maintained, gutters running with water. I could hear the shrieks of children splashing, see their disembodied feet kicking up a spray. The ghosts of mothers hushed them, shop owners shooed them, stately, robed figures ignored them completely, a stark processional down a bright promenade.

"Eiren, wait!"

Gannet's voice was too loud as he grabbed my arm, only just preventing me from walking forward into nothing, a yawning pit before us where the street had collapsed. I fell back against him, dizzy, trying to see both worlds at once. I could see the crush of revelers, advancing into the shadow cast by a domed structure, the light spilling around it, stark as an eclipse.

What do you see?

Gannet's question was a stabilizing touch. I closed my eyes, breathing hard, before opening them and seeing only the world as it was, silent, the pit before us as wide across as ten arms linked and beyond it, all but obliterated by time, the temple of Dsimah.

Look.

He held me still, and I lifted a hand to gently turn his face away from mine and ahead, to the temple. The weight of the dome had been too much for whatever had once supported it for it lay now on its side, broken like a round of bread or a crescent moon. It was clear even from this distance that the whole of the temple was exposed to the elements, many ages of sand spilling out of both the temple's original entrances and those created by the wind.

"Now how are we going to get over there?" I asked, leaving no room for arguments that we couldn't, or wouldn't. I cast around, studying the ruined buildings on either side of the emptiness that had once been a bustling street. These structures appeared no more stable than any we had passed, but there was one, at least, that was still mostly intact, three stories and rounded windows vacant as sightless eyes. Gannet followed my gaze.

"That's a good enough place to start," he said, echoing my earlier sentiment. It was a tense attempt at humor, but I appreciated it all the same.

We skirted the pit, Gannet keeping a hold of my hand, lest I stray into the past again. But the shade of what had been was distant, and I felt for the moment, thankfully, anchored in the present. As we drew near the structure I saw the ghost of color around each blank window, as though the stone had once been brightly painted in bursts of red, pink, and gold. An outbuilding affiliated with the temple, perhaps? That would be lucky.

When we passed inside we both stopped, allowing our eyes to adjust. There was nothing but sand and stone within, twists of desiccated wood that might once have been furniture. Still, our steps were cautious, our eyes as much on the stone below as the ceiling above, hoping that both were strong enough to withstand intruders after centuries alone.

Inside, series of small rooms were connected by a narrow corridor, and I wondered at the purpose of the building, if it had been a home, a place of confession, a storehouse. We entered each room, Gannet bending to examine the walls and floors while I watched, waiting to be shown something.

I didn't have to wait long.

When we reentered the corridor after another fruitless search of one of the rooms, I noted that it lengthened toward where the temple had stood. Rather than the harsh glare of the sun where it should have opened onto ruin and sand, there was a soft light, bobbing like a lantern in darkness.

"Gannet," I murmured, catching his sleeve with my fingers, assuring myself of the warmth of his presence before I let go again. "Don't leave me."

I moved toward the light, not surprised when it took shape, the muted outline of a woman in a voluminous headscarf, the folds skimming her shoulders and obscuring arms, hips, legs. She turned when I drew near and I saw nothing but her eyes, glowing, a demand in their ghostly depths. From beneath the scarf a knife flashed, and I felt it sear hot against my skin, the flesh of my exposed forearm. It wasn't pain that claimed me but something else. I felt myself slipping again, as I had in the corridor with my sisters beside me. I was claimed by another time, another mind, and I didn't resist. The light that I had seen blossomed gold and familiar, and I allowed myself to become the other woman, to see not with Eiren's eyes but Ji's.

"Dsimah's light be with you."

Mara lifted the brazier, arms steady, and two acolytes approached with blazing torches. One of them was even male, though it would take a great deal more than ambition to rise in the temple ranks with his sex to discredit him.

I had little interest in the lighting ritual, though the temple was the ideal place to observe loyalties. From behind my veil I watched those of the First Blood open their veins into the offering bowl, filling it to the very brim with hot, red tribute. More acolytes rushed to bandage the wrists of courtiers and wealthy merchants, the strongest of them tasked with heaving the offering to the head of the temple where Mara stood, still as a statue, holding the now-smoking brazier. To spill even a drop would have resulted in grave punishment. But Mara was strong. I saw the slight quake of her legs only because I was looking for it.

I didn't offer my arm, and in my current garb, it would not have been welcome. From head to foot I wore the charcoal-dusted covering of the mortally ill, and I stood with the poor, doubly disguising my heritage as one of the First Blood. It was the perfect cover. There were no First Blood among the poor, and precious few among those who had to work for their living, even if that work was supervising the work of others. We were esteemed by the gods and so lifted above others.

But to be at the head of a line of sheep bound for slaughter did not seem so great a privilege to me, which was why I hid who and what I was.

"Speaking of," I muttered, noting the robed figure who was now being led forward by armed and armored soldiers. My utterance caught the attention of the long-haired youth who stood nearest me. I met his eyes, knowing mine would appear watery with sickness from the oil I had rubbed beneath them. He looked away quickly. Long hair was usually sign of devotion, but many who hoped to hide their allegiance took on the appearance of the devout. But I wasn't here to determine friend from foe. Recruitment was not our mission, Mara's and mine.

It was rescue.

The robed figure was considerably smaller than those who had laid hands upon her, and when she reached where Mara stood and was turned to face the crowd, I could see that she was very young, perhaps fifteen, and likely eight months gone with child. My heart threatened to rattle right out of my chest, and my nails bit into the soft flesh of my palms when I clenched them under my veil. I had a very good view of the girl, the best, as did all of those without the coin and influence to pay for distance from this unpleasant spectacle.

"Before you stands one of the First Blood, the youngest daughter of House Frai," Mara intoned. "Her child was got on her by her family's horse handler."

At this a second figure was thrust forward, more roughly, and with far less ceremony. The boy was still just that, despite having a few years on the girl, and his surly look was tempered only slightly by the bristling soldiers who stood close.

"They are not wed. They were given no blessing by this temple to be married and will never have it."

I couldn't even tell from looking at them if this was what they wanted. Were they in love? Had she willingly bedded the boy or had he raped her? I wanted it to matter but knew that it didn't—we would save the girl, if we could, but could do nothing for the boy.

"If the child favors the mother, she will be wed as the temple wills, and the infant given to her family to raise," Mara said, steady voice rising. Dalliances were handled always the same. But the next part I knew held special significance for Mara, and though I saw none of it in her face, my own heart pinched in grief for her. "If the infant takes after the father, the babe will be given in service to the temple, and the mother bled."

That infant, in another time, had been Mara. Her mother had been laid upon the guttered table and sliced open.

The girl began to weep openly at this, and the boy struggled, pleading, screeches unintelligible. Perhaps it was love. It didn't change anything.

Mara took a knife, a clean one, the ornamented handle steady in her hands, not even a tremble in her delicate wrist as she approached the young woman. I couldn't help but admire her craft, her pretense of devotion, even as my heart began to pound. The temple wouldn't wait for the babe to be born. If it was of the First Blood, it would survive. If it wasn't, it would have to be strong to live beyond infancy anyway. Gods didn't wait. The poor around me stirred, some riveted, others looking away and hoping that no one would notice their aversion. One elderly woman even retched, the sweet, sickly tang of bile competing with the temple's persistent reek of blood. There were murmurs of discontent even from those of the First Blood who were boxed nearest to us, several still clutching their bandaged arms. Most would not act—even to make a sound of protest was perilous. But I was bolstered by their discomfort, so much that when my cue to throw off the dusted veil came, I did not hesitate.

Rather than plunge the knife into the young girl, Mara lashed out at the soldier nearest to her. She had all the precision of a surgeon when she severed the critical flow of blood between his head and chest, and she leaped over him as he collapsed to take down the next soldier, and the next. She would never be able to return to the temple, but the sacrifice of her place was a strategic one. We had to make a statement. We had to show them that we would not do as they willed, not always and someday, never again.

Sympathizers in the crowd swelled toward the head of the temple, hoping to join the fight against the faithful acolytes and the armed guards, pushing against the tide of those who fought toward the exits. I slipped between the crush of bodies toward the girl and her lover. Even as they struggled to reach each other, one of the soldiers who remained used one of her last acts of life to put an end to his, a lurid spray of blood painting her cheeks before her own throat was cut. I kicked the lifeless body of the soldier, enraged, but met Mara's eyes before we both turned to the girl. She gaped, wordless, one hand reaching for the boy's broken body, the other cradling the swell of their child.

"If you'd see his son or daughter raised in peace, you'll come with us," I said.

I held out my hand. She took it.

The touch of the girl's hand drove me like a strong wind out of the vision and back into Gannet's arm. Or had he been holding me the entire time? We were at the bottom of the corridor, down a slope that ended in rubble and darkness.

"Did you see it? Did you see?"

I was frantic for air, the echoes of terror in my ears akin to those of the opera.

"I didn't see anything, Eiren," Gannet answered, stroking my hair. "You walked down here and you just collapsed."

I tried desperately to hang on to the details of the vision, but again the harder that I tried to hold onto them, the more slippery they became. The stench of blood faded from my nostrils and with it Ji's conviction, the intricacies of the world she knew and lived in, the face of the pregnant girl, the boy, of Mara. Like a dream out of sequence, the narrative of what I had seen lost all sense.

Gannet's mind brushed against mine, and I tried to share with him what I remembered, but there was little more than feeling left, sorrow, rage, the struggle against forces beyond our control. I closed my eyes, pressing my face into his shoulder. I had sought the vision, this time, and I wanted more. But I had to find a way to see, really see, the world before. There were answers there, perhaps more important even than the relic we sought.

I looked up at him and then beyond him. We had reached the bottom of the corridor.

"I don't think there's anything else here for us," I said, once I was sure I could speak without a tremor in my voice. "And I need to know more about Re'Kether as it was before. I need to know everything that you know, every story."

"It would take a long time to tell you every story, Eiren."

"Then you'll have to show me."

CHAPTER FOURTEEN

Gannet stared at me, lips parted slightly as he sought for words.

"I don't think you know what you're asking, Eiren," he replied, at last, lowering me to the ground and squatting in the sand before me.

"The icons share memories, don't they? That's part of how your histories are kept." It was a gamble, a guess, but his sudden intake of breath confirmed my suspicions.

"When one icon dies, those who knew them will share their experiences, their knowledge, with the new icon, when they are old enough. I have only ever been the receiver of memories, Eiren. Never the giver."

"But you've shown me things before. I just need to know what you know."

"I don't know how to choose what I share with you," he insisted, and I felt his discomfort growing despite the barriers he usually had in place against me, against the world. "I don't know what you'll see."

"I'm not afraid."

"And what if I am?"

He leaped to his feet and I remained at a crouch, limbs beginning to protest. But I didn't move.

"This has always set me apart," he said, his eyes a storm when he gestured to the mask, though his hand was steady. "Adah knew me, but only Adah. In every life, I am sentenced without even knowing the crime. I don't want you to see how much that once… troubled me."

"Do you really think that I could judge anyone for being

unwilling to accept a punishment?" I asked, drawing slowly to my feet but not touching him, not yet. "Theba would burn up everything soft in me, every sentiment, every gentle thought. I hate it and my hate feeds her."

"And she would have that same opportunity in me," he said, low as the groan of thunder. "We would be that close. Could you control her?"

Would you control her?

It was a thought we shared, bred of the desire we felt for each other, the uncertainty of what it might mean to give in.

I laid a hand upon his arm, against the skin between his wrist and where he had rolled his sleeves against the heat. But he was cool, and the touch hummed up through my fingers into my arm, my shoulder, to my heart.

"I am stronger than she is." Even as I said it, I knew that to win against Theba I would have to lose. She had tempted me with revenge, with secrets, with the power to have and hold what I wanted, and I had given in to her every time and cursed her for it afterward. If Gannet opened his mind to me, I knew that I would want everything and she could give it to me, if I let her.

But I didn't want to take from him.

"Please, Gannet," I continued, taking two steps forward and willing his arms to open, to embrace me. "I saw something terrible, I think, and I feel like I am playing a game of dice without etchings. Like there's a score being kept and I don't know what it is."

He hesitated, his anxiety stirring the air around us. The burn of rejection had just begun to heat my core when he laid a hand against my neck, pulling my face to his in a fierce kiss, our teeth knocking against each other in a rattle that shook its way down my body. And then his cheek was against mine, the prickling of a hastily shaved face paired with a sensation of another kind: falling, weightless, cradled in his hands, buoyed by the murmur of his words against my cheek and the tidal swell of his thoughts.

Every story of every icon that had come before, generations of lore cataloged as only a man like Gannet might organize memories that were not of his own making. I sensed only Adah's touch in this record, the Adah that we knew and the Adahs that had come before him, each, apparently, the sole carrier of Gannet's icon's experiences. He was the only one who knew who he was, the only one who could see justice done. Each of them had possessed a scholarly interest in the past, and I recognized the details that Gannet had shared with me in his story of the icon of Adah, who had united the Ambarians. I peeled away these layers of memory, searching for what they knew that had come before, of the exodus from Re'Kether, of the city's fall.

Many of the stories that I knew professed that the gods had walked among us, meddled with us, made demands and handed down punishments. I was overwhelmed by the number of histories recorded in his mind, the ledgers of past sins, variations on tales that I knew that were too dark to retell. I needed to focus, and I felt my grip on Gannet's neck tighten as I prowled about in his mind.

I needed to know more about the gods as they had been. They had favored the First People, Shran and Jemae among them, because they were special. The First People had created the gods, and their descendants were both servants and councilors. But how had the gods been driven away? And why did their departure coincide with the collapse of the kingdom we had once shared? For I could see now the great gaps in what Gannet could share with me, the kingdom as it had been, the terror and chaos of living under immortal rule, Shran and his kind merely puppets. The gods had fallen, and when they did the blood of the First People had failed, too. What Gannet knew amounted to little more than lengthy records of births, marriages, deaths, the proceedings of justice, lines of succession, ritual and tradition, but it was enough to provide a frame on which to hang the things that I had seen in my visions. Details from Ji's world glittered like the facets of a jewel passed from hand to hand under a light; with the skeleton of Gannet's knowledge, I saw things I hadn't been able to hold onto before. The visions were of a rebellion, and of Ji's part in it. I felt Ji's hatred for them even now, nearer to the purity of Theba's rage than it was to my own. With Mara, she had fought them, had been party to some scheme against them. Their culture, the central function of the temples of the gods to dispense justice, fortune, food. The children of the First People given over to the temples, their blood a prize, a commodity. But there was nothing in my visions to explain the departure of gods from our world, and nothing in Gannet's mind, either, the fact that they went on to live as icons a mysterious burden.

Icon.

It was a whisper, and the catalog of memory around me dimmed, light from another corner of Gannet's mind pulsing the potent red of a fire waiting to be stoked. I didn't have time to wonder if this was something he didn't want to show me, if this was something he feared, because I felt an umbilical tug drawing me near to that light, that sound.

Icon.

"She is an icon. You must trust me." I saw Gannet in the dark cloak and impractical garb he had worn when I had first met him, standing on the terrace in Jarl with his sister. Though the edges of this Gannet blurred, around him I recognized another chamber in the palace I had lived in as a child. Days before we'd met, then. "We will have to take her with us."

"Is that why you were sent with us? To find this icon?" It was Morainn, and I felt my heart squeezed by the fists she clenched in her skirt. Sweat stood out on her brow. "Did Adah tell you that she would be here?"

"Maybe he knew, I don't know," Gannet's tone was impassive despite his words. "But I don't think so. I can sense her, her every breath, every thought, every gesture. They're getting close. I've never felt anything like this."

Morainn's face clouded, and I realized Gannet hadn't recognized the emotion on her face, did not remember this as accurately as I might have done.

"That sounds dangerous."

"You have no idea." I drew near to Gannet, studying him,

looking for the twitch of alarm or longing in his pursed lips. I could still feel his true lips against my cheek, the soft, meditative breath, as though he slept.

"What happens when we take her back?" Morainn's question was a practical one, but her tone demanded many answers.

"The world ends. Or it begins."

"And if we don't?"

"We have to," Gannet insisted, looking away from Morainn, one hand brushing the lip of the mask above his brow. "*I* have to. It's the only thing I've ever felt I had to do."

Now Morainn seemed truly shaken.

"Which icon is she?"

He looked at her, and when he opened his mouth to speak, a cruel mockery of my own voice emerged.

"*Theba.*"

My voice, first, and then my face, pushing forward through his, shredding skin and breaking bone. I was screaming, scrambling back as though I could escape this memory and Theba's invasion of it. He reached out for me, the fine points of my own fingers twined before me as they burst through his, spraying blood. I heard her laugh, high and cold, like the strike of a blade against stone. I felt it shaking me out of the memory, rattling my teeth and tongue as I was returned to myself, when I captured Gannet's mouth with mine in the corridor of the temple where our bodies crouched still.

"The only thing you've ever felt you had to do?" She spat his words back out at him in between the fevered press of my lips against his. She made me bite his lip so hard I tasted blood, and worse, I felt his hands slide down to my hips, pulling me against him. I felt his need and though I wanted to cry out that it wasn't me, I remembered the night before, when he had left me wanting.

I had promised I would control her. Even if she offered me what I wanted.

"Gannet, no," I ground out the words between my teeth, my arms leaden as I tried to draw away from him. Theba made my blood sluggish, my muscles weak.

Gannet's eyes were closed behind the mask and still he held me, so tightly now I thought he might bruise me. When he spoke, it was as though he wasn't even with me, was lost in a memory of his own. "Adah said I can't hide from her. The mask hides me from everyone, but I can't hide from her."

Theba's words were wine on my tongue, a sip taken but not yet swallowed. "And why would you want to hide from me?"

She was easing me against him and even through our clothes I felt dizzy at the contact, the pressure of my own need, of his, of *hers*. I didn't want it to be like this.

But if we couldn't have each other any other way?

I had promised him control and I was losing it. A shout and a crash of stone and sand drove us apart as the ceiling above us shuddered perilously. Gannet's eyes snapped open, but they were unfocused.

"We need to get out of here!" I hissed, grabbing for his hand and attempting to haul him to his feet. But he was far heavier than I was, and I nearly fell over, scrambling as the ceiling's rattling was joined by unsteady stone beneath us. Whether it was my family's forces or the enemy outside, we would be buried alive if we remained here.

Gannet pressed a hand against his face and though it was only a few seconds, it felt unbearably long before he rose. We raced back up the corridor toward the light, but another explosive crash sent us sprawling. The Ambarians were launching stones from somewhere behind the ruined temple. I could see a small force ahead, my family's soldiers, attempting to maneuver between the stone missiles and the lethal whirring of arrows. They were being driven back.

And there was no way we could safely reach them.

"Eiren, here," Gannet hissed, pulling me into one of the small chambers we had explored previously. The earlier impact had shifted the thick stones in the wall here, revealing an opening. He bent down and I joined him, noting the ancient plate that we had missed before that, when pushed, revealed the false floor.

"We don't even know what's down there," I said, wary.

"But we do know what's out there," Gannet returned, looking back over his shoulder. We heard shouts now, the clang of weapons in close combat. I could've called upon Theba, perhaps driven them all off, but her fire was not merciful, and I'd already proven today that I couldn't control her. I ducked into the opening, choking on the dust and the stale air, and he was quick to drop in behind me.

I was relieved to learn that it was no cellar we had discovered but another path that wound toward the temple, a deep, secret way that went beneath the collapsed street we had entered this building to avoid. They had stopped launching the stones above us, no doubt because they didn't want to endanger their own forces, and I was grateful: my dark sight illuminated for me every stirring mote of dust, every crack in the tunnel's ceiling. Gannet strode ahead and as the path widened, I moved to walk beside him. I wanted to apologize for losing control of Theba before, of perhaps seeing something he hadn't meant for me to see, but he began speaking first.

"I saw what you saw, when you were in my mind. Did you learn anything that will help us find what we're looking for?"

I grimaced, eyes on the floor.

"I understand their world better. But I think the visions must hold more answers, if I can find a way to remember them more clearly."

"So we're hunting for ghosts now, too."

There was a touch of amusement in his voice. I stumbled with surprise and he steadied me with his hand, a slight pressure that he immediately released as though the touch had burned him. When I opened my mouth to thank him, the start of a story came out instead.

"I feel like blind Cassia, lost in the dark," I said, nerves live as quivering strings in my voice. Gannet didn't look at me, but his posture softened.

Who?

I realized he wanted me to tell a story, that as much as I needed to hear myself in this place to ground myself again, he had missed hearing my stories as much as he had once pretended to dismiss them.

"Cassia was the daughter of two famous court musicians.

They made music so fine common folk were not permitted to hear it, only those lords and ladies with wealth and influence enough to win a seat at one of their performances. The king and queen kept them as permanent retainers at court, and so Cassia, too, was raised in the palace.

"But Cassia had no talent for music. No matter the instrument they put in her hands, no matter what song they bid her sing, she was far more likely to leave an audience weeping for wanting her to stop than she was to move them to any sincere feeling. Though her mother and father bemoaned her lack of skill, and the king and queen, too, no one felt the disappointment more keenly than Cassia herself."

Gannet's mind touched lightly against mine, sharing a hazy picture of the girl taking up one instrument and then another and the next and the next, the lines of sorrow in her face drawn as tightly as strings. As it had been in Jhosch, sequestered with the icons, I considered how full and wondrous something like telling a story could be when in the company of those who had the capacity to contribute to the telling without speaking.

"Cassia determined that the only way she could develop an ear for music would be to deaden one of her other senses. Maddened by her need to prove herself, she heated a dagger in the fire and plunged it into one of her eyes, and then quickly into the other before fear and pain overcame her.

"It was her dearest friend and lover, Denia, who found Cassia in a wounded stupor in her bedchamber, all but bled to death. Denia cleaned the blood from Cassia's face, her own tears softening the medicinal waters she used to sterilize the wounds. She tucked her into the bed they had secretly shared and begged another servant to bring a healer, and Cassia's mother and father.

"It was four days before Cassia woke, and though she could no longer see her, the contours of Denia's face were fine and familiar when she reached out to touch the girl.

"'You idiot,' Denia scolded, weeping-wet kisses pressed to Cassia's wan face. 'What were you thinking?'

"But Cassia would not explain, only begged for a harp, for double-reeded pipes, for a drum. Denia was reluctant to comply, sure that she was only putting disappointment into the hands of her dearest friend, but she did as she was asked. The pipes were lifted to Cassia's lips, and as the young woman took a breath and hesitantly blew, dulcet-sweet tones issued forth, circling the pair like a cooling breeze. Next came the drum and the harp, finger cymbals, the long-necked lute. Every instrument that had refused to yield to Cassia's clumsy handling despite hours and years of practice, she picked up again and was its master. Her smile cracked so wide the sockets where her eyes had been crinkled and began to bleed anew, and she seemed to weep red tears.

"When Cassia's mother and father came at the glorious sounds teased out by their daughter, they banished Denia from the room. Their daughter would play as they did, only ever for the noblest of ears, and never for Denia again."

I wondered then, and Gannet, too, at the unnecessary order of our lives, why things must be so, and not so. In a story it was easier to see how such things were foolish, but we had as many boundaries to our own behavior as folk in tales; we only lived them and did not think them as strange.

The tunnel widened further, but I saw no intentional breaks in the stone, no sign of doors or what this way might once have been used for. We walked on.

"Cassia would play for the king and queen in a week's time and was kept busy performing with her parents and suffering fittings of headdresses that would disguise her disfigurement. She could only see Denia at night, and secretly, and was now so protective of her new gifts that she brought no instruments to their meetings. She feared, and perhaps rightfully so, that the gods would take away what they had given, no matter the price she had already paid. But Denia was sorry for it—she had loved the way that Cassia's face lit up when she played, how her whole body seemed to bend into the music, even when others could not appreciate her playing. She had often told Cassia as much, but just as Denia's heart was stubbornly set on the happiness of her lover, Cassia's was blinded by a lifetime of disappointment.

"So desperate was Denia to hear Cassia play again that she snuck into the performance, covering her face with a rich silk she'd taken from Cassia's own stores so that she would not be recognized. She swayed rapturously as Cassia's hands danced across a lap harp, folded herself against the wall in a swoon when Cassia beat her heart's rhythm into the pliant skin of a drum, felt herself lifted to the rafters on the wind of Cassia's breath blown through a set of pure silver pipes.

"But Denia, in her rapture, tripped and fell, dragging the scarf away from her face, revealing plain, unpainted features and the stark, unadorned collar of a servant. She was seized immediately and dragged before the court. Though Cassia could not see her, she recognized her cries and rose to her defense. But she could not stop the punishment that befell anyone who dared listen where they were not welcome: boiling oil was poured into Denia's ears, deafening her. She was imprisoned, and Cassia vowed never to play again until she was released. But the judgment came from Adah himself and would not be reversed. Cassia begged to be chained up, too, and it was perhaps his perverse version of mercy that he allowed it. They shared a cell, chained to opposite sides of the wall so that they could not touch, one calling out in a voice the other could not hear, one pair of eyes searching and seeing nothing. They could take no comfort in each other, and lost their youth in darkness and silence."

My breath was shallow and sorry, and I could almost feel the dragging weight of manacles on my wrist, the raw sadness of jailed isolation. I wondered now, with what little sense I had been able to make of the visions with Gannet's help, if there wasn't more to this story. Maybe Cassia had been one of the First People, and Denia had not. Maybe the cruelty of that world had been driven by a god's hand, and not a mortal one.

But weren't we just as cruel, or worse, if we acted on their behalf?

"I've fought Adah's judgments in the past," Gannet said, and there was something in his tone that made me think it wasn't just his own punishment, the burden of the mask, that he spoke of. "Being an icon has many privileges."

"I know that," I replied, thinking of our earliest conversations, when he had urged me to accept who I was.

"Including using the power and influence of our station to change things," he insisted, slowing as the terrain grew rocky, more naturally subterranean than shaped by tools. It was cool here but dry, and my steps grew more halting at the smooth, uneven stone beneath my feet.

"Is this your way of telling me to be optimistic about our chances with the Ambarians?" I asked, incredulous. Always Gannet had seemed resigned to his fate, urging me to accept the same for myself, but something within him had been woken. Had it been when he struck out to find me after the fire in Jhosch? At the opera? Or sooner, even? Had the conversation I had witnessed in his mind with Morainn been the start of something neither of us could have anticipated?

Gannet strode forward with none of my hesitation, pausing to inch his way down a deep depression in the stone where the shadows in my dark sight parted to reveal at least a dozen stout, squat casks, each as large as a seated man.

"That depends," he answered, examining the seal on the nearest cask, "on whether this is wine or fire oil."

I crossed to him, holding out a hand toward one of the casks, closing my eyes as I felt for the spark within, not wanting to feed it, not yet. I just needed to know if it was there. I immediately sensed but did not stoke the embryonic fire within the cask, the hungry flame in my heart that recognized fuel.

I opened my eyes.

"We won't be drinking tonight to celebrate your change of heart."

CHAPTER FIFTEEN

Though we considered for a moment going back the way we had come in the hopes that the battle was over, a thorough survey of the cavern revealed four more caches of fire oil and a rotted platform and pulley system that had been used to lower the casks here, many generations ago. There were handholds carved into the rock, leading straight up to the open air. It had grown dark, and I quelled the panic at having lost a full day with the knowledge that we had, at least, secured one small advantage for my family's forces. I didn't immediately recognize the surrounding ruins, but I could see the palace in the near distance, and we moved quickly and quietly in that direction, noting the turns that we took and any features that would help us find our way back to the cache of fire oil. How we retrieved it I would leave to my parents and my siblings. Gannet and I still had work of our own to do.

There were no specters in the streets, no sense that the past would overtake me, though I could see it as before, out of the corners of my eyes. I needed more of Ji's story, needed to know what she knew, and I was as ready to open my mind again to her world as I might open a book and page quickly through it to the conclusion. But no one and nothing appeared, and when we drew close enough to the palace to encounter a patrol, Gannet and I both threw our hands up in the air, baring our faces in the cleansing moonlight. When they escorted us within, only my father was awake, poring over documents in the room where Esbat had shown us the map. He looked up, and Gannet explained quickly what we had found.

"Are you sure the Ambarians didn't know it was there? That

wasn't why they were attacking in that quarter?" My father's face was lined with worry, exhaustion, having aged years, it seemed, in the months I'd been away.

Gannet shook his head.

"If they'd known, they would've used stealth. Disrupting a cache that size with missiles would've resulted in that whole section of the city being sunk in fire, and all the oil with it."

"Then we're lucky they didn't." My father laid a hand upon my shoulder, pulling me into a sudden embrace. I was dead on my feet, but I didn't sink into his arms as I might have before, and I couldn't place my hesitation until he spoke. "You kept her safe. Thank you."

I bristled. Gannet's look was guarded, his words careful.

"*Han'dra* Eiren doesn't need safekeeping."

My father's gaze narrowed, and when he smiled, the expression didn't reach his eyes.

"So I am beginning to understand," he responded, releasing me. I felt his discomfort and had the sense that it had more to do with thinking of me as a woman grown than the icon of a goddess possessed with terrible strength and fury. I didn't like to be so close to his thoughts and took a step back, toward Gannet.

But I knew that hurt him, too.

"We should sleep. It will be another early morning for us," I offered, my tone apologetic. My father nodded rather more enthusiastically than was necessary.

"Of course, of course. I should do the same."

But when we moved to depart the smoky chamber, the braziers burning low, my father didn't follow. I felt the light touch of Gannet's mind against mine, gentle as a nurse's hand might be tending to a wound. It was dark in the corridor outside my small chamber, the lone torch burning several paces away, failing to banish the shadows from Gannet's face.

"You haven't called me *Han'dra* Eiren in some time. I always wondered why you addressed me so formally, and after our fashion, not Ambar's," I said on an impulse, unable to keep my hands from settling against his chest, smoothing the rumpled collar of his shirt. I felt the warmth of his skin beneath, tantalizingly close, but I didn't allow my fingers to stray.

Gannet studied me, head cocked at a slight, quizzical angle.

"I wanted you to know from the first that I respected you and where you came from. I knew you felt conquered and lost, at the mercy of strangers. I assumed it would be a comfort to you."

And now my hands did stray, framing the bones of his jaw.

"You were a comfort to me," I whispered, feeling the jump of his pulse beneath my fingers. "You are."

I leaned forward then against his chest, not wanting a kiss and the inevitable breaking of it. He held me only a moment and I was keenly aware of the huff of his breath in my hair, as though he were gathering my scent. When he stepped away and retreated down the corridor, he was silhouetted a moment in the torchlight, his shadow thinning impossibly long behind him until it was folded into the darkness where the wall met the floor. Gone. He would go to his bed, and I would go to mine.

"What were you doing?"

I jumped, bracing myself against the stone wall behind me. Esbat had emerged from the chamber opposite, twitching the cloth closed behind her. How long had she been there?

"Gannet and I found a cache of fire oil beneath Dsimah's temple." My words came out in a guilty rush, sure that I owed my sister more but strangely resistant to share my feelings with her. "We've told father, and Jurnus will be able to muster a force to recover it tomorrow."

Esbat hugged the shadows, and I couldn't see her whole face. Her mind was quiet, but I sensed her trying to make sense of my actions all the same. So, she had seen something of what had passed between us.

"Gannet is a friend to me," I continued, determined to curb her suspicions. It was bad enough that I had to share him with Theba; I didn't want my sisters passing judgment, too.

Despite the dark, I could see Esbat's eyes widen.

"He took you from us. From your home. You were their prisoner, Eiren."

"Yes, but—"

"They've *slaughtered* our people," she continued heatedly, her reason sharpened like a blade against a stone. "You left and it didn't stop, and it was worse because we didn't know what was happening to you. And then you return here with him and claim he is a friend? How could someone like that ever be a friend to one of us?"

Unless you aren't one of us anymore. She didn't say it but I suspected she knew that I could hear it, and that hurt more. Before I could argue or temper the rage that twisted in my gut, she waved a hand, dismissing her thoughts, or mine.

"Lucky you stumbled on such a find. I found a record detailing how to craft a slow-burning fuse for use with fire oil—I'll be sure to share it with Jurnus in the morning."

And she swept back behind the little curtain, leaving me alone in the corridor. It might have been made of stone for the distance it put between us.

I wasn't sure what I had expected, returning to my family, but the distraction of the war made it easier to ignore the obvious unease between us. We didn't have to reach an understanding, not really, not yet. It wasn't only the Dread Goddess that had awakened within me. I didn't always like who I was becoming, and I was beginning to think they didn't, either.

I didn't sleep in my room, not at first. Someone had left tough bread and bitter wine at my bedside, and I ate every crumb while drinking more than a reasonable share of the bottle. My head was spinning by the time I laid it on the thin pillow, and my body, too, seemed to turn in the sheets, twisting like a corpse in a funeral shroud. There were no windows in my chamber, but the light that touched my eyes come morning was warm as day. I opened my eyes, expecting a torch or a lamp, but it was the sun, breaking through a clever skylight above where I slept. Beneath me I felt the touch of silk, and the air was heavy with fragrant flowers.

I sat up, wondering what dream I had wandered into, or if this were a vision, pressed upon me while I slept. It felt most like the brief encounter at the fountain with the fish, when Jurnus had first brought us into the city. I was still Eiren, still aware that what was happening was not quite real.

But if I was in Re'Kether as it had been, as myself, I should learn what I could, shouldn't I?

I swung my legs over the side of the bed, feeling the thick pile of a rug beneath my bare feet, unable to resist curling my toes into the luxurious weave. There was a fine sturdy door of pale wood where the curtain had hung, and when I tested it, it opened easily.

The corridor was equally bright and happily empty. I sped down the hall, not sure where I was going, only looking out for inhabitants or perhaps a library. Esbat must have gotten her scrolls from somewhere, and what I couldn't learn from Gannet I could maybe learn here.

But several turns brought me outside, and I found I couldn't move for wonder. I was in a lavish garden, leaves as broad as my body and as brightly green as pigment arching overhead, providing ample shade. Vivid pink, yellow, and orange flowers were bedded at the bases of the trees and they stirred in a delicate wind, spilling their heady scent. This place was empty, too, but I felt surely this was somewhere the wealthy would gather to admire and envy each other. And I did hear them, muffled laughter and the splash of water. I followed the sound, moving off the stone path onto tufted, springy grass. The slick blades beneath my feet felt so real it tickled.

There was an opening in the garden wall that didn't lead onto a street but into a narrow foyer. Here I saw someone, at last, a slight figure with his back to me, a child, perhaps, with a dull knitted cap only just containing a mop of dark curls. Beyond him I heard more voices, adult voices, arguing, groaning, and flirting, and the air soured, the cloying perfume of the flowers doing very little to combat the rotten, stony smell that was drifting up from below us both. I thought of retreating, perhaps to find another way in, but he turned then and when his eyes met mine, they were glowing faintly gold. The world listed to the left and I felt like my stomach had dropped right out of my body. My arms flew out, as though I could steady myself, and he caught my hand. His touch was like fire, and he pulled me forward, pulled me *into* him, and I felt myself beginning to unravel as I passed through him. I felt Ji's increasingly familiar resolve, her edges furious, racing toward some rebel's bloody end. I fought harder than I had before to hold onto some part of myself even as her consciousness claimed mine, I wanted so badly to observe, to know, to remember. I even reached out to Theba, as though her strength of will could supplement mine, but though she uncoiled down my legs and arms, she was just as powerless as I was to stop what was happening.

For once, we weren't fighting. We weren't anything.

We were someone else, again.

The bathhouse was a necessary evil. I might've felt differently if I had been able to simply enjoy the water, the occasional splash of a handsome body slipping in, the cautious gossip passed between lovers and friends when their lips broke the surface. But I had business. The priestess I'd been charged with following was rutting with one of the king's courtiers in the curtained pool behind me, and I ducked beneath the water to keep from rolling my eyes at her obviously staged cries of ecstasy. When I surfaced, there was someone worthier of my attentions newly arrived in the bathhouse. Two someones, in fact.

The crown prince, Shran, and his personal god—or so we joked—Tirce, here, in a public bathhouse. Either Shran was slumming it, as his father's courtier was, or someone had displeased his divine shadow. They were both fully dressed and didn't look like they intended to alter that state anytime soon.

I sank to my eyes, watchful.

"Ameth the Radiant. Where is he?" The god's voice was penetrating, causing the marbled stone benches to quake as readily as the bathers who lounged upon them. No one answered the god, but pointed looks were cast toward the many-curtained enclosures where visitors were meant to sequester themselves in pious reflection and cleansing steam but were more likely to engage in deeds both intimate and illegal.

Yet the gods had eyes and ears everywhere, not to mention senses more keen than those of any mortal.

The pair had to pass by the pool where I waited, mouth obscured beneath the surface as I fought to keep the breaths I pulled through my nose measured and soft. The prince met my eyes briefly, his gaze cold and unreadable. Did he enjoy this work, rounding up his own people for scrutiny and inevitable punishment? Did he anticipate the oath he would take as king, which bound his life first in service to the gods, and only second to the people, whose blood and bodies were as vulnerable as his own?

I had hugged the pool's edge to give myself quick exit if I needed one but it also, unfortunately, meant that when the pair stopped, they were too near to me for comfort, and all but blocking my view of the scene. I peeked around Shran as much as I dared to the curtained enclosures behind me, my curiosity momentarily overcoming my sense. Tirce did not wait for Ameth to emerge, reaching behind the curtain and yanking him to his feet with a stony fist. The fool surely knew what waited for him, and while I could only guess at his crime, there were no gentle punishments in this city.

Liquid streamed down Ameth's legs, and I didn't know if it was water or if he had lost control of his body in fear.

"Someone has been putting gold behind the things that they're saying about me!" Ameth squealed, but Tirce wasn't even looking at him, moving back already the way that he had come. "I would never cheat the temples. I give my tithe of blood and coin. It's lies, what they're saying about me."

Shran shifted his weight to follow Tirce and his captive, giving Ameth a brief view of where I sat, partially submerged. Ameth's face twisted into a grimace of glee.

"It's her you want! Ji the sneak, the sly, the gutter-tongued. She has more dark deeds to her name than me! She's a killer. *They say she's running messages for the rebellion.*"

My stomach clenched. Ameth knew me. While my reputation was a comfort in the streets and back alleys where it granted me a wide berth, now only cold dread crept forth from my belly, combating the water's warmth. To speak such an accusation out loud was a desperate move. He further risked his own condemnation as well as mine.

Time to put my so-called gutter-tongue to task. "A man will say anything to save himself. I'm a servant of House Kaliri, reserving a space in the pool for my mistress."

It was a common enough practice for a servant to hold a prime position in the water for her master, and there were enough merchant families in the city that I didn't expect the prince to know everyone. My voice was pitched firm but deferential—an innocent who, though fearful, knows she has nothing to hide.

Tirce made no motion, expression impassive, but I could tell he waited for some confirmation from the prince. Shran's hand tensed on the ceremonial blade he wore at his side. I was sure he'd never drawn it, or perhaps hoped that he had not.

"You'll come with us. Two criminals are better than one," the prince said, at last, expression unreadable.

"But, my mistress—"

"Now."

There were gasps at my questioning the edict, and I wasn't sure the crown prince was entirely taken in by my slow-witted servant's act. I didn't know many idiots, even, who would dare to defend themselves, but to follow the pair was certainly to die.

Still, he left me little choice. I rose out of the water, shrinking with the humility that was to be expected from a girl in the station that I claimed, for I wore not a stitch of clothing. My own instincts trended more toward lunging for the weapon the prince wore and giving it a first taste of blood rather than covering myself.

Tirce's eyes remained fixed on mine before traveling cursorily down my lean frame.

"House Kaliri doesn't waste much food in the keeping of their servants, then."

It was a crude joke, and there were bathers relieved enough not to have been the target of Tirce's attentions to laugh. It was then that I blushed, seething at the insult, struggling to remind myself that there were better causes to die for than wounded pride. Shran gestured then with chin only, a curt command, and I moved past him, angling away. He might look at me, he might judge, but he would not touch me. Tirce did not take my arm, which was a very small comfort. I was unlikely to get far if I chose to run, but I hadn't ruled it out.

It seemed he had no intention of allowing me to recover my garments at the entrance to the bathhouse, either, but to parade me through the streets of the capital with less courtesy than one would a woman whose services could be bought. I conceded that there *were* matters of pride worth killing for.

Ameth took this opportunity to begin to jabber again in his own defense, to draw as much attention to us as possible.

"I'm not a rebel! They're mad, with their talk of god-killing. My life is in service to the temple, to the crown. It's her you want, and those like her. Not me, not *me*!" If he hoped for a distraction, a chance to slip away, he was more of a fool than someone who had simply allowed himself to be caught.

But I had been caught, too.

And his efforts weren't entirely in vain. A crowd was beginning to gather, and it did not take long in this part of the city for a crowd to become a mob. I felt the eyes of the crowd, hungry for a spectacle, the entertainment of cowards. Some men grabbed at themselves, watching me. Women threw cold oils from their cooking, first, and then the contents of their waste buckets. I was their target, for Tirce was too close to Ameth and they wouldn't have risked angering the god. There were soldiers among the crowd, though the crown prince hardly needed additional protection with the god at his side. The soldiers did nothing to keep the onlookers from attacking me, however. I fought to remain calm with every splash and the stink of urine against my skin, my face, their slurs as sour and as sick. But I wasn't tortured, wasn't shamed.

I raged.

My next move was calculated. I knew this part of the city, knew we were near a safe house and an entrance to the warren of the underground where they would not be able to follow without getting lost. I broke from the line into the crowd, hands clawing, legs kicking wildly with every stride. The crown prince and the god attempted to follow me, as I suspected they might, and the soldiers began to push their way toward me, as well. But there was chaos now and rebel sympathizers within the throng began to hurl their abuse more broadly. I cast a quick look over my shoulder to see Shran with a smear of mud, or something worse, in his bright hair. The look on his face was one of cold determination, resignation, as he tried to cleave to Tirce.

With the hands of strangers pawing my body I dove for the ground, weaving between pairs of legs filthier even than my own, my escape assured even as I heard the soldiers calling for order, the voice of the god raised in a divine howl. I saw the sigil carved into the safe house's foundation, the diamond divided. Our sign. I grinned at the risk of having my teeth kicked out of my mouth. They might have all the power, but there were more of us, and more wildness in us, more want, than any unfeeling god and his royal puppet could muster.

My heart beat hot and fast with Ji's thrilling, her anger. My anger. Ji and I, a stranger and a woman estranged. I felt hollowed out, like an empty lamp or a waiting coffin. I came to myself slowly, my heart and head unwilling to relinquish the other world, another life.

"Eiren."

Cold stone, cold as the frosted soil I'd clutched in the woods beyond *Zhaeha*. A stern voice, but warm, too. Warm enough to breathe feeling back into stiff fingers.

"Eiren, where were you?"

My eyes popped open. Gannet's face wheeled above mine before settling into a familiar shape, smooth jaw, a sweep of pale hair, the worried curve of his lips beneath the unfeeling mask. I'd fallen out of my bed. He reached out a hand to help me from where I lay prone, but I didn't take it, using my own instead to be sure that I was whole, unharmed. The smell of refuse faded from my nostrils, so real I could still feel Ji's suppressed gag. Gannet frowned, and when I still did not take his hand, he retracted it.

"Another vision?" His tone was distant, but he couldn't disguise his curiosity.

Already the fine details of Ji's experience in the bathhouse and the street beyond were slipping away, and I scrambled to my feet, scanning the chamber for a writing implement. There was nothing to be had but last night's wine, or the cold coals from the brazier. I snatched one up, beginning to scrawl on the stone floor as much as I could remember of the steps I had taken to the bathhouse, tracing Ji's course through the street. As I worked I could in one moment feel the heat of water on my skin, the slick of pots of emptied waste, and in the next the sensations were as unfeeling as a dream. I couldn't even remember the faces of the god, Tirce, or the mythic Shran, both of whom were far more interesting to me than they had been to Ji. The shock at having seen both appear in the vision stilled my fingers, and I was unsettled by the perversion of the friendship I had believed between them from stories. In the instant I hesitated, I felt more of the vision drifting away.

"Ji was thinking of a safe house, underneath of the city. A warren of places to hide, and to hide things."

Gannet crouched beside me, eyes roaming over the dark, hasty sketch.

"Do you think you could find this place she sought?"

I wanted to promise him that I could, but even the sign she'd seen wavered in my memory. It had been a diamond, but corrupted, somehow. And would such a thing have survived the ages of neglect?

"I think we should try," I answered at length, leaning back to study the etchings on the floor as he had. I was sure that I could trust the visions, though the landscape of the palace and the surrounding ruins had changed so greatly the way might be impassable. I caught Gannet's eyes. "Is that why you came in here for me? Is it morning already?"

He nodded. "Only just. I wasn't going to come in but I heard you thrashing around."

"You probably shouldn't have." I didn't need to elaborate, and Gannet's jaw tightened.

"I've seen the way that they look at me. I know."

"It doesn't matter," I insisted, heaving a sigh as I made an attempt to rise. But Gannet had laid a hand on my wrist, arresting my progress.

"It does matter, Eiren. If we live through this, it matters."

He might have held my heart in his hands.

"I can't even imagine what my life will look like in an hour, let alone what it might be after this," I said quietly, his touch as perilous as the press of a blade. "As hard as it was for me once to believe that I was Theba, now I don't know how I could be just Eiren, again."

"It won't matter what you call yourself," he said, withdrawing his hand, a contrast to the intimacy of his words. "It won't matter what you've done, or what you do to survive between now and then. I want to live to share that day, the day when this is over."

Being so close to him and not touching was like sitting near a fire but feeling none of its heat. I knew there was warmth there, and comfort, but dared not get any closer. I struggled to mirror his restraint.

"I do, too," I replied, at last, keeping my eyes carefully leveled on the partial map I'd scrawled on the floor, as though looking at it could bring back more of the vision's details. I took a deep breath. "Let's find a safe house." Though it was just barely morning, as Gannet had implied, we were far from the only ones stirring. No one was about belowground, so we went above. Soldiers who either hadn't slept, or had been up for some time, stalked to or from some skirmish, carrying messages, delivering reports, ferrying the wounded. It was a short walk from the small series of chambers where my family slept, ate, and received news to an interior courtyard that served as both a hospital and a practice yard. Many of those who served under Jurnus had no military training or nothing more than what they'd learned brawling in the streets of Jarl. As we followed two soldiers supporting a third between them, I heard the cutting sound of steel against steel and was not surprised that they were already being drilled.

Lista, my brother, and a few of the more seasoned members of my family's force were working with smaller groups of men and women. I saw Esbat and Anise at the courtyard's edge, ladling out porridge and discs of hard, flat bread to the soldiers who were not fighting. Esbat met my eyes from across the courtyard and released them immediately. I didn't need her to look at me to feel the force of her thoughts, the scrutiny over how close I stood to Gannet, her wondering over where we meant to sneak off to today. I didn't have to report to anyone, but I resented the notion that I could not be trusted and resolved to speak to Jurnus myself, explain what I had seen and what I hoped to accomplish today.

When we drew near, Jurnus had just disarmed a young man who couldn't have been more than fourteen or fifteen. Both were sweating profusely despite the early hour, and I wondered how long they had been at this work.

"Jurnus," I said at a distance, not wanting to startle him. When he looked up from explaining some military particulars to his sparring partner, his eyes flitted quickly between Gannet and me. A brief, whispered exchange with Esbat was at the front of his mind, and I felt the same suspicion in him that I had in her. My temper flared, and I fought to keep it from my voice. "I believe there may be another cache of some kind nearby. We're going to look."

Jurnus had a definite swagger as he strode to meet us. It was not an affectation I had seen in him before; he must have developed it during my absence.

He carried a spear, which I knew was not his favorite weapon but was the preference of most of the soldiers of Ambar. No doubt he had been observing the enemy's tactics, and hoped to master the weapon.

"It would be useful to know more about what to expect from this invading force," he said, driving the spear's shaft into the sand beside him with some force and cocking a hip against it. Despite his posture, I knew the weapon could be easily readied. "Gannet, you're a man of Ambar. What training have these bastards received? What weaknesses can we hope to exploit?"

The challenge in his voice was plain, and Gannet stiffened slightly beside me.

"Gannet's not a warrior, Jurnus," I began, but my brother raised a hand, silencing any further comment. Jurnus had never known when to shut his mouth, and I'd never wanted to throttle him more for it than I did just then.

"Neither was Lista. Neither was I. We watched, we learned. What have *you* learned in your years of service, Gannet?"

Several of the sparring pairs near us had stopped to observe the exchange, and their attention quickly spread to others. I felt Gannet walling himself up, and I had no idea what he intended to do until he adjusted the fittings of his cloak. Not to remove it, as Jurnus imagined he might in anticipation of a fight, but to tighten it.

"I do not think that what I learned in my years of service will be of much interest to you," he answered in the superior tone that had once been so irritating to me. I hadn't heard it in weeks, and I knew now he did it to protect himself. "Patience, watchfulness, delayed gratification. Useful skills in war, but rarely possessed by those who wage them."

Jurnus's nostrils flared at what he perceived as a subtle insult, though I couldn't tell what Gannet had intended. Whatever passed between them now was beyond me, though I suspected I played some unsought for role in the exchange. Instead of responding, Jurnus swiftly tore the spear from the sand and tossed it forcefully to Gannet. Rather than let it fall, Gannet caught it. Though he shifted it in his hand to hold it properly, it looked wrong, and I didn't like seeing him armed.

"The Ambarians can't have allowed you to come all this way

the first time without any means of defending yourself, unless they spared good men to protect able-bodied ones," Jurnus said with a sneer. Where was this anger coming from? "If that's the case, perhaps we stand a chance, after all."

There were chuckles amidst the soldiers, though many didn't smile or laugh, looking to Jurnus instead for a level of direction I was beginning to believe he didn't deserve. One of the soldiers nearest to my brother passed him her spear.

"That's enough, Jurnus," I broke in, but he wasn't looking at me. Gannet had assumed a posture I had seen on Antares any number of times, and I found myself taking several unwitting steps away from him, heart hammering. I felt Theba's bloodlust burning eager trails up my body and something else, too, at the sight of my brother circling the man who rivaled all others in my esteem.

"You've learned something then," Jurnus said, sweeping out with his own spear before he'd finished speaking. Gannet retreated, shuffling across the sand, but maintained his defensive stance. "What about this one, though?"

Jurnus's next lunge was a feint, easily disarming Gannet who was slow to counter the attack. He smirked and I felt my heart straining against my ribs, a whistle of rage on my lips.

"Maybe you ought to accept that armed escort my father offered," Jurnus crowed, bending to collect the second spear even though Gannet had made no move to recover it. They were close enough together now that he lowered his voice, but I still heard what he said next. "He doesn't trust you alone with her any more than I do."

Many things happened then, all at once.

Something in me boiled over, and where Jurnus stood the packed earth cracked and tilted, launching my brother a short distance away, scrambling and tumbling to the ground. Gannet, too, was knocked off his feet. Neither man had much time to recover, for into the square swarmed armored men and women, swords and teeth flashing. Jurnus rolled but not quickly enough to avoid a glancing swipe at his unprotected side. The Aleynian soldiers who had been idling, watching the encounter between my brother and Gannet, sprang to action, some pulling discarded helmets onto their heads while others didn't pause before launching themselves at the enemy. Lista was among these, engaging two of the enemy without hesitation. A sharp yank on my arm drew me back to myself and the immediate danger.

My father and mother flanked me. Two of the enemy were running at us, and I could not tell if they were men or women for they wore bulky, ill-fitted armor and dark cloth wound over their mouths, noses, and brows. I could see only their eyes, and these were as charged, wild, and empty as only those of a zealot can be.

"Can't you do something?" This from my mother, a shriek that I heard but barely over the clatter of weapons, the growls of battle. I tried to reach into myself, to summon the fire or something worse, but I felt cold, like a hearth after a long, neglected night. There was only terror at the nearness of the battle. I was only Eiren, afraid to be hurt, afraid to die.

Not just Eiren. Never just Eiren.

Time seemed to slow as I took in the weapon strikes, the parrying, the bodies twisted in defense and in falling, too. On instinct I bent and scooped a handful of sand, and when I stood, I blew it into the face of an advancing attacker. My lungs were hot as an oven, and the grains turned to glass as they flew forward, instantly blinding the one who'd dared come at me. It was Theba's doing; she burst from me then, a snake coiled in a nest. I felt her just under my skin and thought I might shed it, so great was the press of her outrage. The next nearest Ambarian she flung away without even needing to use my hands, the others closest to me felt their weapons burn as hot as they had in the instant of their forging. But they could not drop them. The blaze crept from their screaming hands to their shoulders, their bellies filling with fire, their mouths belching smoke. Blackened figures crumpled before me, their bodies broken in a perverse semblance of worship. Theba's leer was on my lips as though strings pulled them back, and I fought to control my expression, eyes taking in each figure, and those still standing, drawing near in shock.

Six at my feet. What I had not finished my family's forces had.

"You did this," Jurnus said, an uncanny blend of horror, relief, and outrage on his face.

I nodded, my chin dipping forward as though weighted. I wanted to look away from the corpses, wanted to drop to my knees before them, wanted to retch. I did none of these things.

"And the stone, before. You broke the stones under my feet."

I nodded again. My face burned as Theba burrowed back within me, satisfied as a glutton after feasting. It wouldn't last.

Behind Jurnus my sisters assembled, and I felt my mother and father at my back. I didn't need to see any of them to know they warred with themselves as my brother did; I could hear their thoughts torn between marveling at my power and horror at seeing it employed.

I felt a hand on my heart, squeezing. They were grateful to me, but I'd finally inspired the fear I'd hoped to when I first told them that I was Theba. It hurt, to see the truth of what I was through their eyes.

Another mind intruded upon mine, but I shrank from him, too. Gannet could not comfort me now. I turned to look at him, standing behind my father, a spare, tidy figure in black. Not a warrior. Not a killer.

I tried to back away from them all and my hem caught against the charred curl of a limb, burned beyond recognition. I felt tears in my eyes, hot as oil.

"Dispose of these corpses," my father called out, directing the soldiers who'd hung back, uncertain. "Figure out how they got in here, and send someone below to check on the others."

"It was a scouting party," Gannet said. "When they don't return, the enemy will send another."

"Then we'll be ready next time." Jurnus wasn't looking at me now, but at our father, his gaze fevered. "We'll need to be ready for an offensive."

"I won't rush to attack." My father's voice had gravel in it, and I heard echoes of this argument in his mind, tackled from many angles by my dogged brother. "We risk leaving our people leaderless. We are safe enough here for now."

"It is obvious that we're not," Jurnus muttered, eyes on the corpses that others had begun to drag away from the courtyard. "If we don't press what advantages we have, we will lose them."

He wasn't just speaking of the knowledge of the terrain, of the capacity to surprise our enemy, but of me. My father sensed it, too, even without my gifts. They were all thinking of it, of what I could do and how I might be used. My mother was resigned. Esbat's gaze, on the other hand, was critical, a scholar's consideration of what must be done. What sacrifices should be made for the preservation of all.

I met Lista's eyes then and she searched my face, her own marked with blood and sand. She didn't recognize me. She wondered over what it was she had seen—the fire, and if Jurnus had merely tripped, if Gannet could be trusted…if I could.

"I already told you I can't," I said hoarsely, turning my back on her, on all of them, and exiting the courtyard. Let more of the enemy come. I would burn myself to a cinder torching their flesh from their bones, and then what? What place could there be for me in the world they built after?

Gannet caught up with me and kept pace, several lengths removed so that even the hems of our clothes were in no danger of brushing together. "I think you've forgotten everything I've taught you."

"You never taught me how to control my temper." *Or hers.* "In fact, you used to be particularly adept at igniting it."

"It's a gift," he answered, tone severe for all his eyes glittered behind the mask. My laugh was like sand rasping in my throat. Soon it collapsed into a sigh, not of discontent, but of release. We had work to do. I relaxed, only just, and drew nearer to him when we stopped to allow a cluster of older children, their arms full of bandages and salves in squat jars, to hurry in the direction we had come from. The search before us seemed all the more urgent on the heels of the attack.

We moved beyond the perimeter of activity, going more carefully even than the day before. Between following what I could remember of the vision and keeping an eye out for surprise attackers, our pace was crawling. I fought to keep the sight of both cities before me, Re'Kether as it was, and the wonder that it had been. Ji's flight from the bathhouse was messy, an incomplete memory crowded with fright and fury. But I thought I recognized the cobbles here, or the sun-baked ruin that had once been cobbles. I crouched, the fleeting scrape of stone against my hand the same sensation Ji had experienced when scrabbling between the legs of rioters. Wind whipped sand against the stone faces of ancient buildings that stood still in this quarter, and I heard in the howling the animal rage of a long-dead rebellion. Was that the gutter she had crawled to, the worn stoop that had born the mark that promised her sanctuary?

Where there should have been the indifferent glare of the sun there was shadow, an inexplicable square of it between two columns that were all that remained of a once-modest structure. And in the shadow a gloved hand extended, reaching out to me, or to Ji. I shook my head, confusion like heat sickness muddying my thoughts. I gestured to Gannet to come near, my vision blurring as I felt the stones beneath my feet shift. The owner of the hand didn't wait for me to take it, but snatched forward like a viper striking, seizing my wrist. I felt Ji's heart and head eclipse my own, and I wanted it and didn't want it. I turned to look at Gannet, his alarm plain even as he disappeared.

Desecrating a temple was a crime punishable by death. There was no appeal, not for anyone, and certainly not for me. It was rumored Adah was doling out punishments himself of late, rather than allowing his disciples to exercise their own cruel interpretations of justice. While the god could be counted upon to harbor neither human jealousy nor outrage, neither did he possess anything resembling empathy. I wasn't sure whose justice I would prefer, if caught.

The streets were dark, what few lanterns usually maintained in this quarter stolen or smashed to conceal crimes of another kind. There was no moon. Still, I saw the figure that stepped into my path an instant before they did so, and my own limbs roused to defense even as the person raised their arms in surrender.

"I am not your enemy."

I recognized the voice. It was the woman from the temple, the one that had refused to show her face to Mara and me even after we had delivered the message. As she had appeared then, there was nothing to identify her but her voice, featureless under a hood, shapeless in a large, shadowy garment. Still I knew her, and that was all I needed to duck into the open doorway to which she gestured.

Once inside, I stopped, unwilling to go further without answers. "How did you know that I would come this way? Are you having me followed? Have I *been* followed? What is this place?"

She didn't answer at first, busying herself far too long with bolting the door before sweeping past me with an air of importance, angling down a hall. "You're safe, for now. But you're careless. I expect it won't last."

I snorted, quick on her heels despite her advantage in height, the length of her stride. The corridor was dimly lit and stank of disuse, and I began to feel the weight of stone and sand above as it sloped downward.

"Torching a prayer garden from within without being seen takes great care," I boasted, my desire for information wrestling with my desire to save face. "I *wasn't* seen, was I?"

She halted before a closed door, old and partly rotted, but brushed clean. The murmurs of those within ceased abruptly, as though they could sense, if not yet see, our approach. "If you'd been seen, we wouldn't be having this conversation."

The door seemed to pulse, the age-softened wood alive to the tremors perceived in the living bodies that drew near. I watched, fascinated, as it opened a fraction, smooth as a breath, and closed again.

"Go in. I'll wait here for you."

"You're not coming?"

"I'm not wanted. Now go in before I decide to give you up to Adah's hounds."

I shuddered, thinking of those most fiercely devoted to Adah, the unwashed ones who wore the hides of animals scraped only partly clean of sinew and fat. The creatures that lived in the wild had a natural order and no need for crime and were sacred to the just god. His followers became near feral themselves in their pursuit of his favor.

"You don't have to threaten me," I hissed, placing a hand upon the splintered wood when next it opened, the pressure of my touch parting the door from frame like a pair of withered lips. There was a slight pressure on my back—she'd pushed me!—and the door closed behind me as soon as I was within.

It was darker here even than it had been in the corridor, and my eyes took a moment to adjust. The resistance, it seemed, was not in favor of illumination, nor of ample spaces, as the chamber we occupied was hardly large than a wardrobe. Three figures clustered together opposite me, and I recognized them immediately, cursing as I stumbled back against the door. It couldn't be opened from the inside.

"She's betrayed us, but I won't," I insisted, eyes blazing even as I trembled with fear. Mara had been so sure we could trust her, the woman from the temple, but she'd given me up to them, not even remaining behind to see how they chose to punish me.

Tirce, with his great hands muddied and his jaw set like a sharpening stone.

Dsimah, her rounded belly promising fertility, fecundity to barren fields and women both, if we offered the brightest and most beautiful youths to service in her temple.

And Najat, the Dreamer, whose eyes were preternaturally wide and without pupils, glowing with the golds and blues of sweet things realized in the blink of a sleeping eye and in another instant, the blood-dark stuff of nightmares.

It was Najat who spoke first, and her voice arrested me, bade my knees to buckle and my belly to clench. I only just managed to keep from collapsing to the floor in an abject posture of devotion. "She did not lie to you when she claimed she was not your enemy. She led you here because neither are we."

I snorted. I would be daring even in the face of death.

"A madman who does not receive what his dreams promise takes it from the three young virgins in his master's house," I said, voice steady though my heart hammered a ritual staccato against my breastbone. I looked away from Najat, glaring at Dsimah. "And just today I saw a woman outside your temple, her belly heavy with not one child but two, begging you to take one if only the other would grow healthy and strong. She had a knife. She meant to do it herself if her prayers were not answered."

I looked at Tirce.

"And you, I *saw* you, in the bathhouse. You and the crown prince."

No mortal face could rival the frown of a god whose province was earth and stone.

"We do what we must to maintain appearances. Would you look more favorably on me if I told you of that man, Ameth's, ill deeds? He is no friend to you or your kind. It was never meant to be like this," Tirce intoned, shaking his head. His remorse seemed genuine, but gods did not feel. They bade others do it for them.

"It has *always* been like this."

The woman from the temple had entered behind me, but I did not turn to look at her, not wanting to put my back to the three who stood before me. My retort was lost, words stifled in my throat as neatly as Tirce might have crumbled a handful of stones to dust.

"I don't care what it was or was meant to be, only what it is," I insisted. I couldn't trust them. I wouldn't. Would there be time enough to reach one of my weapons? Would it even matter?

"But how do you kill a god?" Alarm sprang in my belly when Najat spoke, answering a thought even I hadn't dared utter aloud. Her expression was immutable. The depths of a cloudless night were in her eyes, moon glow, the edge of a dawning sky that promises an end to dreaming.

To hear her say it shocked me, but the others showed no surprise. What wasn't said did far more to convince me of their truthfulness than what was. This truth was at the heart of what we did, what we hoped to do. The gods walked among us, warm flesh, heavy hands, heavier deeds. In our prayers we could not ask them to leave us be, and so we must put an end to praying. We must give them up.

And I didn't imagine they'd respond to much but lethal force.

"I don't know," I said, at last. I had no weapons now but honesty. I had seen too much. Men who swallowed stones to give themselves the strength of the god who stood before me, his mouth touched with a sorrow I couldn't understand. Wild-eyed dreamers whose herbal abuses induced sleep, or prolonged wakefulness so as to control Najat's visitations. Lives lived out only in part because of devotion, or fear, or both.

"We have little time for you to learn." This from the woman who stood behind me. If I'd know her name, I'd have used it as a curse.

"What is it you do for the rebellion, exactly?" I rounded on her now, temper blazing, searching the blank darkness of the hood for eyes and finding none. "How is it you don't have to risk your life?"

"I take a great many risks you would never understand."

"Try me," I growled, but even as it seemed she intended to speak, her shoulders rising and her chest, too, with an angry puff of breath, Dsimah interceded.

"Enough. You both have secrets."

I started at her words, sure that at least part of the diffusion of feeling in my breast was divine in nature. What did she think she knew about me?

And what didn't I know about the woman who'd led me here?

Dsimah's gaze leveled on us both. "It is best for now, for all of us, that you keep them. There is something you must do together."

The mention of a task grounded me, though knowing now that my orders came from those I purported to fight was unsettling.

"I'm listening," I said.

"If you have any hope of succeeding, if *we* have any hope," she insisted, "there's something we need. Something old. Something powerful."

The hooded woman circled behind me. They had our undivided attention now. Even as I leaned forward into the response, it didn't come. Her lips moved and slid away from her face, eaten up in a blaze of light. Gannet held me, the pressure of arms arresting. We were tucked against the remains of a stone wall, taking advantage of what little shade it provided.

"What did you see, Eiren? What are you seeing now?"

I closed my eyes, desperate to hang on to any memory that I could. Already Ji's world was losing color and distinction, the edges like sand dunes slipping into unrecognizable shapes. Ji aspired to put an end to the wicked reign of the gods, and I did, too.

"She was sent to recover a weapon," I said. "What we're searching for, she sought, too. And I saw—I saw the gods. Their true faces."

I was delirious, squeezing my eyes shut against Gannet's chest and pressing my face forward into the shadow of his cloak as though I could return to Ji's world by will alone. But it was impossible to hold on to more than an impression and nothing to sketch in the sand this time. After a moment Gannet freed a hand to hold a water skin to my lips, and I took a few sips to oblige him.

"Where was she sent, Eiren?"

I shook my head, feeling the rough brush of his shirt against my cheeks, my nose.

"I don't know. There were two gods, no, three. They told her, they told her—"

Quiet.

Gannet's hands tightened on my frame, and I looked up at

him, following his gaze to the gutted ruin of a building some distance away, where the sun's light was captured by a glass and reflected out again. Three quick blinks of light, a longer exposure, and then two more blinks. My heart sank.

One of yours?

I don't think so.

The message was being broadcast out toward the city's edge and the Ambarian encampment. Had there been one among the scouting party who had escaped, or were there others secreted away in the city already? Was the Ambarian daring increased by the imminent arrival of the imposter's army?

Or had they arrived already?

We were running out of time. We needed to hide, to run, something to guide us beyond instinct and vision.

But we couldn't go anywhere when, their thoughts racing ahead of their boots, the force that had been signaled began to advance into the city.

CHAPTER SIXTEEN

Gannet sensed them, too, and we both pressed back against the wall, as though we might be able to merge with a scrap of shadow the ruined building provided. They'd be on us within a few minutes, and there wasn't cover enough to be had in this quarter. They'd have to be cautious, too, anticipating my family's forces, which meant they'd be drawn to the same corner that we occupied to disguise their entry into the city. I met Gannet's eyes, my own wild, questioning.

Can you do it again?

I knew what he asked, and what it meant for him to ask. Theba's hunger sprang in my belly, too quick, too eager. Every time I gave in to her I felt that I lost a part of myself. I had stopped counting the bodies, stopped actively regretting the carnage. We were at war. But there would be a cost, and I wouldn't be the only one to pay it.

It wasn't a question of whether I could use my power, but whether I would.

Even as I closed my eyes to stoke the fire within, I heard the skittering of arrows striking stone, the cries of alarm, the slump of at least one body collapsing in the sand. My thoughts scattered in the chaos of many minds all at once shrieking, searching, seeking defensible positions. One figure ducked through the doorway for cover, a woman of middle years boasting a festering wound on her neck and bare shoulder, a naked blade in her hands. I threw myself at her legs before she could move, beyond her surprise, and Gannet was quick behind me, striking her in the forearm and causing her to drop her weapon. Together we wrestled her to the ground, but she was crying for help, and I panicked. I could smell her sweat, her fear, the sourness in the wound. I felt her pain, saw in her the lover she'd already lost to this war and the maddening grief that had driven her to follow the imposter this far. Not since the opera had I laid hands physically upon someone I meant to kill. Then I had relished it, but when I reached for this woman's throat, to stifle her scream forever, Theba's glee turned my stomach. I scrambled away on my hands and knees, heaving. It was Gannet who recovered the woman's blade and struck her, hard, against her head, silencing her. I didn't know if she lived or not, but she'd stopped moving.

They were fighting all around us now, in the street beyond the structure where Gannet hastened to drag my cowering form back into the corner, away from the battle. I didn't look but could hear them, sense their thoughts driven to manic regret, fury, and disbelief as they died by arrow, spear, and poisoned dart. Theba raged at my weakness, but I could only shake in Gannet's arms. In the same instant that I considered the necessity of killing, I was undone by Theba's needless wanting to kill, knew that no matter how I justified it, she would twist the deed done by my hands and grow stronger for it. I felt that need bleeding over into me, the lines between us blurring. War was ugly and one became ugly to win—there was no other way, and there was no going back.

Gannet was pulling me to my feet and I allowed it. There were no more cries, only the shuffling of the living.

"Gannet?"

The voice broke between the syllables of his name.

"Morainn?"

He let me go and we stood, our shadows stretching out to meet the figure who approached us.

Her hair was pulled back from her face, but no circlet split her brow. Instead, a scar bubbled from her hairline over one of her eyes, a sweep of puckered skin that terminated above a shapely cheekbone. The eye in its marred socket did not drift, but neither did it focus. It was snow-gray and still, sightless.

The cry of grief that crowded my throat escaped in a ragged

moan, and I leaned against Gannet, unable to tear my eyes away from his sister.

"Morainn, what are you doing here?" he said, but she held up a hand, in it the little reflecting glass the Ambarians had been using to signal each other.

"Not here. It isn't safe. We're only a day ahead of the force that's riding to join this one, and I won't lose an hour of it."

Gannet nodded, struck as dumb as I was, as Morainn was joined by a number of others, perhaps twenty, all with lethal weapons in their hands and countenances to match. I didn't recognize them, and neither did they recognize me. But they knew Gannet.

"We found an entrance to the sewer system. It's extensive. We should be able to move unseen underground," one of them said to Morainn, a man whose scars and deferential tone made him seem older than he was.

"Good. Let's go," she responded. She dared then to meet my eyes and I hers, one sightless, the other brighter, wilder, seeming to see more than the pair had done before. I thought fleetingly of Cassia's blindness, the gift that it had given her at the loss of her sight, and wondered what Morainn had gained.

I could sense that she hadn't been sure until this moment how she would feel when she met me again, if she had forgiven me, if she could. Feelings flashed across her face like lightning strikes, anger, sorrow, resignation, the final thunderclap of unsteady relief. There was no darkness in me that could eclipse her light, no foul feeling that could overtake the good.

We followed after Morainn and the small group at her command until we ducked into what had been an alley. I felt the closeness of this passage as it had been, high walls wet with humidity, washing water and waste underfoot. Now there was only heat, glare, and sand, but there was a shaft, partially obscured by a crumbled wall, that promised the cool darkness of the subterranean. Several of Morainn's people went first, followed by Morainn, while Gannet and I were urged ahead to let others take up the rear. I descended in a daze to torchlight and stale but breathable air below.

Morainn waited only so long as it took for Gannet to gain his footing before she turned and hugged him, arms tightening fiercely around his shoulders.

"You asked me what I was doing here. I could ask the same thing of you," she began, still holding him fast but drawing back to look at him. She searched his face, and he hers. Observing their exchange of worry felt strangely intrusive. "When I woke, you were gone. Mother and father were dead, and Jhosch in chaos."

I noted and Gannet did, too, that she didn't hesitate to speak her mind in front of those who accompanied her, to speak the truth of his parentage. We exchanged a look, and she was quick to explain.

"The false Theba compelled all but the most loyal into her service, made promises she won't be able to keep, threatened further destruction. The heretics enforce her will, now. These men and women remained behind for me. For us. For Ambar. And that's why I'm here," she continued, breaking away from him now and turning her attention to me. "I'm willing to share everything we know about her forces with Aleyn. Before I left Jhosch, I spared an envoy to Cascar, promising them their sovereignty if they joined this fight. I pledge all of those loyal to me to your family, Eiren."

She paused to take a breath, her features transformed by more than the fire that had touched her. Conviction blazed there, born of a duty she'd chosen, rather than one she'd merely accepted.

"I will not be my father's daughter. If we are going to rebuild a kingdom, I will not put greed at its heart."

I nodded, determined not to cry at her courage, at the fact that she *lived*.

"They're in the palace. We can take you," I said. She studied me a moment longer, then turned to the scarred young man from before.

"Can you scout ahead? See if we can get nearer the city's center before we have to go above ground again?"

He set off, and when Morainn sat to drink and remove a few strips of something from a pouch to eat, the others took that as a signal that they, too, had earned a brief rest. Gannet and I crouched beside Morainn, and I thought of the last time we three had been together, how little resemblance there was between that moment and this.

"You haven't told me yet how you came to be here," she said softly, meeting my eyes. I read her thoughts—she offered them to me without hesitation or reproach.

I don't know who leads the army.

I don't blame you for what happened to my parents.

I don't blame you for this.

And now I did turn away, eyes burning.

"We went through *Zhaeha*," Gannet answered, eliciting a look of shock from his sister and from the guards seated near enough to her to hear. "I do not doubt that your aid and Cascar's will be most welcome, but there is something in this city that has the power to end this war. Forever."

"And you're not talking about Eiren," Morainn interjected, a ghost of the smirk I remembered flirting with her lips.

"No," Gannet continued, ignoring her attempt at levity. "Some kind of weapon. I think it's what we've always meant to find for Theba. Something to bring back the gods."

"Or something to kill them." The words felt heavy in my mouth, weights I dropped into the conversation.

"And you're looking for it?" Morainn removed the gloves she'd been wearing, pale fingers working at a bandoleer of darts strapped to one wrist. She hadn't gone armed before, but I wasn't surprised to learn that she had some skill to call on when necessary.

"Yes. And—and Shran's golems."

Her look was incredulous at Gannet's admission.

"That's just a story, Gannet."

"So were the *kr'oumae*," he insisted. "And we saw them. We passed through their waters in the center of the world to arrive here."

Morainn gaped, hands falling away from her work. This response seemed to satisfy Gannet.

"We've been looking for temples, and for Shran's tomb. It seems unlikely to me that the location of his tomb was forgotten, but rather, hidden."

"It makes sense," Morainn admitted, recovering her senses, "considering the turmoil that followed his death, the bloody years under his sons. How do you even know where to look?"

Rather than answer his sister, Gannet looked to me. He sensed my discomfort, the guilt that filled me when I looked at Morainn.

If she can forgive you, you can forgive yourself.

I swallowed.

"I have had visions of Re'Kether as it was, a rebellion against the gods. We've been following them, but they're difficult for me to remember, and we haven't had anything else to go on."

"I might be able to help with that." Her grin now was every inch the one that I remembered as she slipped a pack from her back and began to rifle through its contents. "I have something for you. I couldn't bear to leave it, when I found it in your chamber." She held out a slim bundle to me. The fabric was stained with travel, but inside a tome lay undamaged, the worn marks upon the cover familiar and old. It was the book Gannet had given me, the one that he had entered the burning barge to recover, the one I had unwittingly abandoned in Jhosch. I hadn't intended to leave, or to leave it behind.

I took it from her hands, marveling at how right it felt to hold it again.

"It revealed the way through the Rogue's Ear," she continued. "It may hold more secrets still."

"Thank you, Morainn," I murmured, running a finger down the spine before opening it. The pages made no more sense to me now than they had the first time Gannet had opened it with me, but perhaps now that we had a purpose, a reason, we could learn something.

Gannet looked over my shoulder, eyes hooded as he watched my hands move over the book.

"I found the book in Rhale's library many years ago. He has many treasures of the old world, though he does not part readily with them. He told me to take it, that the book would be mine, for a time, and then it would be yours."

Sweat beaded suddenly on my spine despite the chill.

"He knew about me?"

"Not exactly," Gannet replied, looking away, thoughts distant and guarded. "He didn't tell me who was meant to have it, only that I would know, when the time came. And I did."

I'd thought Rhale's claim to Charrum's ancestry laughable then, but now I wondered. Surely someone who had that man's greed in his blood would possess great mysteries, many of them intangible. There was more value in knowledge, in secrets, than in objects. Charrum would have learned that, in time.

The scarred young man returned, speaking in low tones to Morainn. It seemed there was a way forward, for a distance. We stood, readying ourselves, and I stowed the book in my own bag. We were still near the shaft that led to the surface, and I could see there were lavish carvings even here. I stepped forward, brushing sand from a curling vine, leaves still baring a trace of green.

"I am always finding things are not as they seem," I said quietly, working my way down the carving until under my hand, small insects sprang into relief, their lines so fluid I flinched, stumbling back suddenly into Gannet before I realized they were not real. His hands went to my shoulders instinctively, steadying me, lingering after.

"Some things are, Eiren."

His voice was low, breath threaded through my loose hair, he was so close. Morainn's guards were already moving down the passage with her sequestered at their center. Gannet's hands traced hesitantly across the plane of my shoulders before falling away. I felt them still, as though web-thin threads connected his skin and mine. The heat that stirred in my heart had no relation to Theba's ember-potent fury, but it felt just as dangerous.

"I could've helped, up there. But I didn't. I'm afraid if I call upon Theba's strength again, I won't be able to stop her," I said suddenly, turning to face him before he could advance after his sister. Morainn had slowed, peering back over her shoulder to locate us.

"I don't think that's true," Gannet said after a long moment, brushing my hair back over one shoulder with a touch so fleeting I nearly leaned into it. "I think it's you who can't be stopped."

My breath caught, but even as we stood there, peering into each other, teetering on the edge of something unsaid, Morainn raised her voice.

"I am very close to losing a hard-won hour." There was a warning in her tone, and laughter, too. Gannet and I turned, hurrying toward the promise of both.

CHAPTER SEVENTEEN

"It doesn't look like any map I've ever seen." Esbat leaned over the book, laid bare like a body at a funeral viewing on a long, low slab of stone. Cooled cups of tea circled the busy pages, long forgotten as we thirsted for insight instead. Morainn crouched next to my sister, an incongruous sight, my fair and dark sisters of spirit and flesh. My mother was opposite, characteristically silent save for the occasional murmur of agreement. Gannet hung back, perhaps preferring the shade of the interior wall and the sanctuary of his own thoughts. We had returned to the palace less than two hours before, Morainn's proclamations as powerful for my assembled family as they had been for me. She had risked her life coming here, and offered them what Gannet and I could not: a true ally in herself, and in the Cascari, if they agreed to her terms. She and father had already crafted a missive to smuggle out of the city and to Cascar at the earliest opportunity. Jurnus, upon learning that the imposter's forces were less than a day away, set out immediately to bolster our defenses.

"It wasn't meant to be read by us," Morainn interjected, tone diplomatic despite her exhaustion and her frustration that this was a puzzle she couldn't solve. She curled the page into the spine the way the wind once had while I read on horseback, revealing to me the path made between pages. Neither she nor Gannet had recognized the shape created by this curious way of reading. He explained that it had been through a code of archaic characters that he had discerned the location of the Rogue's Ear, and both were skeptical of the path I pointed out being indicative of the location of the tomb.

"Then who was it meant for?" Esbat asked, but she looked at me when she said it. Morainn followed her eyes, a slight frown wrinkling the bridge of her nose, extending the waxy scar tissue that covered one of her eyes.

"The gods, perhaps? We can only guess," Gannet answered. Everyone considered this for a moment in silence. I moved to sit beside my mother, our knees touching as I, too, regarded the text. I wished for the gown I had worn in Ambar, the one embroidered with the characters that had identified me as Theba, that told the parts of the goddess's story that had come before me. I was sure they were here, too, that their trail would, perhaps, reveal the way to the man whose mortal life she had sullied.

As I considered Theba's corruption of the love between Shran and Jemae, a thought occurred to me. "Where was Jemae laid to rest?" I glanced sidelong at my mother. If anyone here would have the answer, it would be her.

My mother's brows crept toward her hairline at the question.

"I'm not sure. She was always a figure cast in the shadows of her husband and sons," my mother returned quietly, commanding everyone's attention in an instant. "She began her life that way, and I expect she ended it that way, too. It was common among the First People, who numbered few in his time, to arrange marriages for their children almost upon conception. Families schemed to prolong their gifted lines, their lives unnaturally long and their abilities unique to an ancient time. Shran's mother was the daughter of one such house, as was Jemae's.

"A fortune-teller laid her hands upon each woman's belly and spoke of the fish-little ones within, hands reaching for each other before they had even been born. She claimed that they would weather the ages together, that more than the bonds of blood and marriage would unite them.

"As is the way of fortune-tellers, of course, she could not say what or why. But it is also the way of those who elicit the attentions of such folk to believe without reason, and both mothers carried her words in their hearts. Jemae and Shran shared a birthing day, which was considered doubly lucky, and a formal betrothal was arranged for their eighteenth year. Jemae passes largely out of history until their marrying day."

My mother's silence stretched long enough to indicate the short tale's conclusion, but already I was dwelling on what she hadn't said. It had never occurred to me before how unfair it was, and Morainn's snort confirmed that she felt the same. We had so many of Shran's stories, but so few of his bride, who had been so wronged by the life they had shared. But it was his life we remembered, Shran's histories that we told.

I reached out to stroke the pages again, turning and turning.

"What would Jemae's name look like, written this way?" I asked.

We had already pored over the text, noting every mention of Shran and finding little to recommend him, let alone reveal the location of his tomb. It was Gannet who answered me now. He strode forward, dipping his fingers swiftly in his long-neglected cup of tea and tracing the outline of a relatively simple character on the smooth surface of the table. It would require careful reading to spot.

Even as I studied the symbol he'd traced on the table, Gannet thumbed through the pages, landing upon one we had visited earlier. There was Jemae's name in a large, florid script. He circled the table, observing from a different angle.

"Look, curled into her name, here," he said, pointing. I leaned forward. We all did.

"*From mild depths loveliness springs,*" he recited, and my eyes followed his tracing finger in the air, on the page, the unfamiliar characters suddenly taking on the countenance of water lilies. I felt it had always been this way with the book: where at one moment there were only scribbles and mystery, the next, sense could spring from chaos. When he continued, my breath caught in my throat.

"*Where I have bathed in love, let me forever rest.*"

"There used to be a river north of the city," Esbat announced. I saw another map in her mind, different than the one we'd been studying the day before. She must have uncovered something new. "Jemae was fond of swimming there. Perhaps she is there, or Shran. Or both."

I was standing and Gannet, too. We knew we didn't have the time to waste.

"Go," my mother said, reaching for her cup, her grimace of worry disguised when she lifted it to her lips to drain it. "Please be careful."

She looked small to me then, diminished, and when I picked up the book, I laid a hand tentatively against her shoulder. It was a touch that might once have comforted me, and the reversal of the gesture left me with a strangely heavy heart. Gannet and I hadn't gone more than a few steps outside the chamber before I felt Morainn behind me. I stopped, catching his sleeve between my fingers and arresting his progress, too.

"There are icons with the imposter," she said. "Why would they follow her? They must know she isn't Theba."

"You said she made promises she couldn't keep," Gannet answered, a cold edge in his voice. "We're just as susceptible to hope as anyone else."

Morainn's lips parted in surprise, her eyes wide with it.

"You never used to be." Her gaze slid from her brother to me, and the brow above her sighted eye cocked in interest. I flushed. "I'm going to have a chat with your brother. I was told he has an interest in Ambarian battle tactics. I may be able to help with that."

She was moving in the opposite direction before I could ask if she meant herself, or the guards she had brought with her. Or both.

"Do you think that Ji found what we're seeking?" Gannet asked once we were above ground, moving toward the increasingly armed perimeter that surrounded the palace. "That she used it?"

I shrugged. "There are icons for every god I know in stories. If she had, I would think we'd have stories of the god, but no icon."

We passed a line of pikes, their tips coated in oil that would either poison, or burn. I didn't stop to determine which.

"Maybe not," Gannet countered, his imagination dark. "If

you kill a god, will they ever have been? Will their worship be undone, as well?"

I considered his words as we passed under an archway, a discreet vessel of fire oil fixed to the ancient keystone. When struck with a flaming arrow or other projectile, it would carry that fire to whoever was unlucky enough to be passing this way. Our forces had been at work, then. I hoped it would be enough.

"I'm more worried that if she never found it, we won't, either," I replied, lowering my voice to a whisper as we moved into the ruins. It was an hour's walk, at least, to the city's northern edge, and without having to creep for fear of discovery. It was too slow, too much of what little time we had left eaten up in silence and worry.

Finally, the ruins around us began to thin, the lower and lesser buildings of the city's outer edges having given up their shape and substance to the sand long ago. We were more exposed, but there was nothing to be done for it. I had trouble even here separating the two worlds that wavered before me. I saw the phantoms of once-bright market tent fabrics flapping, heard the creak of the carts of tea vendors, my nostrils flaring at the long-absent scents of horse and camel traders.

And the water. I heard the splash of boats and the thump of sandals against a muddy bank. Gannet had drawn close to me the fewer buildings there were to disguise us, and I touched a hand to his arm, wishing that I could share what I saw. He soaked up my disappointment instead, for rather than the sloping bank of the river that had once run here, swift and blue-green with life, there was bare rock, the sweep of a dune. We couldn't even see the ancient bed, and there was nothing that resembled a structure, temple, tomb, or otherwise.

"We've wasted hours," I moaned, shading my eyes against the sun, regretting the distance it had made toward the horizon. "If there's anything here, I wouldn't even know where to begin looking."

Gannet moved behind me, searching my pack and recovering

the book. He turned to the page we had read, hands tracing the wild characters.

"Depths," he murmured. "Was there something under the water, perhaps?"

"Even if there was, how would we *get* to it?" I threw up my hands, the wind catching my sleeve, lifting the sand at my feet in an artful dance. My mouth went dry. "I have a very dangerous idea."

"How dangerous?"

"We're very likely to be seen."

Gannet cast around, lips flat with concern. "That could happen at any moment anyway."

It wasn't a rousing endorsement, but it was enough.

"Stand back, then. And you'll want to close your eyes, I think."

I took my own advice, eyes roving behind my eyelids, feeling the grains of sand against my calves, my scalp, beneath my nails. I brushed them away with my mind, feeling them lift and scatter. I pushed out, my hands following the path my mind was making, parting the sands ahead of us like a plow. Creating a path. A sandstorm. A way down, a way back into time. The sound was like nothing I had ever heard before, a thunderclap but smooth, like tearing a great sheaf of parchment and scattering the continent-sized scraps to the wind.

When I opened my eyes, I saw the layers of stone, what had once been sediment lining the river's bottom, and I saw, too, the regular shape of many interlocking stone plates near the ancient river's deepest point. Boats would not have run afoul there, and only the bravest swimmers would have sought entry by this way.

I grinned at Gannet, giddy as a fool who has just demonstrated a new trick. We clasped hands and moved cautiously forward into the riverbed, each of us eyeing the wall of sand pushed precariously up on either side. But even as we considered this danger, I became aware of another. Voices, thoughts, hurried feet. We slid the last few lengths into the bed and onto our bellies. Gannet flattened himself next to me, length to length, but I hardly noticed his touch. My heart was pounding, and I thought I felt a vibration in the stone, in the sand underfoot, in response.

But it wasn't me.

Several minutes passed before a shadow lengthened above us, then many shadows, moving quickly.

"You're certain you saw someone?"

"Absolutely certain."

Low voices, urgent. I perceived their darting thoughts as I would the movements of scurrying mice wanting a hole to hide in. And behind them, a longer shadow, a broader mind, guarded. This voice was low, too, but with the mellow cadence of the aged.

"You cannot hide, Gannet. You cannot hide her from me."

I looked up. Framed against the bleak horizon, I could not see her face at first, only her narrow form, swathed in a great cloth to guard against the sun. It was Najat, the Dreamer, the icon from Jhosch. I could not read her, could not see if she meant us good or ill, only rose slowly when Gannet did, waiting. Behind her, several Ambarian soldiers wavered, weapons raised but frightened eyes betraying their lack of desire to use them against us. They recognized Gannet, and me they guessed at, fearing and hoping that they were wrong.

"Najat." Gannet's voice was measured, the note of caution so slight I might have been the only one to discern it.

"How lucky to find you both together," Najat replied. At first I thought she raised a hand in friendship, or some ritual greeting, but she held it palm open and facing us, closing each finger until she'd formed a fist. Gannet slumped instantly, and I only just managed to break his fall with my own body, catching him in a limp swoon. I strained, Theba's strength little interested in this task, and cast a furious look at Najat. I felt the fire call.

She shook her head.

"If you want him to wake again you'll do just as I say. Kill me, or attempt to flee with him, and he'll sleep until the day he dies," she said, voice funeral-quiet. "I have seen his dreams, and yours, too. Do as I say and I'll return him to you."

Embers roasted in my belly, and I grunted with the effort of keeping Gannet from sliding to the ground. Measured eyes never leaving my face, Najat motioned for the soldiers to approach and relieve me of my burden. I considered fighting, leaving little more than oil-stink smudges of ash to mark the places their living bodies last stood, but I believed Najat. I had seen enough during my time with the icons in Jhosch to know that each possessed skills, different but no less terrible, than my own.

I allowed the soldiers to lift Gannet between them, touching him carefully first, feeling the warmth of his skin, the shallow but steady intake of his breath. I didn't look back at the riverbed but shut my eyes briefly, willing just a little of the sand to obscure our discovery.

My eyes cut to Najat when they opened, brutal as a blade's edge. "You know me and still you serve her?"

"You don't know what you're saying." Najat beckoned with her hands. There was no malice in her voice. She did not enjoy this task but felt it necessary. "I am ready to die. Ready to never come back. She can give me that, can give it to us all."

Najat couldn't hide much from me, and she wasn't trying. She had precious few details to share, besides, but her faith in the imposter's promise was a blaze to rival my own. And she wanted it, wanted to die, wanted it more than I thought I had ever wanted anything. This made her dangerous.

"We want the same thing. Help me, not her," I pleaded. I wasn't sure that I had the whole story, yet, or enough of Ji's to rewrite my own the way that I wished. But Najat was not a madwoman.

"She wants to talk with you before she kills you," she said, ignoring my plea. "She sent us ahead for you, when I saw your dreams."

She guided our small group a little way back into the ruins, but only far enough in to provide cover. We weren't headed into the city, but around.

"It doesn't matter what she wants. Theba won't allow the imposter to succeed," I continued. The Dread Goddess was coiled hot and low, bristling. I had already known she would not let me die easily, and if there were even a chance that it meant her end, too…she'd set the whole world aflame before she'd let the executioner near. For Theba, there was no other way to die but execution. No quiet exit, no final sleep. Only blood and smoke and screams.

"Theba cannot be allowed to possess what we seek," Najat answered, her dreamy tone edged with regret. "The one I serve may be mad, but at least she is mortal."

My heart hammered. I saw the imposter in Najat's mind, hunched in shadow, wound in silks. I wanted her face, wanted to see it burned away to bone.

No. Not me. Theba.

I shook my head, studying Gannet's limp form, heart fretting over the clumsy slope of his shoulders in sleep, the loose knees, the dragging boots.

"So am I," I insisted weakly, feeling my resolve singing at the edges.

"We both know that isn't true."

"Well, whatever I am, I won't be with you long. My family still controls this city."

"No one controls this city."

As if in response, there was the sound of tumbling stone, and Najat and the soldiers dropped, weapons steady. After a moment's hesitation, I joined them, realizing that it would be worse to be seen by my allies than it would be to find my own way out of this. Perhaps Najat was the only one who could wake Gannet, perhaps not. It was lucky for her that my uncertainty was a leash, my love ensuring I showed restraint.

I saw the brief glint of a weapon from a vantage point deeper within the city, high in a window of what I could see-and-not-see had once been a lavish, many-terraced social hall of some kind. The kind of women that Ji had witnessed opening their veins in the temple had come and gone there, forever ago and never again. It was likely a scout there now, one of my brother's, and there was no way to know if we had been seen or not. We were crouched in rubble, upturned street before us, a low wall alongside that provided a little shade from the blistering glare of the sun.

Najat must have seen the scout, as well, or suspected, for our pace quickened. Rather than continue down the once-broad avenue that would have led us beyond the city walls, she turned back into the ruins, raising a hand to shield her eyes so that she could study the stonework on the weathered faces of what had once been homes, shops, houses for worship, for drink, for misdeeds. The soldiers who supported Gannet between them were looking, too, and I took the opportunity to draw just a little bit closer to him, brushing his dragging ankle with mine.

I sensed his thoughts, his consciousness, but he was deep within himself. His mind was night-quiet, dark but for formless musings. I saw his inner self circling one of the flames, his back to me, pale hair unbound. I thought of reaching out to him, but there was a wrongness to his posture, the feeling that even an attempt to rouse him would snuff those lights, one and all.

Najat's gifts were not mine, and I felt an unfamiliar thrill of fear. Theba stretched her senses into mine, eager to meet this adversary, and I fought her. I needed answers, which meant I needed Najat alive, and Gannet, too.

"In here," Najat said as she gestured for me to precede her within an imposing ruin, the stone black with age, the roof of sand-blasted stones sagging under what seemed the weight of the whole sky and sun above. I struggled to see it as it had been, but there was nothing to see. The place felt as insubstantial as a breath, though more than capable of crushing the life out of us.

"If we aren't careful in there, it will come crashing down around us," I said, hesitating. Najat's eyes seemed to shrug, daring me. *Not ready to die, Theba?*

My lips pressed to a thin line and the flash of anger I felt between them, like a smear of color, or blood from a bitten tongue.

"Do you know what happened in this city, many ages ago? They tried to kill gods then, too. It didn't work. I've seen it," I lied, or rather, offered the half-truths that I had. "I've had visions of Re'Kether as it was. A rebellion against the tyranny of gods. If you want to end it, I am closer than anyone else alive to finding out how."

Najat studied me, and on an impulse, I took a swift step closer and pressed my hand against her cheek, sharing the flashes of the visions that remained with me, the muted colors of the past. She gasped but didn't move away.

"Do you see?" I said softly, a wild hope occurring to me. "You could help me, Dreamer. Show me how to return from sleep with every memory intact."

"Are you sure you know what you want?" Najat whispered, but even as she did her hand snaked out of her sleeve to clasp my wrist. "And that you are the one who truly wants it?"

A whisper of something passed into my blood, sped to my heart. In the same instant an arrow whistled through the air, piercing the armor of the soldier whose body partially shielded Najat's. The second arrow reached its intended target, burying itself in her chest from behind. She looked down, for a moment only shock triumphing over pain on her features. We'd been seen after all.

"In!" the wounded soldier called as he pushed Najat ahead of him, taking little care with the feathered protrusion that emerged from her chest. I dropped my hand to her arm, steadying her as he urged us deeper within and down a narrow entry, remembering the moon-eyed woman she had been in Jhosch, a woman who had been a listener, not a teller. A woman I might have befriended, in time.

As I thought of Najat as she had been, she was fading swiftly before me now. My eyes cut to Gannet. He was still unconscious.

"Najat." My fingers closed on her wrist, fine-boned beneath her weathered sleeve. "Will he wake? Will he live?"

She met my eyes, but if a cloud passed over hers, I couldn't see it. There was another figure in the ruin where we crouched, gold-edged, hooded, leaning into me. I was not seeing the world as it was, and the darkness that crept over my own vision had only a little to do with our descent into a deep, secret place beneath the ruins. Najat was going to die, and Gannet, too. A strangled panic warred for words in my throat, my fear robbing me of breath.

But it was because Ji wasn't breathing.

Mara was touching the wall. She was not supposed to touch the wall.

It was dark and we were underwater, but still I whipped my head back to throw a worried glance at the woman from the temple. Her figure and face were obscured by the water and the darkness both, but she had not drifted as Mara had. There was something wrong about her face, though, the features bulky and blurred in the rune glow.

I thought my heart would create waves, pounding as it did against my chest. Mara's fingers were tracing the sigils now as she passed, too precise, too quickly, and where they had only halfheartedly shed their light, now they blazed. She should've known not to do that. Something was wrong with her. When Dsimah, Tirce, and Najat had charged us with this mission, they had said we would need someone from the temple, but I hadn't told Mara the identities of our leaders. But now, watching her strange behavior, I wondered if there was something she hadn't told me, too.

Mara didn't dart up for air when we came to the fourth and final breathing place, but I did, taking a quick, desperate gulp before ducking below again to peer downward, not wanting to let either of them out of my sight now.

The woman from the temple was struggling with Mara. She was trying to force her to come up for air, but Mara was fighting forward. Their bodies writhed in the water, Mara kicking, the woman from the temple attempting to lift her toward the ceiling, toward me. The muscles in my chest tightened in sympathy. I considered diving down, assisting the woman, but I wasn't sure I could trust her, either. The hood drifted in a lazy pattern behind her head, bare for the first time, and something just seemed *wrong* about her. I could have gone on, but the task that lay ahead was not made for one. It was daunting even for three.

Finally, Mara relented, and the hooded woman was pumping her legs and one free arm, the other fast around Mara's chest, but not toward me, and the air I knew they both desperately needed. She was forging ahead.

Reckless. I couldn't stay where I was, and if I didn't follow I would quickly lose them both. With a curse, I dove down and after the pair.

The woman clearly intended to force Mara to finish what we'd come here to do. Her skills were needed, and mine, and whatever it was the hooded woman could do for us, too. That was why we had been chosen. That was why we all needed to be here, and with our wits about us.

It was clear from Mara's behavior, however, that hers had fled, and mine were soon to follow if this wretched place had seized her.

I ached for lack of air and didn't know how the hooded woman had the strength to propel herself and Mara both, but then she was rising and I was behind her. We emerged from the water mere seconds apart. She'd thrust Mara forward into the shallows, a sweep of her bent head slogging the sodden hood back into place. She was quick to take hold of Mara again, however, for no sooner than my friend had been freed did Mara begin to advance, eyes blazing. Mara's face was ashen, jaw slack, and I felt mine loosen, teeth chattering from fear and from the cold.

"What's happened to her?"

"She'll live, but we might not," the hooded woman said testily after she'd taken several gulping breaths. Mara's jerking form and the temple's many sigils beginning to glow about us should have encouraged me to hold my tongue, but my head was reeling.

"Tie her up," the woman said.

She struggled to maintain a hold on Mara while also loosening a length of rope from under the sodden cloak she still wore. Mara began to wail, a keening song that caused the already glowing runes to blaze brighter still.

"And gag her."

I didn't hesitate. Mara was my friend, my ally, but the wild, distant look in her eyes was not one that I recognized. She'd been corrupted. I refused to believe that she had betrayed me. It was said there were some among the gods who could commandeer the minds of mortals—it had to be that. I needed it to be that.

Even if it meant both the hooded woman and I were going to die down here.

Mara snapped at my hands when I drew near her mouth, her loose, snapping jaw slick with subterranean water and spittle. When I swooped around behind her to bind her arms, the hooded woman edged out of my way.

I felt my skin grow hot as I bent to strap Mara's legs together and we lifted her between us. The hooded woman and I were nearly the same height, which was a surprise and a boon. Not many women were as tall as I was, and it made the work of carrying my struggling friend deeper into the temple at least less physically taxing.

"We don't have a lot of time," the woman insisted as I scouted around for a dry place to secure Mara.

"I'm not just going to dump her somewhere she might drown. If we get what we came for, it won't matter."

There were crooked stairs angling toward what I hoped was the temple's sanctuary, and every few steps, deep, carved openings intended for housing artifacts long since stolen. With a grunt, I hefted Mara into a hollow I deemed safe from whatever tides touched this place. The hooded woman secured Mara's feet while I turned her face to the wall. She wasn't moving now, but her eyes were open, distant. It was as though she wasn't with us anymore.

"We should hurry," said the woman, but her voice was uncharacteristically patient. Perhaps she realized how hard it was for me to leave a friend behind. Or perhaps she rightly guessed that I was as predictable as a mule when pushed to act outside my own wants and time.

We pressed forward, the stairs widening, and I didn't allow myself to look back at where Mara was all but entombed. I couldn't help her. I could only do what we had come here to do. When we reached the stone doors, they were thick as three men and twice as tall. Blind faces were carved at eye level, bodies hung without arms or legs and swaddled as babes, level with our own. It was as the hooded woman suspected. This was an ancient place of Adah, whose followers were as inhumanly cruel as their divine master. When one served justice, one was privileged to define it.

Blood would be needed to pass here. Skilled though I was, my blood had been my entry into the rebellion, this had been why I was so desirable. Only the First People could get close enough to the gods to be useful.

I loosened one of the daggers I wore in a belt at my waist. The faces before us suddenly blazed as though they could sense the coming offering, eyes now appearing white and searching where there had been none before.

I sliced open my palm and blinded the figure in the stone before me once more.

CHAPTER EIGHTEEN

Clutching my hands together against the dull stroke of pain, I didn't feel the warmth of newly spilled blood that I expected to feel. My palms were dry, sand-dusted, and I looked wildly around at the temple-that-wasn't as I came to my senses. Mine. I was Eiren again.

My heart hammered a rhythm not unlike Ji's. I wasn't sure how they'd done it, but the imposter's soldiers had managed to drag both Gannet and me into a chamber so deep beneath Re'Kether that there was a chill in the air. I half-expected to see my breath before me, my next words captured in a false fog.

"Were we followed?" I wanted to ask if they had killed anyone to secure us, for I saw no signs of a struggle here. Najat was clutching at her wound, the shallow shuddering of her shoulders alarming. Gannet was crumpled next to me, his head upon my ankles, the cold metal of the mask smooth and foul-feeling against my skin. I saw all of this by dark sight, though one of the soldiers, stationed well away with his back to us near the chamber's mouth, held a small, dim torch. I didn't wait for a response but seized upon the arm of the nearest soldier, amplifying my capacity to read her thoughts. She drew her weapon but dropped it when I squeezed.

We had been seen. We weren't going to be alone down here for long.

Maintaining my hold on the soldier, whose face was frozen in a look of terror that mirrored what I felt in her mind, I rose to my feet, an otherworldly grace in my movements.

"Najat," I said carefully, for it wasn't just the soldier I held. Theba, too, was plucking at my limbs, teasing my heart. But I would take only just enough to do what I wanted, what I needed to do. I wouldn't allow her to control again. "You're dying. I can't help you. You should remember me well enough to know that I would, if I could. Please wake Gannet. Undo whatever you've done."

Her shoulders shook with sound of another kind, a rattling chuckle that sounded as though it began in her bones.

"Know you? I know you," she managed, her voice a wheeze. "Everyone knows you but *you*, child."

I could feel her slipping away. I'd been near enough of the dead now, enough of the dying, that I fancied I could even see her spirit begin to free itself from her flesh. I wanted to weep. Theba hungered for the fleeing wisp of life, bravery, deep feeling, confidence and regret. There was a clattering of weapons and a shout, and I heard rather than saw the first of Najat's soldiers fall. I thrust the one that I'd held away from me, then dropped to my knees before Najat.

"Please, I'm begging you," I began, but she was lifting her hand, touching it with a firm finality against my brow.

"Theba doesn't beg."

And she used the last of her strength to push me away.

Najat fell back against the rocky floor of the chamber. Neither she nor Gannet stirred, and I howled. I did not see but sensed the bristling of spears at my back. My scream deepened, melting them in their shafts. I couldn't see anything but the pulse of my own blood purpling my eyes, tears streaming hotly as my trembling hands sought Gannet's slumped form. He didn't move. My fingers fumbled at his chest, shaking but sensing nothing. No heart, no breath.

More soldiers swarmed at my back, and I felt a cruel tightness in my chest. Taking, always. The world was always taking from me.

I rounded on the faceless followers who crowded behind me. Najat's forces fought with those of my family, one group sought to secure me, the other to kill me, and it didn't matter. It was all the same, to contain what I was in death, or in a mortal cage, with words or false, familiar feelings.

There was a pulse in the soil beneath my feet, and the fighting, for a moment, paused. I felt the ground splintering and shaking. I seized the soldier nearest to me, no notion of his alliance, and no interest in it. Weapons flashed like lanterns around us, but between him and me, time seemed to stop. I moved my hands down the plane of his chest, parting the dark layers of fabric there, the armor plates, inexplicably dry despite the heat of the air, of the skin beneath. There was hot blood there. I thought of drinking it, bathing in it, or sipping, only, like little kisses planted between lovers. But I could only destroy, never create.

I felt the soldier's heart, powerful, beating hotly with fear and strength in equal parts.

And I turned it to ash in his chest.

Another came, and another, all of them silenced, my will thrust into their bodies like one might a gag into the mouth of an unwilling hostage.

"Eiren."

Gannet. How could he be speaking to me now? From death? I would join him. I would break open my own mind and pour it into someone else. My struggle began and ended in a cloud of stone dust, the smell of smoke, eyes unmasked. I couldn't see him. I would never see him again.

My hands clasped like irons around another throat, choking words, cries, breath, all.

Eiren, no.

Shrieking, I felt hands upon me, pulling me free of the stumbling figure before me. The soldier was doubled over but drawing ragged breaths, resolved to live. A muscled arm fell into the light of many torches, a tangled head of dark hair.

It was Jurnus.

I screamed again, fighting the one who held me, but their arms were strong, steady. Even as I saw Jurnus straightening, his breath reclaiming evenness with each gulp, time seemed to slow as my eyes crossed from one end of the chamber to the other, neck craning as though inviting a blade. I wanted to see the face of the one that restrained me. I knew his touch, but I needed to see.

I wept then against Gannet's shoulder, the dark fabric cool despite the living warmth of the body underneath. His hands tightened around me. I didn't have a thought for Jurnus, who was bleeding above one eye. Neither did I care for those who staggered behind him, shaken, my sister, Lista, my father, among them, nor a thought even for the wet, sticky substance that met my sandaled feet: blood from the soldiers I had slain. I kept opening and closing my mouth against Gannet's chest, trying to speak, but what could I say that he could not sense?

Jurnus stepped forward, his face lit by more than torchlight. Twilight streamed in from behind us where before there had been only darkness. Gannet's arms tightened around me protectively when I peered around him to look.

It was as though a great scythe had bisected the ceiling, a scar wide enough to allow twelve men across to penetrate the chamber. I could think of nothing that possessed the power to destroy so completely; no weapon, no construct of war.

Nothing but me.

"You attacked me, Eiren." Jurnus's voice was ragged, wary, as though he were not sure whom he addressed. And he had every reason to fear. There was a madness in his eyes that quickened my blood, the flood of it that responded to Theba, that belonged to her will. "Why? What happened here?"

I felt Theba pulling me away from Gannet, toward my brother.

"You have eyes," Theba said in a hiss, gesturing with my hands at the carnage. "I killed here. I'll kill here again."

I was drifting, strangely calm, but knew it to be the sort of stillness we saw in the sand-sick: those who wandered so far and so long in the desert that they surrendered to the elements, to the death that exposure swiftly delivered. Theba seized greater control of my limbs until I felt hardly anything at all. Gannet reached for me again but she stepped away from him, hungering for violence.

"You are my *sister*," Jurnus screamed, shrill terror in his words, his eyes. He gestured at Najat's corpse, and I saw the suspicion spiraling out of control in his mind. This seemed a surreptitious meeting to him, a gathering of spies. "Have you been acting against us this whole time?"

Theba leered, and I struggled to return to myself. But I felt deep, drowned.

"Now is the time to remember who our true enemies are," Gannet cautioned.

Jurnus shook his blade in a bloody fist.

"There was never any question who the true enemy was until you showed up," he spat.

His sword was steady, and his intentions were as clear to Gannet as they were to me. Gannet sprang past me, swift to knock the sword from Jurnus's hand. Time slowed and my brother's surprise dulled his reflexes for only a moment before his fist connected with a sickening slap against the broad side of Gannet's jaw. And then things moved very fast. The two men were locked together as Jurnus struck again and again, making no attempt to recover his sword. Gannet evaded him with forearms and elbows, refusing to engage. I began to laugh, manic, as the violence before me escalated, a wicked, tangled shadow of struggle cast into the sand by the flicking torchlight. More soldiers gathered around them, frantic at the sound, my father and sisters among them, trying to tear them apart. I jerked and hiccupped a scream, a cackle, bit my tongue and tasted blood. Theba wanted this, wanted me to want it, and I fought to return her to the dark, to the quiet. She would break the walls, splinter the swords, but her real work was in hearts and bones. Our doubts would be our undoing.

My father fought to get to his only son, shouting for caution. Lista's scream was senseless, the flash of her blade wild. Now Jurnus bent to his own weapon. His face blazed with pride and vengeance. I felt lifted onto my toes with anticipation, the acid touch of rising bile in my throat. My presence, Theba's presence, fed this corruption. I knew that she worked in him as she had other brothers, long ago, brothers whose blood we shared. Jurnus, whose tender heart had always been foolish but never murderous. Never that.

"Enough." Though my whisper was quieter even than the hush of a blade slicing through the air, they heard me, everyone. Jurnus dropped his sword, shaking his head as though to clear it, and Gannet slowly lowered his arms. I let out a breath I hadn't realized I was holding, and with it a tremor chased from my chin to my feet. I needed to be away from them, all of them; I needed to run. But fleeing spoke too much of guilt and blame, for all I shared the responsibility for the ill my hands had wrought.

And those I loved must suffer for it now.

"I'm sorry." This was quieter still. My father's eyes softened on me, uncertain, but there was no forgiveness there. "Gannet isn't your enemy. But I am."

"That's not true," Lista began, but Jurnus held up a hand, silencing her. He had cooled, but there was still fury in his face.

"You should go back. The imposter is only hours away. We don't need you making it any easier for her to get into the city." He pointed above us to the stone my temper had split. He was hurt, his body and his pride, and he was terrified. I saw myself as he had seen me, possessed.

Tears burned my eyes, but still I choked on Theba's laughter, thick as an extra tongue in my mouth, as I climbed out of the chamber and into the ruins. Only when I gulped fresh air again did I feel her retreat fully, sated for the moment with my distress. It was dark and I could move quickly through the silent ruins. I knew where I wanted to go now, and I knew I wanted Gannet to follow me.

The nearer I got to the palace the more urgent the activity. Soldiers worked by touch alone, not daring to light their preparations for the imminent threat of the imposter's army. The innocents, those who could not fight, were nowhere to be seen now, secreted below. But I didn't go down. I went up.

The terrace felt as familiar to me as it had the first time I had walked there, compelled then, too, by Theba. It was empty save for the ghostly rustlings of plants that no longer were, those that had grown here in another time and haunted it still. I walked to the edge, staring out across the dark desert as though the hardness of my gaze could will the sun to rise. Save for the fires of the Ambarian encampments, the dark was unyielding. It was not an unpleasant blackness but rather the sort for keeping secrets in, for restful quiet.

I deserved no rest.

I wanted more of the spectral beauty of the city-that-was, but the moon was new, a cold witness, and my dark sight didn't see the past. I stood there, wanting, for what might have been an hour or an instant before I heard footfalls on the stair I had ascended, and then on the terrace itself behind me. No one could have approached without my being aware, but he made no attempts to disguise his presence. Gannet.

"They are worried about you."

"They should run from me. Steal out of this city. When I meet the imposter, I'll kill her and this will be over."

Gannet moved to stand beside me, not close enough to touch, not near enough even for his cloak to brush my skirts when the wind shifted.

"You know that won't be the end of it, Eiren." He looked away from me, maybe seeing something that I had not, maybe searching, as I had done, for something more.

"Well, then I'll find this weapon, kill myself when I'm done with her. And if I can't, I'll find someone else willing to do it."

He knew my guilt, knew that he could say nothing to change its course.

But he tried anyway, because he loved me.

"An icon cannot resist their nature. I never told you that it would be easy, that accepting who you are would mean you liked it. That there wouldn't be things you wished were otherwise."

He had empathized with me from the first, had judged himself, and had in turn been a harsh judge of me because of something we had both failed to do: resign ourselves to our fate.

"What would you resist, if you could?" I asked quietly, maintaining the distance between us but feeling as though the wind would snatch my whisper and he would hear it still.

He took a long time to answer, his face and mind as guarded and remote as they had been on the day we had met.

"Before I met you, nothing." His voice was heavy and tight, like trying to carry a full jug of wine with only one finger. "Now, everything."

He braced himself against the stone, fine hands splayed as though his words required physical support. I admired his fingers, the pale crescents on his nails moons, neither rising nor falling, but holding steady between the worlds. That was where he stood, always, where I could not join him.

But I kept trying.

I closed the distance between us and laid my hand over his. Mine was much smaller and a little darker, like a gradient of twilight. After a second Gannet's hand turned over, smooth palm pressed to mine, fingers threading through. My heart beat faster, a flutter of moth wings in my belly as his thumb traced the hollow of soft flesh between my own thumb and forefinger.

"I would ask you what kind of life that's meant to be, wanting everything and having nothing. But I don't suppose we're meant to have any kind of life at all." I didn't look at him as I spoke, eyes closing at his touch. I wanted to see less, feel more. If I could have shrouded my ears I would have, to better appreciate his touch.

"You misunderstand me," Gannet answered, but there was nothing of the lecturer in his tone. "There are things I've accepted about my life that I can't wish for you. I want you to have more. I want—"

He stopped and I thought that he would leave me again, distance himself from the temptation, the uncertainty.

But that was not what he did.

Where Gannet's words had failed him, his hands did not. The one that held mine drew me near, the other snaked around my back. There was only a little tenderness in the movement, our bodies crushed quickly together. His mouth pressed to mine, easier work than words, tongue darting behind lips I had unwittingly parted. I could feel the shape of him, the sudden fire that stirred in me in answer to a question he hadn't asked.

It was yes. *Yes.*

Gannet let go of my hand to lower his, gathering folds of my dress as he lifted me against him. A scholar's hands he might have had, brushing coolly against my thighs, but he betrayed a warrior's strength in his urgency to have me closer, and closer still. I swayed against him like a dune reshaped in a strong wind. My hands glided up to his hairline as his pressed forward, hesitating at the thin garments that preserved my modesty until I shifted to allow him greater access. Even as his fingers moved within me and my sighs turned to sounds of encouragement, my own hands found the bindings of his mask, the knots I wished to unravel for him even as his fingers freed something deep inside me. But while I had given him permission, he made no such utterance, no motion. A single finger slipped beneath one of the straps, restless, but not yet moving to free him from this particular bond. Not without permission.

Gannet drew back, only a little, enough for me to see his face. A hand relaxed against my hip and another alighted gently against my inner thigh as he braced me against the low wall of the terrace balcony. His mouth and eyes were unreadable, but there was the trace of something—was it fear?—in the flare of his nostrils below the mask.

"Do it," he said softly, and now I could hear the trepidation in his voice. But there was something else, too, a resolve as firm as stone, immutable as the cold surface of the mask itself.

Now it was my turn to hesitate. The single finger that rested against his scalp, under the binding, did not stir. How was it I feared this intimacy, but not the other?

Gannet's hand was firm on my bare hip, but his lips were soft and light as he bent to brush them against mine.

"Please," he said aloud as he drew back again, eyes locked on mine. New moon or not, his were shining with a fierce light. In my head, I heard him clearer still. *I want you to see me as I really am.*

The blood that had pumped hotly to every part of me only a moment ago seemed to still, as if the whole of my world was held in a single beat of my heart.

I already do.

The knot was simple, the work of only a few seconds. My trembling hands moved to his temples, cradling the crude rim of the mask even as I withdrew it. There were no clouds to obscure the stars, which seemed to shine all the brighter as I lowered the mask and Gannet's features leaped into focus.

His eyes seemed so large without it, depthless, framed in pale sockets touched just a little with the blue of sleeplessness. His countenance was softer without lines of iron to harden it, and younger, so much younger. A long brow sloped down to a nose that was a touch severe, and below it, a mouth I knew, a mouth seeming far more ready for a grin without such a weight above it.

But Gannet didn't smile, and I could see now as well as sense his uncertainty at being so exposed. And his hope.

The mask I lowered to my lap, free hand smoothing his youthful cheek, a finger sliding down his serious nose. I leaned forward, kissing the bridge of it, his brow, the soft swells of his eyes when he closed them. I felt his shiver of pleasure in his hands, still flush against my skin.

"Thank you," I said softly, unsure of what code he had broken, but certain that this was a gift.

"No," he insisted hoarsely, catching my mouth with his, "thank you."

And now there was nothing between us. Gannet's kisses deepened with surprising ferocity. Again he lifted me, drawing away from the terrace to a close circle of low stone benches, smoothed with age. He bent over me, and between us we made quick work of the folds of cloth that kept us apart. Without thinking I used a hand to guide him inside of me, a gasp of pain hastening to a song of pleasure. We moved together, lips meeting and parting again to wander over flesh, my hands tangling in his hair even as his found anchor at my hips. Here was something he had chosen, a path that had not been laid down before him but one he knew all the same. And I knew it, too. I knew the way that it would end, and still I held on and on, hoping that we could walk the path forever.

CHAPTER NINETEEN

We dozed together on the terrace with none but the moon to witness our tender gestures, the kisses planted in secret hollows, limbs waking to join again when a little sleep was had. Sometime later Gannet rose and retrieved the mask, but when he went to replace it, I stayed his hand, taking it from him and fitting it to his features only after I had kissed again the eyes and brow and cheeks it would cover. We shared the memory of his mother, when she had put the mask on him for the very first time, and I knew that it had been too long since it was done in love.

It was a gesture that brought us back to the world we belonged to, the urgent, immediate present that demanded so much of us. The imposter was coming. Our work was undone. I wanted to resist, to remain lying there with my body and heart bared to the stars and the man I loved. But the sun would rise and with it, every horror, every unrealized fear, if we did not find what we sought. I hastened back into my clothes and Gannet did, too.

He looked at me, and though his mask was firmly in place, he did not draw the cloak about him again. Even darkly clad he seemed less imposing without it. Something about him had changed, or something in me as I looked upon him.

He met my eyes, his a storm of tenderness and resolve.

"What happened, with Najat?"

He had slept through it all. Our flight, her death, the vision of Ji in the temple. I had almost forgotten the last vision, given what happened after, but I was shocked to find the details falling lucidly into place in my mind.

"She gave us both a gift, before she died," I said, marveling at the clarity of what I had seen. Rather than try to explain, I reached out to hold Gannet's hand, sharing the full picture of the last vision with him. It was my memory now, and I was able to share it as I hadn't been able to before.

"Maybe this was the place hidden beneath the river," he mused aloud, and I nodded.

"I'm sure they were sent to recover the weapon. We need to get back there," I continued. "Najat said that the imposter has promised them true death. Never to return as icons."

"And who would defy even an imposter when she possesses the power to kill gods," he murmured. I nodded grimly. We had to reach it first.

A sudden battering crack of stone against stone sent us both sprawling in the accompanying quake. The bombardment continued, and I scrambled to my feet to see great missiles, cobbled together from desert rock and ruin, launched deep into the city from just within the collapsed walls that had surrounded Re'Kether.

The imposter was here, and with her, a force that vastly outnumbered our own.

I saw half a stone head, the wind-worn visage of an ancient god, hurtling toward us, and I threw my hands up. The projectile shattered instantly, shards falling harmlessly against the terrace floor, sand roughly kissing our faces. I seized Gannet's arm and pulled him toward the stair and down. I wasn't sure that it would be any safer on the ground, but we needed to move, to find my family, to find the weapon, to do more than simply witness our own destruction.

When we reached a corridor that had been partially blasted open to a courtyard where centuries-dry fountains whipped only sand onto the stone, Gannet squeezed my fingers before releasing me. For all the urgency of battle, I felt lit up from within at his touch, that the glow of my skin or the fierce flame in my belly and heart would rival not only the sun when it rose, but outshine that glaring tyrant at its zenith.

"The golems, Eiren." His eyes sought a deeper darkness

within the ruined palace, his thoughts obscured from me. "We need them."

And I need to find them. He didn't need to say it; I knew, just as I knew I needed the next vision.

"Eiren!"

It was Jurnus, flanked by several soldiers, shouting from the courtyard. The sharpness of my eyes in the dark showed that all were bloodied, but whole.

Gannet had made up his mind. He kissed my hand when I wanted him to kiss my lips and stole away into the ruins. I told myself that the unsteadiness I felt in my legs was only from the crash of another rockfall in the city's center. This palace had stood for centuries, inhabited by ghosts only, and the imposter's army would bring it down around me, around us all, if they didn't get what they wanted. Jurnus was racing up to me now, face flaming.

"What are you doing here? Where is he going?"

I blanched, clutching at my collar, wondering if my skin bore some guilty mark of Gannet's attentions. It was the right of brothers to rage over their sisters in the midst of war, was it not? Gannet had been quick, and Jurnus's sight at night was not so keen as ours. How could he know? Did I seem changed as much on the outside as I felt from within?

"He's going to find the golems," I replied. "And I need to find the weapon."

"It's too late for that!" Jurnus said sharply. I noted now that he favored his right side. Deflated though he was, my brother's eyes were wild. I put my hands on either of his shoulders, gazing tenderly at him even as distant screams wedded with the sounds of exploding stone outside the palace. I smelled fire.

"I'm sorry, Jurnus. For disappointing you. For frightening you. But I need to go—there is still time."

"You're wrong," he answered, manic laughter bubbling beneath his words even as he stumbled back. The blood in my veins crept coldly toward my heart, sluggish with fear.

"What happened, Jurnus?"

"I'll show you."

We moved quickly into the streets, where the corpses of several Ambarian soldiers were crumpled. My brother stooped with some difficulty to collect the sword of one of the fallen, and his compatriots retrieved the weapons of the others. Even I could see that the swords were finer than most our forces carried, and it was a wonder these men had been bested at all. If Gannet couldn't deliver on his promise, if I couldn't make sense enough of what I'd seen, our people wouldn't survive to see the end of this, whatever it would be.

We didn't go far. I could hear the sounds of battle, distant but growing closer, and for a moment the bombardment had stopped. Perhaps our forces had reached their machinery. Perhaps they merely gathered more ammunition.

We crept low, hugging the shadows as we approached one of the city's many ancient places of worship. I could see it in another time, ghostly lanterns hung to welcome supplicants at all hours, the scent of brazier smoke and sweat at every door. High above us, we had the perfect view of a temple edifice, remarkably intact, and my eyes at night were sharp enough to see what Jurnus wanted me to, without needing to go any nearer.

Strung up between the broken, pockmarked bodies of two unrecognizable stone figures, another figure was suspended, naked and limp in death. Najat looked small as a child, her skin pale in the starlight, her eyes open, sightless, never to rest. They had not cleaned the wound in her chest, and blood had congealed thickly down her breast and belly, terminating between her legs. When I had fled and my family, too, they must've come back through. They must've taken her body. They'd had orders, and they'd followed them.

"Morainn said you would want to see this. That you would know what it meant."

Najat might have moved against me when given the opportunity, yet she had vowed to do what I'd never been brave enough to do: to die. But death had come for her too soon; even now a babe somewhere could be squalling, lungs filled with the breath that would sustain the icon, the prison that would house her again.

And the imposter had done this, for me. To show me that she had power. Not the power of the gods, but mortal power, always to take. To use. To discard. Najat had been tasked with bringing me to the imposter. She had failed.

Najat would not be the first to die.

"Take me to our father," I said to Jurnus.

"I understand what you can do now, Eiren. I'm not afraid anymore. You should fight with us. We need you."

"Just take me to our father."

Jurnus hardened at my words, unreadable but for the furtive questing of his heart. It didn't matter what he said; he wanted to use me as much as Theba did. I remembered, what felt a thousand years ago on the day that I had met him, Gannet telling me that I was no tool. I knew his words now for what they were: the first of the many lies he'd told me, and to himself.

Around us, the city wavered between new and old in my sight. I heard the babbling of fountains and children at play, a chorus of screams, the groans of the dying. Cook fires, herbs growing richly in pots outside rotted doors, and streets that welcomed only sand mingled in my nose with the scents of long-undisturbed ruins disturbed anew, of fires running rampant, their colors wild and angry and growing closer. At one point, there was an explosive flare before us, an Ambarian soldier silhouetted in the wild blaze of fire oil. Without thinking, I threw my hands out, upsetting the earth beneath his feet and sending the figure tumbling.

I couldn't hear the scream over the sound of my brother's thoughts, his thrill, his horror.

At last, we ducked into a familiar ruin, and our own soldiers leaped out of the shadows, swords raised, waiting for Jurnus's confirmation before lowering them.

Everyone waited inside. My mother, my father. My sisters with tall, pale Morainn among them, like an accidental arrangement of desert blooms. She met my eyes, and I wanted more than anything to speak to her, to offer her an explanation for every question that crossed her features. Even her sightless eye seemed to penetrate me.

My brother was immediately tended to, and I noted that Lista was wounded, as well, leaning on Anise for support. My father seemed relieved to see me, but there was a new darkness there, after what he had seen where Najat had died.

"I am more afraid for the Ambarians than I am for you. But we weren't going to leave you behind," he said, looking me over. His pause was weighty. "Gannet wasn't with you?"

"He is still looking for the golems."

"It's a little late for that," Lista hissed, her words ending in a whimper as she lowered herself to the floor. Anise laid a worried hand against the bandages that bound Lista's thigh, even the slight pressure causing them to blossom with fresh blood. "There are too many for even mythical creatures to fight. More than we counted. How did they get more siege weaponry into the city?"

Morainn's laugh was hollow and hard, like a stone rattling in a cup.

"They didn't." She met my eyes. "It is Tirce who launches these stones."

I released a breath I hadn't meant to hold, feeling light. Of course it was Tirce. How many more icons had the imposter wooed with promises of freedom in permanent death?

"We have a weapon, too," Jurnus began, and I wasn't the only one to raise my hand in objection. Their voices, their thoughts, were crowded, manic, senseless.

"Your sister isn't a weapon."

"Your sister's life isn't worth the risk."

"Your sister isn't stable."

Your sister can't be trusted.

Your sister is an enemy, too.

Where Gannet had lit a fire in me there was a coal only, now. But I had not cooled.

"It's me the imposter wants," I said quietly, but they were arguing now. The only person who wasn't talking, who still looked on me as though she waited for something, was Morainn. She knew, of course. And she knew me, too.

Don't.

She couldn't project into my mind, not as her brother did, but she knew that I could read her thoughts. They were plain enough on her face, too, if my family had bothered to see. As were mine, no doubt, when I made up my mind.

"We need to take one of the secret ways, one that hasn't been compromised yet. Retreat and regroup," my father was saying. "We may lose this city, but we will not be captured again."

He sounded more certain than I knew he felt, but even my mother, who knew his true heart from their years together, only nodded. Jurnus seemed for a moment like he might protest, but Lista was already struggling to her feet with Anise's aid.

"I can't leave. I have to find what the imposter seeks, and then I must seek her. Gannet and I were nearly there, at the river."

Esbat regarded me, eyes sharp, but looked away before speaking. "There is a passage through the sewer that will get you close to that part of the city. I can show you," she began, a tremor in her voice that quickly vanished when my family began to protest against her offer to help me. "We shouldn't go together, anyway, or all in the same direction. We'll attract more attention that way."

"She's right. I'll send word to the captains and go with Anise and Lista," Jurnus hastened to agree, and I could see already how he plotted to part from them, to fight. "Esbat, you'll be safe with Eiren, and Morainn, too. Mother, father, you must go with Visash and Hale." He indicated the two soldiers who had accompanied us this far. "Make for Cascar, once you're clear of the ruins."

I saw the deep, ancient way that Esbat intended for us, and felt the chill of the Rogue's Ear about me, the snatches of dream that slithered between what was real and what was imagined, like oil on the watery surface of our reality. I had a momentary crystalline thought from the vision, of Ji feeling she had walked into another world.

My mother drew me fiercely to her when the moment of parting came, and it was as though she reached for me in every year of my life, hugging to her the pensive babe, the cautious child, the curious girl. For her, I was still all those things. She did not recognize the monster, or chose not to.

"You are still my daughter," she said into my ear. She didn't need my gifts to know my heart, only those gifts that are the burden of every mother of a living child. "And I will see you again when this is over."

There was the chime of a funeral procession in her words. I pulled back and searched her face. Hers was still and certain where mine was wet now with tears.

And then I was touching hands and faces with each of them, drawn away toward the end of everything.

CHAPTER TWENTY

Esbat scouted a fair distance ahead of Morainn and me. She was smaller than Morainn, and less likely to draw notice, she insisted. I didn't argue with her, though I was as wary of being alone with Morainn as I was desperate to talk with her again. Our path took us away from the fighting, provided the illusion of safety and secrecy. I stretched my mind outward all the same, hoping to sense an ambush before it was upon us, a small part of me monitoring what felt like every quarter of the city, and leaving little to probe my friend's mind.

It was better she speak her mind to me, anyway, than have it taken from her.

"I feel like we've just been reunited and are parting again," she said quietly. "I can't even ask you to tell me what's happened with my brother."

"It's as I said," I whispered, skin prickling. "He's looking for the golems."

But I knew what she asked, and she knew that I knew.

"Eiren," she said, laying a hand on my arm. We couldn't stop, couldn't even slow, but I met her eyes in the dark, one shining with concern, the other milky with secrets. "Do you know what you're doing? With him? With this weapon?"

My smile was all edges. "As much as I ever have."

Morainn looked ahead and I followed her gaze, noting Esbat's quick wave for us to hurry, her movements growing more visible as dawn approached. I didn't know how it could be a new day. It felt to me as though I'd lived a dozen lives in the last twelve hours.

"He loves you, you know," she said, circling a crater that had once been a fountain. We crossed here, where Tirce's efforts were visible. "And so do I. No matter what happens."

I stood opposite her, exposed as a star, wishing for more time and better words. I wanted a story that I could tell in an instant, a moment of connection to rival the fear that gripped us both.

But even as I opened my mouth to speak, there was a rumbling, a whistling, and the world shattered. Flurries of sand and shattered stone from the last enormous stone projectile made it impossible to see more than a few feet ahead of me. My dark sight was of no use, for it was debris that challenged my senses. I tripped madly along a dark slope as the grumble and roar of crashing stone grew more distant. I felt forward with my feet, uncertain of the damage and not wanting to fall. When my toes butted up against something soft, I bent to trace my hands up and down the frame of a body: Morainn's.

Her breath was steady, only unconscious from the blast. I struggled to lift her, cursing Theba's selective aid.

I sucked in a cluttered breath, coughing and stumbling. I tried to speak her name, to rouse her, but I seemed only to hack dust. My lungs were choked with it. I lost my balance again as the world shifted, shuddering, and I only just kept from sliding into what felt like the deepest center of the world. I held fast to Morainn, doing my best to drag her away toward what I thought might be the square's edge.

"Eiren?" Esbat's familiar face emerged from the dust, and I gasped relief.

"Esbat! I need help. Morainn is hurt, I think."

Esbat's expression was unreadable, and when she moved, it was to take a step away from me, rather than nearer. I felt as though I had swallowed a lump of ice, a sudden cold stealing down my throat, frosting my heart and belly.

"Esbat, we need your help. Please."

It was then, only then, that she shook her head, a movement so slight I might have missed it if it weren't for the torrent of emotion that I sensed within her. The haze shifted around her hand's sudden movement, the readied blade within it. My own mind exploded in the colors of revelation, the blood red of betrayal. I felt Theba's temper surge in me, and I bit into my cheek until it bled, trying to hold her back. To hold myself back. I could be wrong.

"Esbat!" There was a tremor in my voice, answered by a tremor beneath our feet. "What are you doing?"

She froze. The ground where we stood was crumbling bit by bit, my shaking limbs setting the stone to shake, too.

"Why didn't you die?" Though her face remained still, it was ashen, and her voice had the cracked quality of someone who should have been weeping. I gaped at her even as we were knocked to the ground by a great crashing from below, all around. Whole sheets of earth were being swallowed up. We scrambled to our feet, she still holding the knife, and me holding an unconscious Morainn, barely avoiding sliding into a growing chasm where the square had been. "I wasn't supposed to see you again. I can't see you. My sister is dead," she continued, voice hollow, high and desperate, her feet exploring as she spoke, grappling for safety. "I read the old texts. I know what happened here. They won't leave until they get what they've come for, and we'll never know peace while we shelter Theba. We'll never deserve it."

Her thoughts skittered like spiders, crazed, furtive. My skin crawled with them. How long had she been working against our family, against me, against hope? I wasn't sure that it mattered. Even if she had betrayed them before I had arrived, I didn't want war any more than she did. My arrival only heralded its bloody end.

"You're right."

Fury billowed off me like steam. Esbat launched herself at me, and I released Morainn to grapple with my sister. I wept as the skin of her wrist bubbled beneath my hand, Theba's fire inching toward her elbow. I didn't want to do this. I wouldn't do this. I let go, arresting the black progress of the flames on her skin. She roared and came at me again, eyes burning with tears of her own.

And then Esbat stopped, stumbling away from me in shock. A small, black-feathered dart stuck out of her neck. I saw her mouth gape open and close, like a fish for water, her hand reaching to pry the dart free. She thrashed about, struggling for air. Her terror lanced through me and I dove after her, tried to hold her. There was a rhythmic quality to the quakes of the ground now, and she lost her footing only an arm's length from me, falling, her hand waving a faint plea before she disappeared into the abyss.

I howled. I had the power to reduce a score of women to smudges, the stink of grease, but could not save even one. I felt wild, a weapon that would not be tempered no matter how skillful the smith. Arms locked around me, drawing me away from the edge, and Morainn's gray face came into focus, a little pipe used for projecting poisoned darts falling from her lips.

"She's dead!" I screeched, not caring if the enemy was near enough to hear. "You killed her!"

"I had to. I had to," Morainn murmured, cold shock pouring from her body into mine, dulling my fevered panic.

There was a blaze of light and I thought the world might fracture in two as yet more fragments of ancient street clattered into the chasm.

Eiren.

Gannet.

I wheeled around, my eyes struggling to adjust to the abrupt change in light, from twilight to dawn's fury diffused in a haze of stone dust. Gannet's narrow form was dark, his pale face slashed with the unmistakable bruise-black of his mask as he came into focus. And behind him, rows upon rows of silent watchers, eyes glowing, twice as tall as he was, and considerably more than twice wide. Their expressions became clear to me as though through water or memory, vision or dream.

I felt weak everywhere, my mouth falling open in bald disbelief. Each golem wore the same stoic expression, eyes hooded, nose rather too long and sharp, mouth etched in a line that was not made for smiling, even though *I knew that smile*, knew it formed a handsome one when coaxed. Each had been made in the guise of the man they had served both in life and in death, Shran's visage remembered in the chiseled contours of their faces. They all looked exactly alike.

They all looked exactly like Gannet.

I thought I heard a laugh. Theba's, surely, but the charging of the golems drowned out everything. My mind felt shattered by Esbat's betrayal, by the revelation of Gannet's identity. Not a god, but a man. The best of men. How was it even possible?

The golems were advancing around Gannet, converging on us. Morainn and I nearly lost our footing with their thundering, sliding near the edge of the chasm once more.

"Gannet, tell them to stop!"

He was the icon of Shran, and so must be their master, but he couldn't stop them, even if they would have heeded him. There were Ambarian soldiers filling what was left of the street. The golems lowered spears, pikes, and wicked, curved swords, meeting the enemy in a flurry of weapons. They'd kill us and the Ambarians, too.

I looked wildly about for some means of escape, but there was only the charging of men and golems, the pit and the broken body of my sister somewhere deep below. And then my eyes set upon a glowing sigil in the stone beneath where the fountain had been, the shock of recognition settling in me dark and deep. I had seen it before, though the eyes had not been mine. One of the golems, felled by one of Tirce's missiles, toppled into the pit, the last flash of his eyes exposing a tunnel, an intact darkness, pointing away from the ruined square.

Protect her.

I had to trust that Gannet heard me, could heed me. I used Theba's strength to charge across the chasm to the sigil and what it promised, leaving Morainn behind. When I laid a hand upon it, the sigil lit another and another, driving deeper below the city, a blazing path for me, and me alone, to follow. I had been here before, with Ji.

I walked in a daze, touching the sigils as Mara had in the vision, mind cloudy with regret, with revelation, with resolve.

There was no water underneath the city now, not as it had been in Ji's time. Still, the ghost of a current snaked between my toes, whipped my bare legs as I slowed, as the tunnel narrowed and then, after a time, widened again. I had been here, too. It was different with the many ages between Ji and me, but the heavy feeling of old power and ancient privilege was the same. If I found the weapon, would it make up for my sister's betrayal? Would it make her right about me, and my monstrous will?

Mine, yes. Theba unfolded like a flower in spring, her will like deadly perfume clouding my senses.

The tunnel's opening was lurid as a mouth, and I saw nothing but shadows in the chamber beyond. I sensed her suddenly, the imposter, alone, watchful, smug in the cloud of some pain-numbing opiate. She was close, she had known the way. If I killed her, would it stop this? Would it stop me? I could almost taste the tremble of sweat on the imposter's lip, and then I saw her. The cadence of her fevered whispers stirred the ragged hem of my gown; my nose and brow felt, too, the ritual touches of her fingers. The imposter was bent in prayer. It did not amuse me that she would die in penitent repose, but a laugh raked through my throat all the same.

I stepped forward.

When I drew near to her, there was a medicinal odor mixed with the rank of refuse, unwashed hair and skin, illness. I could see from the crooked slope of her back as she bent that she was not well, and the slowness with which she moved to meet my dark gaze was that of a crone, or a cripple. Her mind was churning, a storm of senseless anger.

She was pitiable, but I was pitiless.

"I knew you'd come." Her voice was raw, and I caught snatches of a twisted expression beneath the folds of a wintry hood. Much more of her face I couldn't see, but what flesh was exposed was shiny, tight, warped as though someone had taken a sculptor's knife to it.

Or a flame.

She couldn't see me, but she *knew* me. There was a flash of hollow, milk-white eyes in sunken sockets before her hands shot out, grabbing me by the wrists. There was a fever in her, and I felt the weak pulse in her hands. It called to me.

Theba, Theba, Theba.

Was it a warning? A conviction?

She held me more tightly, and I recognized something of Theba in her, crazed and indomitable. I felt the Dread Goddess rising in me to answer this madness.

I would get the weapon.

And then I would kill her.

"You will answer for what you've done," I hissed, my words edged as a blade.

The sound of my voice changed her. The thoughts that raced like blind horses in her mind slowed, gathered. The drift of her head ceased and she jerked chin-first, as though led by a line, to face me. She threw back her hood and I knew why she didn't fear me. She knew the fury of Theba. She'd felt it firsthand.

"Imke?"

Much of her bright hair was gone, twisted folds of flesh streaming down her scalp in a mockery of the pale locks that had once lain there. Her face retained only the smug twist of her mouth, full, fleshy lips too gruesome and strange in an otherwise savage visage.

"I do not go by that name anymore," she hissed. "Not since I was chosen. Since she touched me. *Theba.*"

She was in a reverie, lifting my hand to sweep it down her ruined brow, over one opaque, sightless eye. I shuddered. I had robbed Morainn of her sight, but Imke, of her sanity.

"So you wage a war in her name," I said, struggling to retain control enough to search her mind. "Why?"

I felt the warm glow of contentment in my belly, Theba's anger at Imke's masquerade dissolving as it became clear that this was yet one more bloodbath in the Dread Goddess's name. In her honor.

"Because *you* won't. You're weak. Unworthy. I see that now."

How many of her friends had she slaughtered? What else had my touch, Theba's fury, caused her to betray?

"But you need me."

"I need what's within you. When Theba sees how I have served her, what I can offer her, perhaps she'll bury you in that coward's heart of yours once and for all."

I didn't know if this was something that Theba could do, take me over completely, permanently. But I felt a surge of strength at Imke's touch, as though her devotion powered the monster within me. I fought it, fought them both, thinking of what I wanted, why I was here.

"Where is it, Imke? Where is the weapon?"

She smiled, lips wrinkling her savaged cheeks like paper, squeezing my wrists until I thought my bones might snap.

"It's here."

Imke seemed to feed on my struggle, and a flame was pulled from me, an unwilling thing that began in my fingers, licked at skin puckered already by its touch. Theba's will was like a scorpion under sand, waiting to strike, to shake free and feast. I would be discarded. I stomped, I shook, I twisted to lay my hands, now consumed in fire, on Imke's forearms, but she was changing.

We weren't alone, around us the blur of gold limbs, bodies realized from the air, ancient faces lined with sorrow. They laid their hands upon me, through me.

Imke's face darkened unnaturally, an invisible hand drawing the hood over it again. Her leer became a shadow and my fear, my fight, a distant dream. Suddenly Ji's needs eclipsed my own. I was pulled under into another vision.

"So what are we looking for?"

I couldn't see the hooded woman's face, but her posture tensed, and she stopped midstride.

"I assumed you knew."

It was my turn to feel shocked. The keening of whatever watch we had roused in the subterranean temple was reaching a crescendo, and I almost wanted to be caught just to silence the dozens of voices crying out in fear, or pain, or the pleasure that the wicked take in such things.

"Do you mean to tell me that we've been sent here to find a weapon and we don't even know what it looks like?"

The woman didn't respond, and my belly constricted in rage. We'd been betrayed by those who'd posed as our allies, by gods I should have known that I could not trust.

"Perhaps Mara knew," she began, but she didn't sound as though she believed it. I also did not like the way she had given up on my friend, speaking as though Mara had no future.

Even if it was beginning to seem that we might not.

I charged ahead, brushing past her, sandals squelching.

"We'll find the sanctum. It's bound to be there. I've been in dozens of temples. They're not exactly hidden," I insisted, tone more confident than the panic in my erratic heart. "Gods do not believe us capable of penetrating their secrets, and so I haven't known them to keep any."

She didn't argue, and I would've left her behind if she had. We were running out of time, perhaps spending some that did not belong to us, and I wasn't going to waste it trading bad ideas with an uppity courtier, no matter her allegiance.

The walls were slick with growth, glossy fibers that hung together as the weave of a tapestry might, giving off a starlight glow. Here there were no torches, no touch of the sun, only the ancient sigils pulsing with light, the strange vegetation glowing dully. The passage was uncomfortably narrow. In the city our temples were made for great throngs to worship at once. Here the hooded woman and I could barely walk abreast, and had to, at last, approach single file, sharing a begrudging moment where she condescended to let me go first.

Or perhaps she hoped that I would be eaten and sate the hunger of whatever waited for us at the corridor's end.

But no beast waited, and no gods, either. The careful stone underfoot gave way to slick rock, the temple turned to a natural cave that was never truly dry. The flow of the water was evident here, a sluggish path winding beneath our city. The lichen-green lights twinkled here, as though countless unnaturally bright eyes winked at us. I wondered if we were even under the city anymore.

If we were even in the same world.

"Here or nowhere," the hooded woman said almost to herself, striding forward hurriedly, but failing to register the change in terrain in her eagerness. She lost her footing in a shallow, slippery dip of stone. I reached out a hand to steady her but wasn't quick enough.

And then there was more to wonder at.

As she crashed, a tangle of limbs and unsteady trunk, the hood slipped back. She was devoid of all that made her as she was in my mind: no longer hooded and never, apparently, a woman.

What was more, I knew the man whose eyes met mine.

The crown prince looked up at me from where he had fallen, sodden clothes newly soaked, expression grim. I couldn't think of a single thing to say, but I knew what to do.

I drew one of my knives from the belt I wore under my clothes, quick as an oil flare.

"Don't move."

My head was spinning. I wasn't sure that I couldn't trust him, though my instinct was immediately not to. While I had betrayed duties and a heritage of my own to support the rebellion, who I was and what I was responsible for were nothing compared to what someone from the royal family risked.

"I won't explain myself. There isn't time," he said, expression as unapologetic as his voice, pitched lower, now. It seemed ludicrous to me that I had ever believed him a woman. We held each other's gaze, and I noted the color of his eyes in the strange light, brown touched with the green of new growth, warm and alive with knowing. I cursed the knife that began to shake in my hand.

"You just have to trust me," he said.

"Why must she do that?" This was another voice, hard as a diamond, as bright and loud in our ears as a thunderclap. Where a moment ago it had just been the pair of us, my shock at the hooded woman's identity turned to realization of another kind: the feeling that we were being watched from all sides, that we had been, this whole time.

"I am very curious why a thief and a faker, a consummate anarchist, should trust one whose loyalty was assured at birth," the voice continued.

I turned, sure my curiosity would be the death of me but incapable of keeping still. Behind us, not so close as his voice made him seem, Adah emerged from the deeper darkness of the cavern. He was flanked by bright figures, human-shaped but featureless, their limbs made of golden, glowing light. Adah had only to incline his head the slightest degree and I was seized, my skin burning where they touched me, just enough to scald the flesh but not to scar. Shran they left alone, even as he scrambled to his feet, and my heart hardened completely against him. Whatever his part in this, he'd been in it for himself.

"Traitor," I spat, but he wasn't looking at me, regarding Adah with a stillness I couldn't read.

When he spoke, his gaze didn't shift from the god. "That's hardly an insult, coming from you."

I laughed. What did I have to lose? I was within moments of execution.

"I'm not afraid to die," I insisted, but my heart betrayed me, returning to thoughts of Mara, senseless and all but entombed, of others we had lost. Fleetingly I thought of my family, none of whom I had spoken to in more than two years, and was sorry that they would not know how I had died. I did not think Adah would make my punishment public. He would not want me to be a martyr.

As if he sensed my thoughts, he drew from behind his back, though I was sure it had not been there a moment before, a gleaming spear. It was unadorned but the edge was potent, the metal there discolored with age and much use. I trembled at the sight of it.

I had seen it before. Just once.

"What surprises me most about your kind," Adah mused, as though we were sitting together over tea, discussing philosophy, "is that you hate us so much for being just as you imagined us. You created gods with your dreaming, your wild needs, your raw feelings, and yet you blame us."

"If we created you, we can kill you," I said, struggling against the bright ones who held me. Their grip only strengthened, beyond any human capacity, and I gritted my teeth against the pain and the realization that we had been sent here for nothing. I saw Shran edging away from us, and refused to allow myself to hope that he might want to help me.

"No, not you," Adah said, nodding, and there was a touch of resignation in his voice, slight as a sigh. "But someone yet may."

I blinked back tears of rage and he was before me in as much time, the bright ones forcing me to my knees. The cool water lapped against my thighs and I wondered for an instant at the contrast between the water's icy touch and the fiery touches on my arms, my shoulders, my back. In my heart the struggle was the same: the furious heat of many centuries oppressed, the blistering cold of regret that I had failed, that I was just one among many who would die with the world unchanged. I pitched and howled, but the golden forms only pressed closer. There were so many, and only me.

"Shran."

Adah was holding out the spear to him and I felt myself go cold over. I wouldn't beg, not Shran, not Adah. I didn't think Adah felt satisfaction at such things as a mortal man might, but it didn't matter. I wouldn't give it to him. I'd never given anything to any man or woman I hadn't wanted to, and I would die as I had lived: as though everything that had ever happened to me had been of my own choosing.

The wide head of the spear threw a shadow over Shran's face, obscuring his nose and brow, though his eyes glowed like coals with the light shed from the bodies of the bright ones. He'd been a choice, a lifetime ago, meant for me. Our blood was the same; even now I felt it singing in my veins and knew his must be, too.

My blood remembered the spear, too. It has been in the hands of a priestess, then. At fourteen years old my parents brought me to the temple, where they opened my veins and murmured to each other over some quality of my blood they didn't bother articulating to me. I had heard stories, we'd all heard stories, of young men and women cut too deeply, wrongly, never returning. But it didn't hurt so much and I thought it was over.

But then they had banished my parents and brought me to the table. One priestess brought forward the spear, another a book, and they stripped my clothes from me, anointed my heart, belly, and sex with pungent oil. I was a gift, they said. I was special, they said.

Jemae, Jemae! How lucky you are.

One of the priestesses readied the spear while another took my hands, my feet, beginning to anchor me to the table with bleached linen. There wasn't room for anything but terror. They meant to kill me. I had been spoiled. But I would never be spared.

Jemae, Jemae! Your luck is ours.

I had thrown my full weight against the priestess nearest me, rushed to a smoking brazier in the corner of the room and thrown the coals at the next who advanced upon me. I ran, I hid, I wept. I knew if they found me they would try again. I had to leave my life, my name, never to be chosen by the one who stood before me now, who took the spear after only a moment's hesitation.

Jemae, Jemae! Your luck's run out.

The memory cleaved my heart open, and the spear in Shran's hands tore through me to finish the work begun years before.

My chest was heaving, whole and mine, a body I recognized though the light was different. Was I with Ji, still—Jemae, it had been Jemae all along—or had her world rushed to fill the void in mine? I felt like my head would burst open. How could she have died, and at Shran's hand? Were none of the stories true? Had there been no Salarahan, no gentle father to our people?

The gold glow, the shining limbs, I could see them, could feel their heat. The ghosts of the First People surrounded me now, and I held Imke, still, and she held me. The fire where we touched was pure white, the kind that burns so fast and so hot there's hardly ash to mourn.

And there was someone else.

"Do you understand now?"

Emine stood where Adah had stood in the vision, though I didn't need the correlation to see it, to see her, truly. The child who hadn't died. The child who had never been a child at all. There had never been any Emine, only Adah. Antares had told me the icon could appear as he wished, could manipulate the way that he was seen in the mind of the seer. I had seen him, but I had never seen *her*. Could I even trust that Adah was here now, or did she project herself to this place, a witness?

I released Imke. It was Adah at whom I looked, Adah who demanded my attention. I felt as though I were at the end of all things.

"Why did you lie to me?" I asked, even though I knew she would not believe it a lie. I had taken comfort in the child Emine, prized her attention, grieved her death.

"Paivi told me you would be difficult. If you'd seen me like this first, you would have trusted me even less. You needed the man to make you wary so that the girl could disarm you. I can be both. I can be all."

I thought my heart might burst as Ji's heart had at the spear's thrust. Adah, Imke, Esbat, Jemae, Gannet. I could not trust a face, could not trust my own heart. The mask Gannet wore seemed suddenly a warning for me: not just that I could not know him, but that I could never know anyone again. Not in this world, not in the world of stories. I did not think I could trust even death.

My breathing was shallow.

"Jemae died. How can she have died? How are we even here, if she never lived to bear four sons?"

Adah's smile was like that of a snarling dog, a mountain predator. A mouth made only for killing.

"Did she? *Think*, Theba. Why did you really come here? Aren't you ready to end it?"

Theba's presence was a greater pressure than it had ever been, summoned by Adah's words. I felt suffocated, as I had been, underwater after the storm in Cascar. I felt I would die waiting just behind my eyes, my lips, the joints of my fingers and limbs.

Theba took control.

"Not for this reunion," Theba hissed with my lips. "And you know it will never end, not while Salarahan still lives."

"That depends on how you define life," Adah intoned, smile coy, "and circumstances may change. Salarahan will kill you. Or you will kill him. That is the only way."

Adah's eyes seemed cut from crystal glass, ageless, remote as stars, so haunting in her young face that I thought they must have been carved from a crone and placed there.

"I won't," Theba managed to say. I felt, for the first time, her giving in to me. Like veils parting and lifting, retreating and assembling, I perceived the shape of things, the boundaries of the stage and the players within.

"When the time comes, you won't have a choice." Adah was as cold as a shadow, as dark as I imagined the first moonless night in the world must have seemed. "Take what you came here for, Theba."

We moved together, Theba and I, past Imke's stooped form to the altar where she had been praying only moments, an age, before. I bent my knees, and Theba used my hands to trace around the edges of broken stone, reaching around, below, finding a secret hollow that just fit the shape of my hand. The great, flat stone where Imke had kneeled groaned, retreating to reveal a shallow cavity.

Empty.

"*How?*" I seethed, I shook. Theba had believed it to be here and so I had believed it. But the spear was gone.

"I suppose Salarahan will have to wait," Adah observed, the

slightest edge in her voice, like a drop of blood in a bucket of water. She was surprised, too, to find it gone. "He is very good at waiting."

Adah withdrew and the gold ones circled her, blinding me as they gathered, concentrating their light so that Adah's features were all but obscured. She was a faceless girl. She had always been.

"You should attend to this mess, Theba, before you go. It's entirely of your making."

"My name is Eiren."

I felt Theba rattling behind my ribs like a crazed bird, retreating in an agony I was only beginning to understand. There was a love in her so fierce it had teeth, tearing a hole where my heart had been. But I wasn't empty, my heart wasn't gone. Only swallowed up, sunk deep, changed.

I was no longer afraid of her.

I wondered at the weapon that wasn't, the stories that weren't as I'd always been told them. Adah had challenged me, when I said that Jemae was dead. There was something that I was missing, a story left untold, or changed to suit the teller. The ghosts of the First People retreated, and Adah with them, their hands passing through me but offering no more visions now. They had shown me everything that I needed to know: I was the icon of Theba, but I was descended from Jemae. I shared in the passions and the secrets of both. I had seen her because I was her, as certainly as I was my mother's daughter, as much as I was the icon of Theba.

And now we were alone, Theba and Jemae and I, with the imposter. Imke was at least one woman that I could truly free. I crouched beside her, waited for her to do what I already knew she was going to try to do. She had the little knife tucked against a wrist that looked more like wax than flesh, and I caught her in the moment of driving it toward my throat and turned it gently back against her.

"Rest, Imke. Be glad you won't come back."

Blood gushed thick and slippery against my hands, my arms, my clothes. It wasn't Theba that had killed her, but me. There was none of Theba's rage in the act, only mercy of the kind that Theba and I might never earn. I lowered Imke's body gently to the ground and stood again, observing the temple as it was, peopled with new regrets. The battle raged still in the city above, and a new one, within me. I felt Gannet descending the tunnel first and then saw him, dark cloak whipping like the hangings of a funeral barge bearing the dead into the desert to be forgotten. But we would live to fight another day. The visions had led me here but I had the feeling that they were only the beginning, that I'd been wrong about so much. There was another ending for me ahead, a lost truth. The weapon was out there, and Salarahan, too.

I would hold them both.

ACKNOWLEDGMENTS

There are few things in this world I enjoy more than writing and making lists, but conveying my gratitude without the use of an oven does not come naturally to me. Also, people generally appreciate warm scones more than words.

This book would not be without Jaime Levine and Eliza Kirby, who are patient and wise and ask all the right questions, and the rest of the massively talented, funny, and quirky crew at Diversion Books. Thank you for giving my work a home and helping me to keep it so very tidy.

To friends who responded to innumerable e-mails and wild texts at all hours, you are so loved. Kelsi Dick, Mara Stokke, Alexandra Lucio, Traci Auerbach, thank you for reading, breathing, and dreaming with me.

And to my husband, my girls, you inspire and delight me. There's no world I could write that's sweeter than the one we create between our arms.

As a girl, JILLIAN KUHLMANN preferred writing stories to admitting that there wasn't any such thing as fairies or actually mustering up the courage to talk to boys. She likes to read, a lot, and wear red lipstick. She maintains an untidy house, a husband, two baby girls, and a wicked costume collection in Cincinnati, Ohio.

Visit her on the web at **www.jilliankuhlmann.com**

Printed in the USA
CPSIA information can be obtained
at www.ICGtesting.com
JSHW031956150824
68134JS00062B/3517

9 781682 303474